Praise for the

"Snow in Vermont, soup,
cozy? . . . Charming."

—Julie Hyzy,

Mysteries

"[A] soup du jour of mystery that cozy lovers are sure to enjoy."

—MyShelf.com

"An engaging amateur sleuth due to the troubled heroine and the delightful Vermont location."

—Genre Go Round Reviews

"Plenty of small-town New England charm."

—The Mystery Reader

"A 'souper' idea for a cozy mystery series!"

—Escape with Dollycas into a Good Book

"The way cozies should be written. A small town with lovable characters and a plot that leaves you satisfied at the end."

—Girl Lost in a Book

"A good read from beginning to end. The mystery kept me glued to the pages and the writing style had an easy flow that made it hard to put down . . . I can't wait to see what happens next in this delightfully charming series."

—Dru's Book Musings

"An action-packed page-turner with memorable characters I look forward to revisiting again and again!"

—Melissa's Mochas, Mysteries & Meows

"A great series based on one of my favorite things: soup. Connie Archer gives readers a likable heroine and a great mystery."

—Debbie's Book Bag

continued . . .

"If you already love this series, you're not going to be disappointed. If you haven't read this series, please do! You will fall in love with the characters, the location, and with author Connie Archer herself!" —Lisa K's Book Reviews

"I'm looking forward to reading more books in this series."
—Cozy Mystery Book Reviews

"I adored the characters . . . I wanted the pages to keep going and not end. The series has taken hold of me and doesn't want to let go." —Babs Book Bistro

Berkley Prime Crime titles by Connie Archer

A SPOONFUL OF MURDER
A BROTH OF BETRAYAL
A ROUX OF REVENGE
LADLE TO THE GRAVE
A CLUE IN THE STEW

A Clue in the Stew

Connie Archer

BERKLEY PRIME CRIME, NEW YORK

An imprint of Penguin Random House LLC
375 Hudson Street, New York, New York 10014

A CLUE IN THE STEW

A Berkley Prime Crime Book / published by arrangement with the author

ISBN: 978-0-425-27312-8

PUBLISHING HISTORY
Berkley Prime Crime mass-market edition / April 2016

PRINTED IN THE UNITED STATES OF AMERICA

10 9 8 7 6 5 4 3 2 1

Cover illustration by Cathy Gendron.
Cover art: *Gingham Pattern* © by Maria Dryfhout/Shutterstock;
Soup Love logo © by Miguel Angel Salinas/Shutterstock.
Cover design by Diana Kolsky.
Interior text design by Kristin del Rosario.

For my mother,
who loved libraries

Acknowledgments

Many thanks to agent extraordinaire Paige Wheeler of Creative Media Agency, Inc., for her hard work, good advice and expertise; and to Katherine Pelz and copyeditor Joan Matthews for their invaluable insights and editorial suggestions. My thanks also to Danielle Dill for her enthusiasm and support of the Soup Lover's Mysteries; and to everyone at Berkley Prime Crime who contributed their talent and energy in bringing this series to life.

Special thanks as well to the writers' group—Cheryl Brughelli, Don Fedosiuk, R. B. Lodge and Marguerite Summers—for their criticism and encouragement. And an extra special thank-you to Paula Freedman, R.N., and Romeo Robles of the Los Angeles County Fire Department for their knowledge of emergency treatment.

An additional thank-you to Elise Varey, who can take credit for suggesting a last name for Meg! Meg Findly thanks you and says she is thrilled to be playing a much larger role in *A Clue in the Stew*.

Last, but certainly not least, thanks to my family and my wonderful husband for their tolerance in living with a woman who is constantly thinking about ways to kill people.

CONNIE ARCHER
CONNIEARCHERMYSTERIES.COM
FACEBOOK.COM/CONNIEARCHERMYSTERIES
TWITTER: @SNOWFLAKEVT

Chapter 1

"WHAT?" MARJORIE SHRIEKED. "You haven't heard of her?"

Lucky continued to lay placemats along the countertop of the By the Spoonful Soup Shop. She smiled and shook her head. "Sorry, Marjorie. I haven't. Who is she?"

"Well, Hilary Stone is just about the most famous mystery writer in the world right now. And you know how much I love murder mysteries." Marjorie Winters shook out her copy of the *Snowflake Gazette*. "It's all right here." An advertisement covered the entire back page of the local newspaper. "This ad's been running in several towns. Lincoln Falls, Bournmouth . . . everywhere in Vermont." Marjorie shook her head. "I can't believe you don't know who she is!"

Marjorie's sister, Cecily, sat next to her at the counter. Cecily, always the more excitable of the two sisters, was quiet today. Lucky caught Cecily rolling her eyes in response to Marjorie's statement.

"You can't imagine it, Lucky," Cecily said, squeezing lemon juice into her tea. "There are piles of those horrid books all over our little house. It's revolting. I suspect my sister knows more ways to kill people than Jack the Ripper."

Marjorie sniffed. "Well, the *really* exciting thing is that she's coming here . . . to Snowflake! Our little village. I'm just beside myself."

Cecily sighed and remarked in a flat tone, "She can't wait."

Lucky smiled. She had to agree with Cecily. She had never seen Marjorie so voluble. Actually, now that she thought about it, she had never seen Marjorie excited about anything. The two sisters were polar opposites, in looks and in personality. Cecily's dark hair was chopped in an adorable pixie cut. She was chatty and outgoing. Marjorie, every blonde hair of her bob in place, was the cool, calm and collected of the two.

"I really do love to read," Lucky volunteered, "but I never seem to find the time these days, what with the restaurant and all." Lucky turned to the hatch and picked up the sisters' orders of croissants with butter and jam. "Here you go," she said, placing their dishes on the counter.

"You need to expand your horizons," Marjorie remarked severely.

"For once I agree with my sister," Cecily piped up. "Tell that handsome doctor of yours you want him to fly you off to Paris . . . or . . . Fiji." Cecily's face took on a dreamy expression.

Lucky laughed outright. "Paris! That's a good one. Elias would fall off his chair if I ever suggested that. I doubt I'll ever see Paris in my life. Besides, I've forgotten most of my high school French."

Marjorie was about to speak when the bell over the front door jingled. Lucky looked up as Barry Sanders entered. "Morning, Barry," she called out.

Barry raised a hand in greeting.

Cecily spun on her stool, "Where's your other half, Barry?" she called out as Barry took a seat at his usual corner table. Barry and his best friend, Hank, always arrived together.

Barry shrugged. "Said he wasn't feeling well this morning. I called him but he thought he might have a touch of the flu."

"Coffee, Barry?" Lucky asked.

"Yes. Please."

"Never known him to be sick though." Barry shrugged out of his jacket and hung it on the back of his chair.

"We were just talking about Hilary Stone before you arrived," Marjorie said. "Did you know she's coming to Snowflake?"

"Ah. Yes, I think I read that somewhere. I might buy her book. I heard it's very good."

Lucky shook her head. "I *am* totally out of the loop. Everybody seems to know who this woman is."

"You are, dear. Out of it. Totally," Marjorie added. "It says here . . ." she said, holding up her copy of the *Gazette*, "her book signing will be held in the meeting hall of the Congregational Church. I can just imagine the crowds that will show up for that."

"That's about the only place in town that can host a large group," Lucky said. "Do you think lots of people will come?"

"Oh, I'm sure," Marjorie replied. "You have no idea how famous she is. There'll be people coming from all over the state, maybe beyond." Marjorie reached down to gather her bundles. Cecily followed suit. "I'll have to have a word with Pastor Wilson and find out more. I definitely want to be the first in line. Do you think she'd sign my book? I mean I've already bought one, so I can't imagine she wouldn't."

"I'm sure she would," Lucky agreed.

"Well, we need to be off. We'll see you tomorrow, dear. We have a new shipment coming in today." Marjorie glanced at Lucky's outfit. "Why don't you stop by and see the new things when you have a break?"

Lucky nodded. "I'd like that. Thanks for letting me know." Lucky pushed up the sleeves of the light sweater she was wearing. Ruefully, she realized it had shrunk somewhat from too many washings. Marjorie must have noticed. That's why she had suggested a visit. It certainly wouldn't hurt her to buy a new one.

"Bye, Barry," Cecily called out as the two sisters hurried through the front door with their bundles. "Tell Hank we hope he's feeling better."

"I will." Barry nodded and waved.

Lucky carried a small tray with a mug of coffee and a pitcher of cream to Barry's table. "Anything else this morning? Muffin? Croissant?"

"Nah. Thanks, Lucky. Don't have much appetite. I am kinda worried about Hank though. It's not like him not to get out in the morning. I think I'll just have my coffee and check on him on my way back home." He took a sip from his mug. "Where's your grandfather today?"

"Jack's here. He's in the storeroom. He'll be out in a minute." As if speaking his name caused him to appear, Jack pushed through the swinging door from the corridor.

"Lucky, my girl," Jack said breathlessly. "Pull that sign out of the window."

"What?" Lucky looked up, surprised.

"The sign." Jack was visibly excited. "Hide that damn sign. I spotted Flo Sullivan pulling into the back lot behind the restaurant."

Lucky sighed. "Jack . . ."

"If you don't," he threatened, "I'm leaving and I won't be back."

Lucky hurried to the front window and grabbed the HELP WANTED sign. She rushed back to the counter and slipped the sign onto a narrow shelf underneath.

"What's the matter, Jack?" Barry chuckled. "Afraid of a tiny little woman like that?"

Jack shook his head. "You don't know the half of it," he grumbled as he pushed through the swinging door to return to the storeroom.

The front door of the By the Spoonful Soup Shop flew open, the glass panes rattling in their frames as Flo Sullivan, her mop of neon orange hair glowing in the sunshine, entered. "Hi, Lucky. Where's Jack?" she called gaily.

Chapter 2

A BREEZE RUFFLED the surface of the pond, creating a field of sparkling water. The early April day was cool and windy but the stand of trees nearby offered some protection from the chill air. Guy Bessette followed the trail to the edge of the pond. He glanced over his shoulder to make sure Tommy was keeping pace with him. Guy carried two fishing rods, his well-used one and a smaller one he had purchased for the boy.

Guy smiled to himself and shook his head. Here he was, a single guy, didn't even have a girlfriend, yet he was playing dad to Tommy Evans. When Tommy's mother had fallen ill more than a year ago, Tommy had taken to hanging around Guy's auto shop in the village. *It's funny*, Guy thought, *I've had more fun doing things with Tommy than I ever had when I was a kid myself.*

"Hurry up, Tommy. You've got the bait, right?"

"Yup," Tommy replied, his shorter legs moving fast to keep up with Guy's stride.

"We couldn't have picked a better day. It's still cool. Best time of year to catch trout."

Tommy looked at him dubiously. "You sure we'll catch something?'

"Well . . ." Guy paused at the water's edge. "I can't be sure, but this is perfect weather for brook trout. I've caught 'em here before. One time I even got a bass. This is probably our best chance before the water gets too warm."

"Why's that?" Tommy asked.

"'Cause brook trout like cold water, maybe around sixty degrees. They go deeper if the water gets too warm." Guy dropped his backpack on the sandy soil. He had prepared sandwiches and iced tea for their lunch. Tommy's mother, Karen, looked relieved when Guy had suggested he and Tommy spend Saturday fishing. She was back on her feet now, healthy and getting strong, but Guy suspected she didn't yet have the energy to keep a young rambunctious boy entertained.

"Pass me that can of worms, will ya?" Guy asked.

"Sure." Tommy giggled as he looked into the can of squirmy creatures.

"Now, here's what we do. We put one of these little guys on the end of our hook, like this . . ."

"Can I do that?"

"Okay." Guy held out the end of the line for Tommy. "It's all yours. I'll hold the hook and you can do the bait."

Tommy reached in and grasped a slippery worm. He hesitated and looked up at Guy. "Does this hurt them?" he asked seriously.

"I never really thought about it." Guy's brow furrowed. "I guess it might."

Tommy let the worm drop back into the can. "Maybe we can use something else?"

Guy sighed. "Well, I have some lures but I didn't bring 'em today. I've always used worms 'cause they're cheap and they work good." Tommy still didn't look convinced. "Tell you what. I understand how you feel. Next time we come out here, I'll bring my best lures that the fish might like just as much as worms."

"Okay," Tommy replied regretfully. "I can do this."

Concentrating, he carefully pushed the hook into the worm. "There," he grimaced, "I did it."

"Okay. You did good. Now, we'll weigh down this line and you stand back a little. You want to swing it out like this." Guy demonstrated and then reeled in the fishing line. "Now you give it a try."

Tommy swung his rod and watched as the weight plopped the line into the water. "I didn't get it out as far as you."

"That's all right. You did fine." Guy eyed the short wooden pier with a rowboat tied to the side. "Tell you what, if we don't get any nibbles soon, we can move over to the end of the pier and try there."

"Can we go out in that boat?" Tommy asked hopefully.

"Maybe. We'll see. The man who rents them isn't here. And it's a little early in the season. The other boats are in the boathouse over on the other side of the pond."

"I've never been in a boat before," Tommy remarked wistfully.

Guy smiled. "Really? Well, it's high time then. If we can't do it today, I will definitely take you on a boat ride. You can help me row and we can go out to that little island out there." Guy nodded in the direction of the small parcel of land covered with trees in the middle of the pond.

"I wanna play pirates when we're in the boat." Tommy gazed at the island. "What's out there anyway?"

"Not much. Just some trees and things."

"Can we park our boat and walk around?"

"Sure."

"Have you ever gone out to the island?"

"Uh . . ." Guy thought a moment. "No. I don't think I have. I've been in these boats before but I never stopped there. It'll be a first for me too."

The man and the boy stood patiently, holding their rods for several minutes. Guy remembered he had brought two small folding chairs, which were still in the back of his car.

"Guy?" Tommy asked.

"Yes?"

"I have to . . . I have to go."

"Ah. Okay." Guy nodded. "Tell you what. Reel in your line and we'll go into the woods a bit. Then I want to go back to the car to get us those two folding chairs."

"I can go by myself," Tommy insisted.

"I know you can. But I don't think it's a good idea to go into the woods alone. I won't look. I'll just stay close. All right?"

"Okay." Tommy sighed. Guy was beginning to sound just like his mother.

Guy followed the boy into the stand of trees behind them. Tommy took a meandering pathway searching for just the right spot. Finally, he reached a tree trunk that met with his approval and turned, looking over his shoulder at Guy.

"Okay. I'm not looking." Guy turned his back, waiting for Tommy to give him an all clear. After a minute Guy shoved his hands in the pockets of his jacket. This was taking a while. Finally, he said, "You done, Tommy?"

"Yup."

Guy heard the sound of a zipper and then quiet. Then the rustling of leaves. "Hey," Tommy shouted. "Look what I found!"

Guy turned around. Tommy appeared from behind a bush holding a woman's shoe, high-heeled and black. Guy reached out and took the shoe from the boy's hand. "Where did you find this?" he demanded. The shoe looked almost brand new.

"Over there." Tommy pointed at a spot near a small clearing. "I think it belongs to that lady."

"Lady?" A chill ran up Guy's spine. "What lady?"

"Shhh. I think she's sleeping."

The hairs on the back of Guy's neck stood at attention. "Stay right here, Tommy. Don't move," he ordered.

Guy stepped slowly into the clearing and turned in a circle, carefully scanning the underbrush. Something colorful caught his eye. A bright splash of color. He walked forward a few steps and pushed back the branches of a thick bush. The woman lay on her side as if asleep. Her eyes were closed. A dark purple mark encircled her neck.

Chapter 3

HANK NORTHCROSS SAT in his favorite armchair, the one he always used when settling in with a good book on a quiet evening. His breathing was shallow. The last thing he'd be able to do right now would be to focus on reading anything. Inwardly he fumed. He had drawn the curtains and locked the front door. When the phone had rung, he knew it was his friend, Barry, calling to see if he was ready to walk down the hill to the Spoonful. He had answered the phone, but only because if he hadn't, Barry would have become worried and knocked on his door. He couldn't face Barry or anyone else for that matter. His emotions were in a jumble. He was angry. No, furious was a better way to put it. *How dare she*, he thought. How dare she rip his heart out and ruin the most important thing in his life? And how dare she think she could worm her way back into his good graces? Not a chance in hell! Not if hell froze over. He picked up the newspaper and read the article again. He shook his head. *What colossal nerve the woman had.* Hank flung the newspaper away in disgust and kicked the small table in front of him, sending it careening across the room. He'd show her.

Chapter 4

"WHO?" LUCKY ASKED, leaning over the counter.

"Hilary Stone," Elizabeth replied. "Have you heard of her?"

Lucky groaned. "I certainly have. Just this morning. Marjorie was in here talking nonstop about her and her book." The lunch rush had ended, and Elizabeth Dove, Snowflake's mayor, had come by for a quick bowl of soup before returning to her office.

Elizabeth chuckled. "Well, I'm glad I wasn't the only one who hadn't heard of her. The woman who called me this morning acted as if I had been banished to the planet Mars for the past year."

"Who called you? And why? Sure you don't want half a sandwich or anything?"

"I'm sure, dear. I'm fine." Elizabeth took a last sip of her cream of asparagus soup. "This is fantastic. Something new from Sage?"

"Yes, his latest invention. I love it too." Lucky leaned over the counter, "But tell me about your phone call."

"Well, apparently, Ms. Stone is the hottest thing to hit the publishing world in the past two decades. She's the author of *Murder Comes Calling.* Her publicist called me from New York last week and acted as if I had been in solitary confinement for not knowing about her or her book. It's number one on the bestseller list and has been for several months, which, I guess, is quite an achievement."

"Why did her publicist call you, of all people?"

"The author, now that she's so famous and popular, has decided to purchase a home in Snowflake. She's looking for a quiet place to write and avoid her public. Her people at the publishing house want to smooth the way for her and they've set up some sort of a book event, book signing for her. I'm sure you've seen the ads."

"I still don't get why they'd call you," Lucky replied.

"I don't either. Maybe because I'm mayor of Snowflake and Hilary Stone is such a big celebrity." Elizabeth shrugged. "But I referred her to Eleanor Jensen at the realty office. They've already been in touch with her for their venue. I don't know why they just didn't call her again if the author's decided to purchase a home. I'm sure Eleanor will be able to show her several properties," Elizabeth continued. "She and her retinue are all staying at the Drake House rather than the Snowflake Resort. Barbara Drake is thrilled. I know she can use the business now that the ski season is over."

The bell over the door jingled. Horace Winthorpe, now one of the Spoonful's regulars, stood on the threshold. "Hey, Horace," Lucky called out.

Horace held the door open, leading Cicero, his dog, inside. He approached the counter and took a stool next to Elizabeth.

Elizabeth turned to Horace. "I was just telling Lucky about the phone call I received from Hilary Stone's publicist."

"Ah, I heard about all that. Imagine a famous writer like that coming to Snowflake."

"Not just visiting, Horace. She plans to purchase a home here," Lucky offered.

"Oh. Really? Hmmm. I'm not sure how I feel about that."

Lucky passed Horace a hunk of chicken meat wrapped in a napkin for Cicero, who gobbled it instantly.

"I hope it doesn't bring hordes of fans and followers to our little village."

"I think that's why she picked Snowflake," Elizabeth said. "She wants peace and privacy."

"Good. Let's hope that continues," Horace replied. Retired from teaching, Horace had moved to Snowflake for the very same purpose. Now that he had the time he had always yearned for, he was working steadily on his book about the Revolutionary War years in Vermont. When Lucky's parents had been killed in a car accident a little over two years before and she wasn't able to pay the mortgages, Horace arrived in town. He needed a place to live and she was happy to rent her parents' home to him.

"I should be on my way," Elizabeth said. "I have to get to a town council meeting." She smiled at Lucky. "I'll chat with you soon, dear. Bye, Horace."

Horace stood as Elizabeth rose. "Good-bye."

Lucky blew a kiss in Elizabeth's direction as the older woman left the restaurant. Elizabeth had been her parents' best friend and had offered so much help when she had first returned to town to take over her parents' restaurant. Elizabeth had truly become a second mother.

"What can I get you, Horace?"

"What do you have for specials today?" Barry asked.

"We've got a fantastic tomato-based Southwestern chicken soup and a cream of asparagus, and Sage also made a chicken and almond soup this morning."

"That sounds marvelous. I'll try a bowl of the cream of asparagus." Horace swiveled on his stool and spotted Jack taking a break at the front table. "Maybe I can talk Jack into a game of chess before he gets busy." Horace rose from the stool and headed toward the table where Jack sat reading the newspaper.

Lucky finished laying placemats and silverware on the counter as a few more customers arrived and took seats at the tables. Meg, the Spoonful's young waitress, returned from the kitchen and took their orders. It was shaping up to be a busy day. The bell over the door jingled again and

Lucky saw a tall figure and a shorter one on the threshold—Guy Bessette and Tommy Evans. She waved a greeting.

Guy smiled and sat at a counter stool. Tommy hopped up on one next to his friend. "Hey, Lucky. How's everything?"

"Fine, Guy. What would you like?"

"Well, let's see"—he glanced at Tommy—"we were up real early this morning. So this is way past lunchtime for us and we're starving. How about two bowls of the carrot and ginger soup and half sandwiches of chicken salad? How's that sound, Tommy?"

Tommy nodded eagerly.

"We'll grab a table, since it's still quiet." He turned to Tommy. "You want to set up a game of checkers at the corner table?"

"Sure," Tommy agreed and slid off his stool, heading to the same corner where Hank and Barry sat every morning.

Guy's expression became serious. He leaned closer to Lucky. "I had to cancel our fishing plans this morning and call Nate."

Lucky raised her eyebrows. "Why? What happened?"

Guy sighed. "We got to the pond early. I wanted to take Tommy out for the day, but . . ." Guy glanced over his shoulder to make sure Tommy couldn't overhear. "See, Tommy found a shoe. Almost new. He came back and told me he saw a woman sleeping in the woods near the pond. Only, she wasn't sleeping, Lucky. I think she was strangled."

"Did Tommy see that?" Lucky asked, shocked.

"He did. But I'm not sure he realized what he was seeing at first. I went further in to have a look around. Something about the shoe . . . it looked too new and it wasn't the kind a woman would be wearing to go hiking around the pond or anything. Thank heavens Tommy didn't see anything more gruesome."

"What did you do?"

"I told him we couldn't fish today. That the woman had been hurt and we had to call Nate at the police station and wait there for him. I took Tommy back to the car and then stepped away to call Nate so Tommy couldn't hear. He was real disappointed our outing got canceled just as we were getting started."

"That's so horrible, Guy. But it sounds like you handled it with minimum trauma. Why should the poor kid have to see something like that? Any idea who the woman is?"

Guy shook his head. "Nope. A total stranger. Never seen her before. Attractive, maybe middle-aged or a little younger. Hard to tell. I didn't want to take a closer look."

Lucky shuddered involuntarily. "Maybe Nate will come by later and chat with Jack. He might know more by then." More customers were arriving. Lucky picked up Guy's orders from the hatch.

"I'll take care of it, Lucky," Guy said, taking the plates from her.

"Thanks, Guy."

Guy carried the dishes to the corner table to join Tommy, who had already prepared the checkerboard.

Jack placed his newspaper to the side, returning to his seat behind the cash register, and Horace moved across the room to join Guy and Tommy. A few tables had filled but the counter was still unoccupied. As Meg walked by, Lucky signaled to her that she'd give her a hand if needed. Meg nodded curtly in acknowledgment. Lucky had noticed that Meg didn't seem her normal self today. It was no surprise. Janie, the Spoonful's other young waitress, had left a few months before to attend college in another town. Since then, Meg had handled all the waitressing duties, with Lucky pitching in as much as she could. Lucky had advertised anonymously in the local paper, the *Snowflake Gazette*, for a replacement for Janie, and the HELP WANTED sign was propped in the front window, but so far, she had had no nibbles. Lucky had made sure to replace the sign in the window as soon as Flo Sullivan had gone. Flo, years before, had been an employee when Lucky's parents ran the Spoonful. Ever since that time, Flo had set her cap at Jack and had made his life a misery. So much so that Jack always made a run for it when he saw Flo approaching. The last thing Jack would be able to handle was Flo resuming her waitressing duties at the restaurant.

Sage, the Spoonful's chef, was busily lining up orders on the hatch behind the counter. Lucky grabbed the prepared dishes and carried them to the first table. She double-checked the orders and delivered food all around. When she slipped back behind the counter, she heard Meg's raised voice in the kitchen.

"I didn't ask for a tomato and chicken. I wanted a tomato and turkey salad," Meg argued.

Lucky peeked through the hatch. Sage's eyes were wide at Meg's outburst. Meg, normally shy and quiet, seemed to be on her last nerve. Her face was red and her glasses had slipped down her nose. Meg had nursed a not very secret long-term crush on Sage. And Sage, always gallant, had treated Meg in a friendly and courteous manner, careful not to encourage her feelings. Since Sage and Sophie had married, Meg had adjusted to the new reality, making her outburst of the moment even more shocking.

"Okay. Okay," Sage said. "Musta been my mistake. I'll fix it."

"Good, glad to hear it," Meg grumbled. She turned away and pushed through the swinging door, slamming it loudly against the wall. Lucky caught Sage's eye through the hatch. He shook his head and shrugged, indicating his surprise at Meg's behavior.

Several more patrons arrived and took seats at the counter. Lucky busied herself filling coffee cups and orders for the next several minutes. When she'd finished, she realized that their customers were looking around, wondering when their food would arrive. Lucky peeked through the hatch. Sage was hard at work in the kitchen and Meg was nowhere to be seen. Lucky grabbed the next few orders and bustled them to the tables that Meg had deserted. When everyone had received their food and the counter was quiet for a moment, she hurried down the corridor and peeked in the small office. It was empty. Where had Meg gone? The only other rooms in the restaurant were the bathroom and the storage closet. Lucky opened the door of the storage closet first. Meg was on a stool, her head on her knees.

"Meg, what's wrong?" Lucky touched her shoulder.

Meg stood. At her full height, she barely reached Lucky's shoulder. Meg's round face was blotchy and flushed. She took a deep breath. "I quit."

"Whaaat?" Lucky asked in alarm.

"You heard me. I quit. I can't do this anymore. I can't handle everything in the front, not without Janie," she wailed.

"Oh." Lucky sighed. "I know. It's tough and you're right, but please don't quit. I'll find someone, I promise."

"When?"

"Soon. I swear." Lucky had no idea how she was going to keep her promise, but she'd absolutely have to find a way. The only person who was always asking about openings was Flo and that would be impossible where Jack was concerned. Hiring Flo was out of the question. Not unless she wanted to watch her grandfather have a nervous breakdown.

"I swear. I will, Meg. I'll hire the next person who inquires."

"And if nobody asks about the job?" Meg crossed her arms, a sullen look on her face.

"Then I'll . . . I don't know, but I'll figure it out. I promise you."

Meg tossed her head. Her glasses were steamed up from crying. "Three days. That's my notice. If there isn't someone else here in three days, I'm leaving." Meg pushed past Lucky and stomped down the corridor to the front of the restaurant.

Lucky rubbed her temples. She could feel a pounding headache coming on. This was so unlike Meg. She hurried to the front room in Meg's wake and returned to the counter. She had no idea how she'd be able to find another waitress in the village so soon.

Chapter 5

LUCKY SAT AT the table by the front window with Jack. The restaurant was quiet. The dinner rush was about to begin. She nibbled on a grilled cheese sandwich to fortify herself for the rest of the evening. Meg had disappeared again, probably hiding out in the office or the closet. The girl hadn't spoken a word to anyone since her earlier outburst. Lucky couldn't blame her one bit for the way she was feeling. It was just that Meg's recent behavior was so uncharacteristic. If Lucky had to name one person who never became ruffled or upset or cranky, who was the sweetest person in the world, it was Meg Findly.

The bell over the door jingled. Lucky sighed. Not even ten minutes for a break. She glanced up. A rather plump fortyish woman with brightly dyed carrot red hair, packed into a flowered dress and wobbling on high heels stood in the doorway. She reached over and grasped the HELP WANTED sign from the window. Her sharp eyes darted around the restaurant and finally settled on Jack. She made a beeline for his table and plopped down on a chair next to him, sidling as close as possible.

Jack looked up in surprise.

"*You* must be the man in charge," she gushed, batting what looked to Lucky to be false eyelashes.

Jack's eyes opened wide. He sat up straighter in his chair. "Well, not really . . . Lucky here . . ." He trailed off.

The woman shot an appraising glance at Lucky then turned back to Jack. "I always like to deal with the man of the house if you don't mind." She smiled widely. A miasma of heavy perfume bathed the surrounding air. "I saw this sign in the window and I thought, my Lord, the angels are watchin' out for me. I am *meant* to be workin' here."

Jack was transfixed by the strange woman. Lucky cleared her throat. There was no way she'd hire this outrageous person. And rude too. After all, this was her restaurant. The woman could at least have had the courtesy to be polite and not ignore her.

"We . . . uh . . . we have several applicants we're considering . . ."

The woman turned to look at Lucky. In a harsher voice, she said, "I doubt they'd have *my* experience."

"And that is?" Lucky struggled to keep a disbelieving tone from her voice.

Jack was staring at Lucky, as if to say, *Don't be so rude.*

"I've been waitressing most of my life." The woman shook her head and the red curls wiggled. Bright yellow plastic hoops hung from her ears. They matched her patent leather shoes and purse.

"Really!" Lucky responded. She glanced at the counter where Meg stood, staring furiously, her arms crossed. Lucky backtracked quickly. If she turned this woman away, Meg would never forgive her. "Uh, well, in that case why don't you come into the office with me and fill out an application if you're interested in working here."

"Apply?" The woman's voice rose two octaves. "Apply? Honey, I'm here. Now." She turned back to Jack, who still sat staring at the strange woman. A flush had crept up his cheeks. "I'm Nanette," she smiled coyly. "Nanette Simms." She wiggled her shoulders, allowing an ample amount of cleavage to show. "I've been livin' in Bournmouth but"—she batted her eyes a few more times—"I'm sure you can tell I'm a Southern Belle . . . originally, that is." She smiled more seductively this time at Jack. He, in turn, stared at the woman as if he had never seen a live female in his life.

Lucky groaned inwardly. *What a floozy*, she thought. She glanced at Meg once more, aware that Meg had heard every word spoken at the table. There was no choice. She stood. "Why don't we go into the office and I can take down your information. We usually require a month's probationary period before a position becomes permanent," she lied. She glanced quickly at Jack but he hadn't heard a word she'd said.

Nanette wiggled her curls once more. "If you insist, darlin.'" Lucky heard her heels clacking against the floor as the woman followed her down the corridor and into the office.

Chapter 6

"JENSEN REALTY," ELEANOR announced brightly as she picked up the phone.

The voice on the other end of the line introduced herself. "Hello, I'm Audra Klemack. "I'm the publicist for Hilary Stone at Lexington Avenue Publishing. As you might know, Ms. Stone is the author of the bestselling thriller *Murder Comes Calling*."

"Oh!" Eleanor replied. "Yes, I have certainly heard of her. I've spoken with her assistant to arrange the venue for her book signing in Snowflake. In fact, I can't wait to read her book. What can I do for you?"

"This is somewhat confidential for now, but Ms. Stone is looking for a property to buy in Snowflake. She's hoping to find a home that's private and secluded while she works on her next novel. You were recommended to me by your mayor, Elizabeth Dove."

"Oh, how nice of Elizabeth," Eleanor said, knowing full well that her realty was the only one in Snowflake. "I'm sure I can show Ms. Stone several properties that she'd be interested in." Eleanor hoped against hope that the Stone entourage hadn't heard of the body discovered at the pond earlier this morning. *Oh, how could they?* she thought. The news had spread like wildfire through town in no time at all, but there was no way someone calling from New York could possibly know. Besides, whatever had happened, had happened at the pond, outside of the town proper. It hadn't actually happened *in* Snowflake.

"That's terrific," Audra Klemack replied. "I'm on the road now but I'll be in town in a few hours. I'd like to see what you have available."

"Today?" Eleanor barely kept the squeal out of her voice. She wasn't really sure what state some of the listed properties were in.

"Yes. Ms. Stone is already in town, but I'll be arriving later this evening. I'm charged with selecting the best of the best for her to look at."

"I see. Well, can I ask you if there are any special requirements?"

"There are. Ms. Stone, you see, is a rather particular person." Eleanor groaned inwardly. "The house must have *at least* four bedrooms, a private drive and a wood-burning fireplace, and of course, an up-to-date kitchen with all new appliances."

"All right." Eleanor mentally reviewed the listings she had available. "I'm sure I have a few homes that will meet her requirements."

"Thank you."

"And please tell Ms. Stone she'll be very welcome in Snowflake. She has many fans here."

"Good to hear. This event has been publicized all over the state and beyond, so we expect a very large crowd. Have all the arrangements been taken care of?"

"Oh, my! Yes. Everyone in town is very excited," Eleanor remarked. "And everything's been taken care of. As I'm sure you're aware, I've arranged the use of the meeting hall at the Congregational Church, which should certainly be adequate."

"Your town doesn't seem to have a bookstore. And I've been told the library is very small?"

"That's correct. Sadly we can't boast a bookstore in Snowflake."

Audra sighed loudly over the connection. "Very well. We'll just have to make do with the church.

Eleanor wondered if Hilary Stone had the slightest idea just how small their village was. But best not to question their good luck in attracting business.

"Thank you, Ms. . . ." The publicist trailed off.

"Jensen. Eleanor Jensen, but please call me Eleanor."

"Thank you, Eleanor. I'm looking forward to getting together with you. I'll call as soon as I reach town. Hilary will be very happy to hear she has local fans."

"Very good. I'll see you soon. Please call my office when you arrive. I'm right off Broadway and I'm easy to find." Eleanor hung the phone up. She sighed and reached for the folders containing flyers for all the available properties for sale. There'd be nothing in the main part of town, but there were two homes in the Lincoln Heights area of Snowflake and a few more closer to the Resort near Ridgeline that were larger. It would be wonderful to make a sale this week, she thought.

She placed the folders in the center of her desk and slipped on a sweater. She checked the clock. Pastor Wilson should be in his office right now. She'd just run over and make sure that everything was clean and ready to go at the meeting hall. She grabbed her purse and locked the office door behind her, hurrying the few blocks to the Village Green and the Congregational Church.

Chapter 7

LUCKY WAITED PATIENTLY while Nanette filled out the employment application. She had had to rummage through the file drawer and locate the forms, since no new employees had been hired at the restaurant for a long time. Not since Meg had joined them, right after Janie had started working there.

"Let me find you a pen."

"Oh, no need. I have my favorite lucky pen right here." The woman pulled a small ballpoint pen out of her yellow purse. It was topped with a plastic flower in the same color.

"Did you mention you're staying in Bournmouth? Won't that be rather a long commute for you?" Lucky asked.

"Oh, ah'm stayin' with relatives over there but it's just temporary. As soon as I can, I'll be looking for a place to stay in town. Can you recommend anything?"

"There are a few small apartment buildings in Snowflake. I don't know if there are any vacancies, but there's a very nice building over on Chestnut that you could inquire about." Lucky wasn't about to mention a vacancy in her own building around the corner on Maple Street. This woman caused her to grit her teeth. She certainly didn't want to run into her in her very own building. Sage, their chef, and Sophie, her best friend, who had married last spring, were renting an apartment in the building on Chestnut. If Nanette ended up there, hopefully they would forgive her for recommending it. She couldn't put her finger on exactly what it was about the woman that annoyed her so. Right now, she had to admit, she was feeling like a judgmental snob and she couldn't afford to be choosy, not if it meant losing Meg.

"I'd like to make a copy of your driver's license and identification for our records. And whenever you move, please let me know your new address. As I mentioned, we have a probationary period of thirty days before a hire is considered permanent."

"That's fine," Nanette replied. She signed the form with a flourish and pushed it across the desk to Lucky. "Ah'm afraid I don't have my big wallet with me today." She smiled, holding up the tiny yellow purse.

"You don't have a driver's license with you?"

"No. But I promise I'll bring it in as soon as I possibly can. Should I start tomorrow?"

"Uh, well, if you like, you can start today. Meg can show you around and show you where everything you'll need is stored. How does that sound?" Lucky did her best to put some warmth into her voice. She really hadn't liked the way this woman had been looking at Jack.

Chapter 8

ELEANOR TAPPED ON the door to Pastor Wilson's office.

"Come in," the pastor called out.

Eleanor turned the knob and peeked through the door. "I hope I'm not disturbing you?'

"Oh, hello, Eleanor. Not at all." Pastor Wilson rose from his chair, knocking several books to the floor. "Don't mind all this . . ." he said, waving his arm over a desk buried in books and paper. "You've saved me from writer's block with my next sermon. An interruption is gratefully appreciated."

"I just wanted to make sure everything was set with the church hall for Wednesday evening."

A confused look passed across the pastor's face. "The hall?"

A frisson of fear traveled up Eleanor's spine. "Yes. Don't you remember? We talked about booking the hall for Hilary Stone's author event."

The pastor's face looked completely blank.

"You do know who Hilary Stone is?" Eleanor demanded.

The pastor furrowed his brow and stared into space for a moment. "Is she one of my parishioners?"

"No." Eleanor's heart sank. "She's a famous writer. We talked about this a few weeks ago. She wrote *Murder Comes Calling*. You've heard of that book, I'm sure."

Pastor Wilson shook his head. "I don't believe so. What was that title again? *Murder Comes Calling*? What sort of a book is that?"

"A very popular murder mystery."

"Ah. Well, that's not my usual reading fare." The pastor smiled. "And frankly it's not something I'd want to read, not with the news I heard this morning about a dead woman found up at the pond." A sorrowful look passed across his face.

"Yes, terrible," Eleanor replied impatiently.

"But what were you saying about Wednesday night?" The pastor looked at her quizzically.

"I arranged the use of the hall for the event that night with you," Eleanor replied patiently.

"Wednesday night?" Pastor Wilson squeaked. He looked down and rummaged through a pile of papers for his calendar. "I thought . . ."

Eleanor waited, a knot of dread forming in her stomach.

"I thought that was *next* month." He continued to shuffle papers around. "Oh, here it is." He held a small calendar up triumphantly. "Let me just check."

Eleanor took a deep breath to stay calm.

"Oh, my mistake, I'm afraid. I wrote it down for next month."

"But . . . I've told them they could have the hall for their event."

"Oh, dear," the pastor replied.

Eleanor felt an urge to rush across the room and throttle him. She quickly suppressed the thought. Pastor Wilson was one of the kindest people on earth. "What do you mean?"

"Well, it's not possible," he replied.

"Why not?" Eleanor's panic was almost full blown.

"Come. I'll show you." He held the door open and indicated Eleanor should follow him.

Eleanor followed the pastor dutifully out of his office and down the long hall to the double doors that gave entrance to the meeting hall. He pushed the doors open and stepped inside. He gestured to the chaos in the large room. Waterproof coverings were laid over the entire floor. The plaster ceiling was stained with large dark spots. A huge scaffold stood in the center of the room, taking up most of the available space, and heavy cloth tarps hung over the tables and benches.

"What's all this?" she asked.

"We've had a terrible leak. It's rained and, of course, with all the snow melt . . ." He trailed off. "We can't possibly hold any events here right now. The roofers are just starting their repairs. We can't risk any more water damage." Pastor Wilson shrugged. "We could certainly use a donation for our coffers, but it's just not possible until these repairs are finished."

Eleanor groaned. "This is a disaster."

"I'm so sorry about the mix-up. Had I realized the event was this month, I would have called you right away."

"I have no idea what I can tell them. What am I to do?" Eleanor moaned.

"I'm sure you'll think of something," the pastor replied brightly.

Eleanor nodded. Her stomach was in knots. "Never mind then," she replied. She turned away and left the hall by the side door without another word. She half walked and half stumbled around the building to the Village Green. *This is absolutely dreadful*, she thought. The author and her entourage had arrived early and were already lodged at the Drake House. If she let the Stone group down, they might decamp for the Resort and its large conference rooms. And if the book signing took place at the top of the mountain, the Drake House would lose the business, the town would lose the business and she might lose a sale. If there was going to be a popular event, then Snowflake itself should host it, not that corporate monstrosity at the top of the mountain. A thought occurred to her. The Spoonful! Why hadn't she thought of the restaurant before? It had a large front room. Glass windows where, even if people were lined up to wait, they could watch the activities inside. That just might solve the problem. She pulled out her cell phone and dialed the number of the restaurant.

Chapter 9

ELIAS SLID HIS desk drawer open and stared at the small velvet-covered box. He reached in and pulled it out, lifting the lid to stare at the jeweled ring. An antique diamond in an old-fashioned square setting nestled inside. He touched his finger gently to the gem. Then he closed the box and replaced it in the drawer. He took a deep breath and told himself he wasn't nervous. There was nothing wrong with sliding the drawer open and looking at the ring—only a few times today. He wasn't exactly sure why he had brought this to his office at the Clinic. Perhaps because this spot was a few yards closer to the By the Spoonful Soup Shop and Lucky Jamieson. He had finally worked up his courage and decided that this was the right time to propose and he wanted to do it properly. He was sure he wasn't nervous. It needed a romantic setting, dinner and candlelight. Was that too mundane? Maybe at the top of the mountain overlooking the village? No. Too chilly and damp still. A special weekend out of town perhaps? New York? A hansom ride in Central Park? Now, that would be something to think about.

He pulled his calendar closer to him on the desk and tried to calculate dates. Next weekend might be a possibility, if he could talk Lucky into taking a few days off. He knew things were tight at the Spoonful. She had been trying to find a replacement for Janie, but maybe he could talk to Sage and Sophie and enlist their help. They would certainly understand and keep a secret. Perhaps Sophie would be willing to cover for Lucky for a couple or three days. He checked his calendar again. No, that would never do. He had three patients scheduled for upcoming surgery and he'd need to see them over that weekend. It wouldn't be right not to check in on them. Two were elective surgeries that could be rescheduled, but the third was rather serious. He didn't want to leave his patients in the lurch, wondering why he hadn't made his rounds.

Frustrated, he took a deep breath. He really had no idea what Lucky's answer would be. There was no doubt in his mind that she was the right person for him, and no doubt that she loved him. But would she say yes? He had been wanting to pop the question for months, but somehow the timing was never right. And then, of course, they had had that dustup over a year ago when he was sure it was all over between them. It was his own stupid fault that had happened. But Lucky had reacted strangely. He had been sure she would understand the situation and sure she would know there couldn't be anyone else in his life but her, yet she had bolted like a frightened colt. He wasn't at all sure if her answer would be yes, but it was time. It was high time. He didn't want to spend the rest of his life rattling around an empty house alone. He wanted them to be together, to make a home, to build a life together. He took a deep breath to calm his nerves. He'd just have to find the right spot and the right moment. He wanted everything to be perfect and romantic. Something they could look back on years from now and reminisce over.

The buzzer on his phone jolted him from his daydream. He pressed the button. "Yes?"

Rosemary's voice filled the room. "Mrs. Cartwright's in three."

"I'll be right there." He tucked the tiny jewel box under some loose papers at the very back of the drawer. Then he stood, buttoned his white coat and headed for examining room three.

LUCKY FLIPPED OVER the sign at the front door. The Spoonful was closed. Meg had spent most of the afternoon showing Nanette the ropes, and to the woman's credit, she seemed to catch on quickly to the restaurant's routine. She had been kept too busy to flirt with Jack, who had spent most of the day behind the cash register. Lucky would glance at her grandfather occasionally, aware that his eyes were following Nanette's progress around the tables. Sage had gone home, as had Meg. And hopefully, now that Nanette had been hired, Meg would be in better spirits. Lucky peered through the glass panes of the front door. Nate's cruiser pulled up in front of the restaurant. She opened the door and waited for Snowflake's chief of police to climb out.

"Hi, Lucky. How are you doing?" he asked as he walked through the door.

"Good, Nate. Come on in. I'll fix you something." Lucky locked the door behind him.

"Thanks. I sure could use a bite. I doubt Susanna's had a chance to fix anything for dinner. She's been on the phone all day calling everyone about this mystery writer who's coming to town." Nate shook his head. "Meanwhile, I've got a real mystery on my hands. I'll just visit with Jack for a while." Nate sat heavily in the chair at Jack's table.

Lucky warmed a bowl of chili in the kitchen microwave and fixed a half sandwich of chicken breast and sprouts with mayonnaise for Nate. She arranged the dishes and silverware on a tray and carried it back to the table where the two men sat. She was hoping Nate would fill them in on the discovery of the dead woman at the pond that morning.

"We heard a little bit about it, Nate." Jack said.

Nate smiled gratefully as Lucky placed the dishes on the placemat. "Thanks."

"How'd you hear?" he said, his mouth full with his first bite.

"Guy Bessette came in with Tommy right after it happened. I guess he wanted to cheer the kid up when their fishing excursion got cut short."

"Yup. Guy did a good job keeping the boy away from it all. He waited until I showed up. I had to keep them there for a while to get all the details. Then he took off with Tommy. Bad scene."

"I can imagine," Lucky said. "It's so frightening! Have you been able to identify this woman yet?"

"Not yet, but I'm sure we will. No purse with the body. Looks like she was dumped there. We're looking at vehicle tracks and footprints. Going through missing persons lists, all that stuff." Nate shook his head. "Feels like there's no place safe anymore. Guy tries to take a little kid fishing and what does he find?"

"He said he saw a ligature mark around her neck. He thought she was strangled."

"Most likely, he's right. That'll probably be the cause of death. We found a length of plastic cord nearby, but it may not be related to the crime scene." Nate took a bite of his sandwich.

Lucky shuddered. "Guy told me about Tommy finding the shoe. How was the woman dressed?"

"Well dressed, but sort of casual, maybe what you'd call business casual. Nice clothes. Almost new shoes. Probably works somewhere around, or maybe close by . . . Lincoln Falls or Bournmouth. Clothing didn't seem to be disturbed."

"How old do you think she was?" Lucky asked.

"My guess, maybe mid-forties."

"Any idea how long she'd been there?" Jack asked.

Nate shook his head. "Hard to say, but I'd guess about a day . . . maybe longer. And whatever happened, I don't think it happened there. I think whoever did this thought it'd be a safe place to hide the crime."

Lucky shuddered involuntarily. "It's so beautiful up at the pond. I'd hate to think this would spoil things for all the people who go there."

"I agree with you. With luck, we'll get her identified in the next day or so, and better yet, we'll find out how she got there and who did this to her."

Chapter 10

LUCKY FINISHED LAYING placemats along the countertop, then unlocked the front door and flipped the sign over. The Spoonful was open for the day. She heard voices in the hallway. Meg and Nanette were chatting. The door to the closet gave its customary squeak as they opened it and pulled out fresh aprons. The Spoonful's aprons were yellow to match the gingham café curtains at the front window. Lucky's mother, Martha, had created the design of a steaming bowl of soup outlined in blue on the front of the aprons. It matched the yellow and blue neon sign her dad had hung in the front window.

The bell jingled as Miriam Leonard bustled in. Her face was flushed and she seemed excited. "Lucky! I just heard last night. Susanna Edgerton called me. I couldn't believe it."

"What's that?" Lucky asked. Lucky only saw Miriam occasionally now that Miriam's daughter Janie, the same Janie who had worked at the Spoonful, had left for school.

"Hilary Stone! I couldn't believe my ears. Hilary Stone is coming to Snowflake! She's such a celebrity! Are you a fan?"

Lucky shook her head and laughed. "I've been hearing

all about her, but only since yesterday. Marjorie first told me. I guess everybody in the world knows who she is except me. I must be in the minority not to have heard of her book."

"Oh, that's terrible," Miriam exclaimed. "I'll loan you my copy if you like. It's a fantastic book. Couldn't put it down. No wonder she's such an overnight sensation. It's a real thriller."

Lucky leaned over the counter. "You know, I heard from Elizabeth that she's planning to buy a home here, somewhere in Snowflake. And of course, I'm sure you'll be going to the book-signing event."

"Absolutely. And I've been calling everyone I could think of too. It's tomorrow evening. What a lot of excitement this is for us," Miriam exclaimed.

"I bought *Murder Comes Calling* a few months ago though. Do you think she'd sign a book that's already been purchased?" Marjorie asked.

"I'm sure she would," Lucky offered. "Can't see why not."

Miriam's face was wreathed in smiles. "I'm looking forward to this. Since Janie went away to college, it's been rather lonely for me. I just don't have enough to fill my days. Before, I used to do a lot of cooking, but now with Doug gone"—she smiled ruefully, referring to the death of her husband—"there's no point unless Janie's heading home for a weekend. Maybe I should think about doing something with myself. Volunteering or getting a job doing *something* . . . anything."

Lucky's ears perked up. "Are you serious about taking a job?"

"I guess." Miriam smiled ruefully. "I don't have any real skills except housekeeping and cooking, but maybe I could find something."

Lucky kicked herself. If only Miriam had stopped in the day before. She would have hired her on the spot. Instead, she had panicked and hired Nanette, whose voice and harsh laughter had already begun to grate on her nerves. Lucky only hoped Meg could manage to get along with Nanette.

"Well, I might hear of something. If I do, I'll be sure to call you." Lucky glanced over at the cash register, where her grandfather was making change for a customer. Nanette stood beside him, a proprietary hand on his shoulder. Jack's cheeks were flushed. Lucky was sure he was enjoying all the female attention but her grandfather was eighty-six years old. Everyone loved Jack, his spirit, his outlook on life, but what possible attraction did he hold for a woman at the very least forty years younger? Lucky realized she was staring. Nanette must have felt the focus because she looked up quickly and glared across the room at Lucky. She pursed her lips in a scowl and moved away from Jack and the cash register.

Lucky took a deep breath. Something about this woman kept getting under her skin. Was it her familiarity with Jack? Her aggressive behavior, or just her bad taste in clothing? She wasn't sure but Nanette was really rubbing her the wrong way. She caught Meg's eye. Meg had also been watching the activity at the cash register and had spotted Nanette's reaction. Meg's expression was somewhere between a warning that she would quit if there wasn't more help at the restaurant and at the same time confusion over Nanette's overt gestures in Jack's direction.

Miriam had followed Lucky's gaze. She leaned across the counter. "Who's that?" she whispered.

Lucky struggled to keep her voice neutral. "That's Nanette. She's a new hire . . . well, temporary for now."

"Ah," Miriam replied. Lucky was sure Miriam was too polite to comment on Nanette's skintight and low-cut dress.

Lucky took a deep breath. "What can I get you, Miriam?"

"Well, I'd love to try that new tomato pepper soup and I'll have a corn cake with that too, please."

"You got it." Lucky placed Miriam's order on the hatch, where Sage grabbed it quickly. The counter was filling up and she busied herself taking orders, filling coffee cups and clearing away dishes. When Lucky looked up next, Eleanor Jensen was sitting at the end of the counter, waving to her.

Lucky moved closer. "What would you like, Eleanor? Coffee to start?"

"Yes, please."

Lucky returned with a mug of fresh coffee. "Anything else?"

Eleanor smiled ruefully at her. "Yes. I'm here to beg."

"Excuse me?"

"I'm really desperate, Lucky. I'll be showing properties to Hilary Stone's publicist and assistant, but the venue I had arranged for her book-signing event just fell through."

"At the church? What happened?"

"Pastor Wilson thought it was next month. That's the first problem, but it would still be all right except the roof of the meeting hall has sprung a bad leak and he has workmen in there doing repairs. It's a mess. The floor is covered with tarps. That space is out of the question now. I'm just praying you would please reconsider. I don't know where else to turn."

"Reconsider? I don't understand."

"Well, when I called yesterday, I was told you wouldn't be willing to host it at the restaurant. But your space is the next best thing. The Pub is too dark and the space is broken up by the fire pit and the bar, and the library is way too small."

Lucky raised her eyebrows. "You called here yesterday?"

"Yes. I spoke to someone. Maybe that new waitress you have."

Lucky took a deep breath, "I see," she replied darkly. She fumed inwardly. Nanette had taken it upon herself to make decisions about the restaurant and had not even bothered to give her the message. She would definitely have to have a word with the woman.

"I wouldn't ask like this, but it's just that I could possibly make a sale. Stone's whole group is renting the entire second floor of the Drake House and Barbara Drake can use the business. They're making very generous offers, so money isn't a problem."

"Well . . ." Lucky thought a moment. "We'd have to close the restaurant for the evening. When are they thinking of holding this?"

"Tomorrow evening. From six o'clock to nine. It's been advertised in all the newspapers and they expect hordes of people. Our village is so small, it wouldn't be a problem for anyone to find the event down the street from the church."

Lucky stared off into space. "Tomorrow? Wow, that's

cutting it close." Lucky came to a decision. "Well, I'd have to talk to someone, her assistant maybe, about renting the space, or you can negotiate for me. I'd be happy with that." It wouldn't hurt to give Sage or Meg a night off. She was sure it would be appreciated. They could set up coffee and tea urns and she and Jack could take care of that. "Okay. I'll do it. I'll have to post a sign outside that we'll be closed tomorrow evening, but I think it would work."

"Oh, thank you, thank you! I really appreciate this. I'm doing all that I can to let them know we will handle everything they need in the village. I really don't want them giving their business to the Resort. And your restaurant would be lovely. It has such a warm homey atmosphere. And Barbara Drake will be thrilled to hear you said yes."

"I'm just wondering, Eleanor . . . wouldn't it make more sense to hold this at the Drake House? They have that dining room for their guests."

"Yes, but it's not as large as your front room and Barbara has other guests staying there on the first level. She has to consider them first, even though renting her entire second floor is such a boon."

Lucky nodded, "Okay. I understand. We'll do it then."

"I can't tell you how much I appreciate this." Eleanor reached across the counter and squeezed Lucky's hand.

"You're very welcome. Besides, I owe you. You found Horace and rented my parents' house to him. That was a huge relief for me."

"It's settled then. I'll stay in touch." Eleanor waved as she hurried through the front door.

Meg stood on the other side of the counter, her eyes wide. "Did I just hear right, Lucky? The book signing is going to be *here*? At the Spoonful?"

"Yes, that's right."

Meg's face flushed a bright pink. "You mean I can actually get to meet Hilary Stone?"

Lucky raised her eyebrows. "Don't tell me. You're a fan too?"

"Oh, yes. You know I love mysteries. *Murder Comes*

Calling is fantastic! I couldn't put it down. Do you know where the title comes from?"

Lucky shook her head. "No idea."

"It's because"—Meg leaned over the counter and whispered—"because the victims all received anonymous telephone calls days before they're killed. And they're strangled with a telephone cord. Isn't that clever?"

Lucky blinked, recalling Nate's information about the crime scene. "Yes. Clever."

"Lucky, do you think I could get the night off? I'll be here, but I don't want to have to work. I want to hear what the author has to say about her next book. And I want to get her to autograph mine."

Lucky was sure Meg's help wouldn't be needed, and giving her the night off might compensate her a little bit for all the extra work she had been doing. "Sure, that's not a problem. Enjoy the evening. Jack or Sage can help out if need be."

"Thank you, Lucky," Meg gushed. She pushed her glasses up her nose and headed for one of her tables.

Lucky turned when she heard raised voices in the kitchen. She peered through the hatch. Nanette stood at the worktable, her hands on her hips. Sage's face was dark with anger.

"Ah'm just tellin' you that the asparagus soup would be so much better with a lot more pepper added to it."

Lucky could almost see the steam coming out of Sage's ears. "If I ever want to serve tasteless crap from this kitchen, I will let you know," he replied quietly.

Nanette shrieked, "How dare you speak to me that way! You're nothin' but kitchen help. You can be replaced like that." Leaning across the worktable, she snapped pudgy fingers under his nose.

"Lucky!" Sage hollered.

Lucky rushed through the door to the kitchen, horrified that Sage would take anything this woman had to say seriously. "You"—she pointed her finger at Nanette—"in my office. Now!"

Nanette's eyes widened. She turned and stormed out of the kitchen and down the corridor.

Lucky turned to Sage. "I'm so sorry. She had no right. I'm going to have a word with her right now."

Sage shook his head. His face was beet red. "You better. Because I'm not putting up with this."

Lucky groaned inwardly. First Meg and now Sage. She stomped down the corridor to the office and shut the door behind her as she entered. "Let's get a few things straight, Nanette." She took a deep breath in an effort not to lose her temper and throw the woman out the back door.

"Yes?" Nanette sat with her hands in her lap.

"Sage is the best thing that has ever happened to this restaurant. You are not . . . ever . . . to interfere or comment on anything he does in the kitchen." She knew her face was bright red from anger. It was horrifying to think that Sage might get upset and leave. Sage never said anything, but Lucky was sure he had had offers from the Resort. Even so, he had always remained loyal to the Spoonful.

Nanette began to sniffle. Tears filled her eyes. "I'm so sorry. I didn't mean to offend anyone. I just thought Sage might appreciate my suggestions."

"Well, he doesn't. Nor does he need them. You've been hired to wait on tables, not to cook, not to criticize the chef and certainly not to upset him. Do you understand?"

"Yes, ma'am. I understand. I didn't mean anything by it. I'll go apologize to him right now."

"No. Not a good idea. The damage has been done. Please go out to the front room and watch the counter for a few minutes until I can get out there."

"Of course." Nanette rose from her chair and hurried to the door.

"Oh. And one more thing."

"Yes?"

"I understand Eleanor Jensen called here about renting the restaurant for an event. Not only did you not deliver the message to me, but you told her that wouldn't be possible."

"Well, I just figured you all are so busy that—"

Lucky cut her off. She wanted to reach across the room

and throttle the woman. "Please do not take it upon yourself to make any decisions about anything at the Spoonful."

"Well, I was sure you wouldn't want to be closing up and losing all those customers . . ."

Lucky gritted her teeth. "Please remember, it is not your business to make decisions. If anyone calls, for any reason, you are to tell me about it right away. Is that clear enough?"

Nanette sniffed. "I was only tryin' to be a help. But I understand." Her face had assumed a thoroughly chastised look as she stepped out to the corridor and shut the door behind her.

Lucky rubbed her temples and put her head in her hands. What was wrong with this woman? Flirting with Jack, ignoring the fact that Lucky was her boss and upsetting Sage. This would never do. She was sorely tempted to fire her on the spot but she was terrified Meg might quit if she did that. *Maybe things will work out*, she thought. *And maybe that's too optimistic*, was her second thought.

The phone on the desk rang. "What now?" Lucky mumbled to herself.

"Lucky?" the voice on the other end of the line said.

"Yes. Who's calling?"

"Oh. It's Barbara. Barbara Drake. It didn't sound like you at all, Lucky."

Lucky sighed. She was sure she had sounded like someone had their hands around her throat. "It's me. What can I do for you, Barbara?"

"I just wanted to call to thank you, for hosting the book signing at the Spoonful. Eleanor just told me. I was really afraid it would be canceled and I'd lose all these bookings. You know, Ms. Stone and her staff have rented the entire second floor. And they're really keeping all of us busy too."

"How many people did she bring with her?"

"Well, her assistant, Phoebe, is here already and her publicist just came in. Plus her son, Derek Stone, and his wife, Sylvia, so all four large bedrooms and the sitting room on the second floor are filled. It's a blessing, but I can't let them have the dining room. I have guests on the first floor and I need that for serving meals."

"It's no problem. Hopefully, Hilary Stone is so popular our customers won't mind. Besides it'll give Meg and . . . our new waitress a night off. They'll appreciate that, I'm sure."

"I hope to get over there too and have her sign a book. I wouldn't want to miss all the excitement. Imagine, somebody as famous as Hilary Stone coming to our little town. It's wonderful! She'll really put Snowflake on the map."

Lucky mumbled an agreement. *That's what I'm afraid of,* she thought but didn't reply.

Chapter 11

"WHAT EXACTLY DID she do?" Elias asked as he sliced through the shell of a jalousie he had created with pie dough. The vegetables inside steamed in a creamy mushroom sauce.

"More like what she *didn't* do," Lucky replied vehemently.

"Okay. Okay!" Elias held up his hands in mock surrender.

"I'm sorry. I don't mean to bite your head off. The woman is just so annoying—cloying, that's what she is—with that Southern accent and all the phony gooey charm. It's probably not even real."

"What's not real? The charm?"

"That too," Lucky grumbled. "No, I meant the accent."

"You think so?" Elias scooped a large helping of vegetables onto her dinner plate.

Lucky shrugged noncommittally. "Oh, I don't know. Sometimes I hear it and sometimes I don't. I'm just being critical 'cause I'm so mad at her right now. She gets under my skin. First she sashays in and flirts with Jack and completely ignores the fact that it's *my* restaurant. Like I'm invisible because I'm not the man in the room. You know the kind of woman I mean. Just lays it on thick for every guy around and tries to get one up on all the women."

"Hmmm. I'll have to meet her."

"Are you trying to make me jealous?" Lucky smiled.

"No, just trying to make you laugh."

"Well, I'm not jealous anyway. She might even be young enough to be Jack's granddaughter. Hard to say. And she's stuffed into that low-cut dress like pork sausage in a casing. I just can't stand the way she's so obviously flirting with him."

Elias chuckled. "Maybe Jack's liking it. You ever think of that?"

"Hmph," Lucky grumbled. "Well . . . maybe you're right," she agreed reluctantly. "I guess Jack's flattered by all that attention. I can't blame him. I'm sure he's lonely a lot of the time. He's been all alone for years, really."

"He may be," Elias agreed, "but he has the restaurant, and now you're here. I'd guess Jack's pretty happy all around. He never seems down."

Lucky nodded. "You're right. Let's not talk about that awful woman anymore. She just makes my blood boil."

"Okay." Elias smiled. He knew what was coming. "What would you prefer to talk about?"

Lucky grinned at him across the table. "You know me too well. I am curious, even though I feel so bad for Guy and Tommy. I worry about how discovering the woman's body will affect that little boy."

Elias nodded. "At least it wasn't a gruesome scene. Tommy told Guy that a lady was sleeping in the woods." He sighed and shook his head. "Nate told me that."

"Kids are sharp though. It will filter through. And for all we know, his mother's been ill, he might be deeply affected. There's just the two of them and a small kid would be terrified his mother could die."

"His mother's doing fine now. And don't forget, kids are resilient. Tommy will be okay."

"Who was she? The woman in the woods? Does Nate know yet?"

Elias shook his head negatively. "Not as far as I know. I

haven't talked to him since he called me out there. Nate didn't find a purse or wallet near the body. He was sure she wasn't local so hopefully he'll find a car or figure out how she got there."

Lucky shuddered. "How awful. Strangled in the woods. Maybe she was meeting someone there?"

"I guess that's a possibility. Otherwise why would she be in that area dressed as she was?"

"Nate mentioned a plastic cord near the body. Was she strangled with that?"

"Quite possibly." Elias reached over and helped himself to another scoop of vegetables. "The pathologist will be able to tell for sure, but whatever the murder weapon was, it was something thin, maybe plastic. The mark was very clean. They'll check for fibers in the wound and look at the cord microscopically, but it's likely that's the murder weapon." Elias took a sip of his wine. "But I want to hear about your day. What's the scuttlebutt about the famous mystery author?"

Lucky took a deep breath. "My arm's been twisted. I couldn't say no. Apparently, this woman, Hilary Stone, is very famous. Her murder mystery is on every bestseller list in the world . . ."

"Really? I'll have to check this book out."

"The original plan was to hold the event at the church meeting hall but the church roof has been leaking like a sieve and Pastor Wilson's keeping his fingers crossed that the whole roof won't have to be replaced. Eleanor Jensen was just frantic. They can't really use the dining room at the Drake House, and if they cancel the event, Eleanor could lose a sale and Barbara will be left hanging too. What else could I do?"

"I see your point. So you're closing the restaurant tomorrow evening?"

"Yes." Lucky nodded and took a sip of wine. "We'll close at five, clean up and rearrange everything. They've been very generous in compensation, so I'm not worried about that. We'll serve coffee and tea and pastries from Bettie's Bakery. Jack and Meg and our wonderful new waitress can have an evening off," Lucky replied grimly. "It'll just be me and Sage. Sophie might come by to help if she feels like it. But it really shouldn't be a lot of work."

Lucky took another scoop of the mushroom sauce and smiled. "And it turns out, Meg is a big fan! I had no idea she was such a mystery devotée. She wants to be there to meet the author. That's why she didn't want to have to work that night. I don't mind at all. She's been so upset about her hours and she had a meltdown the other day if you can imagine that. That's the only reason I hired Nanette. I promised Meg I'd hire the first person who walked through the door"—Lucky shook her head—"even though my first instinct was to toss her out on the sidewalk."

Elias smiled. "I can just picture Meg with her nose in a mystery book."

"She's told me all about the characters and the police officer and the clues. She's a huge fan." Lucky's face clouded. "It's weird though . . . I just recalled . . ."

"What?"

"Meg told me the victims in *Murder Comes Calling* were strangled with a telephone cord."

Chapter 12

JACK SAT BY the window reading the morning paper while Lucky moved around the front room of the restaurant organizing everything for the morning. She laid placemats at all the tables with napkins and silverware, straightened the chairs and refreshed the water in the vases of forsythias in the front window. She loved the way the yellow color of the blossoms on their long twigs reflected the color of the gingham curtains. It was still early. Meg and Nanette had yet to arrive. Only Sage clattered about the kitchen, getting pots ready for the day ahead. Sophie had promised to stop in later. Now that the long winter was really over, Sophie's schedule as a ski instructor had finally freed up. She often spent time helping out at the restaurant during the warmer months when her schedule was light. Lucky looked forward to the season and having more time to spend with her friend.

She heard a tap at the front door and looked up. Nate Edgerton stood outside. She hurried over and unlocked the door.

"Hi, Nate. How are you?"

"Fine, Lucky." He smiled. "I know I'm too early, but I

was hoping for a cup of coffee and a muffin, if that's okay. I've been up since the crack of dawn."

"Of course. No problem. Grab a seat with Jack and I'll bring you something."

Sage had peeked through the hatch and overheard Nate's comment. He poured a large mug of coffee and placed a warm blueberry muffin with butter on the ledge. Lucky carried it over to the table.

"You still investigating this woman Guy and Tommy found in the woods?" Jack asked, folding up his newspaper.

Nate nodded. "Unfortunately, yes. Things are breaking though. We found an abandoned car a quarter of a mile away, off a dirt road that verged from the main road. Got a license number and a photo and we've identified this poor woman."

"Really!" Lucky remarked, sitting down at the table. "Who is she?"

Nate shook his head. "The last person you'd expect to find around here, especially in such a state. Turns out she's . . . she *was* a psychiatrist at the Salisbury Retreat in Bournmouth." Nate took a sip of his coffee. "I suspected she was some sort of a professional woman, given her clothing."

Lucky shuddered. "The Salisbury Retreat? Isn't that the place that used to be called the Institute for the Criminally Insane?"

"I think you're right," Nate agreed. He guffawed, "Good thing they changed *that* name."

"How do you think she ended up in the woods?" Jack asked.

"No idea right now." Nate shrugged. "She might have just come from work, or maybe she was heading to her office. Certainly not dressed for tromping around in the woods. Was she kidnapped and taken there? Had she broken down on the road or maybe gave a ride to the wrong person? We don't know yet. We'll have to track her movements. And check the car out. She might have had mechanical problems but . . ." Nate hesitated.

"But what?" Lucky asked.

"If she did have problems with the car, why would she

pull so far off the road? She could've called for roadside assistance, but she'd have to wait where a tow truck could find her. Or possibly somebody else moved that car in an effort to hide it."

"Well, she might not have been exactly local, but Bournmouth isn't that far away," Jack said.

"I'm heading over in that direction now. We're trying to find a next of kin and check her residence and all that. Just real sad. She was a relatively young woman."

"It's so scary, Nate," Lucky said. "Another murder right here in Snowflake."

"I know. Doesn't make anybody sleep easier around here, that's for sure."

Lucky heard the rear door slam. Nanette called out, "Yoo-hoo, everybody." Lucky cringed. She hoped today would go more smoothly with their new hire. She glanced at Jack. He sat up straighter in his chair and brushed some crumbs off his shirt. No doubt about it. Jack was taken with Nanette's dubious charms.

"I better be on my way, folks." Nate stood. "Thanks for the bite to eat, Lucky. I'll see you all later."

Lucky followed Nate to the door and unlocked it for him. He waved once from the sidewalk and headed for his cruiser. Lucky flipped over the sign at the front door to read OPEN. "I better get busy too, Jack." Her grandfather wasn't listening. His face was wreathed in smiles as Nanette, smiling broadly, waggled her fingers in a cute hello from across the room.

Lucky sighed. *What next?* she thought.

THE MORNING FLEW by quickly. Sage seemed to have calmed down after yesterday's upset, and Meg and Nanette were managing to work well together. She allowed herself an optimistic hope that everything might work out just fine. Lucky glanced around the restaurant. The midday rush had just ended and only a few customers remained. Something wasn't quite right though. She had been so busy she hadn't had a chance to notice that their two most regular regulars hadn't arrived at all this morning. Hank and Barry always came in together and were usually their first customers of the day.

"Jack?" Lucky called to her grandfather. He looked up quickly. Lucky realized with a shock that Nanette was standing next to him again as he made change at the cash register. She was rubbing his arm in a very familiar way. Lucky gritted her teeth. What was this woman's game? She was openly flirting with Jack in a way that was inappropriate for a working environment.

"Hey! Lucky!"

Lucky turned. Sophie peeked through the hatch and waved.

Lucky smiled. "Hang on." She slipped out from the counter and pushed through the swinging door into the kitchen. "We missed you here." She gave her friend a big hug.

"I know. I missed everybody too, but you'll be seeing more of me soon." Sophie and Sage had married almost a year ago in May. Their lives had settled into a routine that revolved around work and setting up housekeeping together. The three of them hadn't had as much time to visit and catch up with news.

"I can't stay long this morning. Just popped in to say hello and see how things are going." Sophie leaned closer. "I also want to check out the new waitress. I heard all about her."

Lucky glanced at Sage and grimaced. "I'm sure you did. I'm not happy about all this but I really had no choice. Too much work was falling on Meg's shoulders and she was pretty upset."

"I know, Sage filled me in," she said. "He was telling me about . . ." Sophie trailed off as the swinging door opened.

"Hellooo." Nanette smiled. "Who do we have here?" She stood with her hands on her hips as though waiting to approve anyone who entered the kitchen.

Sophie's eyes widened. She was rendered speechless.

"Uh, Nanette, this is Sophie. Sophie DuBois, Sage's wife." She turned to Sophie. "Nanette is our new waitress." Lucky forced a smile.

"Well," Nanette drawled. "Very nice to meet you, I'm sure." She turned to Lucky. "Ah was just talkin' to your grandfather, dear. I was tellin' him I think our aprons could use a new logo. This one with the soup bowl is kinda old-fashioned, don't ya think?"

Lucky blinked. "My mother designed these aprons," she replied quietly. Sophie and Sage stopped breathing. "And my dad had the neon sign in the front window made to match."

"Oh." Nanette pursed her lips. "I see. Well, Jack's agreed with me. So he'll be talkin' to you about that. I just wanted to give you a heads-up." Nanette turned on her heel and returned to the front room.

"I think we should kill her," Sophie mumbled under her breath.

"I'll help you," Lucky added.

Chapter 13

SOPHIE SAID HER good-byes and Lucky returned to the counter, where she swept up the dirty cups and dishes and slammed them into the plastic bin under the counter. In a determined effort not to lose her temper, she counted to one hundred under her breath. She caught Meg's eye across the room, where Meg had just finished taking an order. Meg raised her eyebrows, aware that something had just happened and that Lucky was upset. She approached the counter and leaned across. "Are you all right?"

Lucky's jaw clenched. "Fine. I'm fine."

Meg looked doubtful.

"Really. I am. Nothing to worry about."

Meg shot a look in Nanette's direction. Nanette was taking orders at another table and talking animatedly to her customers. Her hips wiggled as she talked. Meg looked back at Lucky and heaved a sigh, then placed her order on the hatch.

The bell over the door jingled as Barry Sanders entered. Barry was alone again. Barry waved a hello to Jack and sat on a stool at the counter.

"You're late today. No Hank? Is he still not feeling well?" Lucky asked.

Barry had a worried expression on his face. "I don't know, Lucky."

Lucky's attention was immediately arrested. "What did you say?"

"I don't know where he is. I called him again yesterday and he said he still didn't feel well. I stopped at his house on my way back but he didn't answer the door. I figured he was maybe sleeping. I didn't want to be a pest. But today, I went by on my way down here to see if he was feeling better. He wasn't home. His car was gone."

"That's unusual, isn't it?"

"Sure is. Hank always mentions it if he has an errand to run or goes out of town, so I won't go looking for him. But we always grab our coffees down here every morning. This isn't like him."

"Maybe he had to . . . fill a prescription or something." Lucky shrugged. "You think there's something else going on?"

Barry shook his head. "I don't know. I had a feeling the other day that he was upset about something, but when I asked him if everything was all right, he just said he wasn't feeling too good."

"Well . . . maybe he *was* sick. Maybe he went over to the Clinic. I hope he's not at the hospital in Lincoln Falls. I mean, I hope it's nothing serious."

"Me too."

"I'm sure he'll call and let you know he's okay."

Barry nodded. "I'll keep calling him too, just to make sure."

Lucky laid a fresh placemat in front of Barry. "What can I get you today?"

Barry looked up at the blackboard. "Why don't I get a bowl of that carrot ginger soup and a croissant."

"Coming right up." Lucky quickly placed the order at the hatch and saw Sage's hand grab it.

"I heard all about the big book event tonight. I had mentioned it to Hank when I first saw the ads. Thought he'd be interested, especially since he's always reading mysteries and thrillers. And he used to write for a living too, before he retired."

"Oh, I think I had heard that. What exactly did he do?"

"He worked at a newspaper in upstate New York . . . Albany, he once said. But he never talked too much about it." Barry swiveled on his stool. "Maybe I'll chat with Jack a bit if he's ready to take a break."

"Sure. Go right ahead. I'll bring your order over to you."

"See you got a new waitress."

"Yup," Lucky replied noncommittally.

"Quite a looker. Where'd you find her?"

Lucky's eyebrows raised. "You think so?"

Barry nodded. "Sure is. She live around here?" Barry checked the buttons on his shirtfront that always threatened to burst and sucked in his ample gut. He smiled and waved at Nanette, who returned the greeting in kind.

What was it about this woman that every man found so charming? Personally, Lucky found her voice grating and her behavior over the top. "I think she's looking for a place here. But Nanette actually found us. She just walked in one day and grabbed the sign. And we really needed the help, now that Janie's off at school."

Barry laughed. "Jack was real lucky Flo Sullivan didn't march in here demanding her old job back."

As much as she hated to admit it, Barry had a point. Jack would have taken to his bed and disappeared from the restaurant. Things could have been a lot worse.

Chapter 14

SAGE MOVED THE last table to the side of the room. "What else do we need to do, Lucky?" he asked. The Spoonful had closed a half hour before. Sage had cleared away everything in the kitchen and set up two large urns for coffee and tea, with cups, saucers, spoons and small plates. Lucky had spread pastries of various kinds and cookies on their best trays and covered them with linen napkins in preparation for Hilary Stone's book event.

Lucky turned when she heard a tap on the front door. Marjorie Winters stood outside. She hurried over to the door and unlocked it.

"Oh, Lucky. I'm so excited." Marjorie rushed in. "I just can't wait to meet her. This is the most thrilling thing that's *ever* happened in Snowflake. Imagine . . . a famous mystery writer right here in our little town!"

Lucky smiled at Marjorie's enthusiasm. Marjorie's cheeks were flushed. She was almost hyperventilating. "Yes, I suppose it is," Lucky agreed.

"Well, I can't believe you haven't read her book yet. I'll have to get you a copy tonight."

"Don't worry, Marjorie. I've heard so much about her, I'll have to pick one up for myself." Lucky fidgeted, anxious to get on with the task of preparing the restaurant for the event. "Did you want to come in? We're actually closed right now, trying to get ready."

"Oh," Marjorie breathed. "Would you mind? I'd love to be here to meet her when she arrives."

"Uh, well . . . sure. Just be careful, we're going to mop the floor and we're still moving things around."

"I won't be a bother, I swear. I'll stay out of the way."

"If things get hectic, just grab a seat in the office until we get started."

"Thanks, Lucky." Marjorie tucked her purse under her arm and took a seat at the counter, surveying the room.

Before Lucky could lock the door again, a florist's van pulled up. The sign on the side of the van read GARDEN DELIGHTS. *Are they heading here?* she wondered.

A man in a delivery uniform climbed out of the van and opened the double doors at the rear of the vehicle. He lifted out a four-foot-tall arrangement of exotic flowers and headed for the front door of the Spoonful. Lucky opened the door.

"This is the By the Spoonful Soup Shop, isn't it?" he asked as he reached the threshold.

"Yes. Are these for us?" Lucky asked.

"Sure are. Where should I put them?"

"How about on the counter for now."

"Okay," he replied and carried the heavy vase close to where Marjorie sat. "You want the rest to go here too?"

"The rest?"

"Yes, ma'am. My van is loaded. I have nine more just like this one."

Lucky's eyebrows raised. "You're kidding!"

"Nope." The man shook his head. "I guess you're hosting some big celeb tonight. This order came from her assistant."

"Oh, well, all right. Bring them all in." She turned to look at Sage, who stood shaking his head in wonderment.

"I guess we're just not used to life in the fast lane," he remarked.

Jack came through the swinging door from the corridor as the last bouquet was lined up at the counter. "What the . . ." He stared at the huge vases. "Looks like a damn funeral."

"Shhh, Jack. I agree but don't let anybody else hear you."

"What happened to my table? I was just gonna have some tea."

"I'm sorry. We need to move everything around tonight. I'll get you a cup of tea. Have a seat at the counter with Marjorie, why don't you?"

Jack sighed and slid onto a stool.

Marjorie leaned closer to Jack. "This is so exciting, Jack, don't you think? Did you ever think you'd be hosting someone as famous as Hilary Stone?"

"Never heard of the woman," Jack mumbled.

"Oh, you must read her book. It's fantastic. And she's working on her second book, right here in Snowflake. I can't wait to get it. I wonder if she'll talk about that tonight."

Lucky hurried to the kitchen and grabbed a mug. She heated some water quickly in the microwave for Jack's tea and carried it out to the front counter.

"Thanks, my girl," Jack said when she placed the mug in front of him. "Uh . . . where's Nanette?" he asked, looking around.

"She's off tonight. We really didn't need her. Sage'll be here. And Sophie will probably come by later."

He smiled widely, "I'm real glad you hired her."

"You are?" Lucky reminded herself to keep her response neutral.

"She really livens the place up a lot, don't you think?"

Lucky nodded noncommittally. "That's one way to put it."

"You know, she was tellin' me about some of her ideas."

Lucky cringed inwardly. "Oh, really?"

"Yup. She's got lots of good ideas about making our restaurant better. She thinks our aprons could use a new design too."

Lucky felt her blood pressure rising. "Is that so?"

"And she wanted to change some of our recipes too. She's

from the South and she thought our menu might be getting a little dull."

"Dull!" Lucky exclaimed. Sage looked up from the corner where he was rearranging some chairs. He caught her eye.

"Well, I'll have to have a little chat with her now, won't I?" Lucky said darkly, but her intent was completely lost on Jack.

"I'm glad you agree." He finished his tea and placed the mug on the counter. "I'll be takin' off now. It's gettin' late. It's almost two bells." Jack, a Navy vet, had always told time by the bells. Only Lucky was able to translate.

As soon as Jack left by the back door, Lucky stormed into the kitchen and filled a plastic bucket with hot water and cleanser. She lifted it and, grabbing the mop on her way out, headed back to the front room. She dipped the mop in the liquid and began in the far corner of the room, working her way toward the front door. The activity helped calm her.

Sage tapped her on the arm. "Why don't you let me do that?"

Lucky closed her eyes and took a deep breath. "Okay. Maybe you better. I just might put this mop through the front window." She passed the handle of the mop to him.

"Did I hear right? Jack agrees my menu is dull?" he asked quietly.

Lucky turned to face him. "Your menu is not dull. I meant what I said to Nanette. You're the best thing that's ever happened to this restaurant."

"You told her that?"

"Yes. And I told her a few more things too. I told her she was hired to wait on tables, not to offer her opinion about food or anything else for that matter."

"Good," Sage replied. "Lucky, can you pull those tables away from the wall? I'll mop there and then we can push them back."

"Sure," she replied. "Don't worry about Nanette," she said as she dragged the first table to the center of the room. Sage quickly mopped the area and continued on to the other side of the room. Marjorie, still sitting at the counter, clutching her purse, lifted her feet as Sage moved past. "You just let me know if she even looks at you cross-eyed."

"Well, it sure sounded like Jack agrees with her."

Lucky dragged the table back to its place. "Jack couldn't care less what design is on the aprons, to tell you the truth. He's just smitten."

"I'll say," Sage chuckled.

"It's pathetic really."

"What is?" Sage asked. He had reached the far side of the room near the door to the corridor.

"The way men go all gooey when she's around. What is it about her they find attractive? Do you find her attractive?"

Sage shook his head. "Me? No. She's not my type. Plus I'm in love with my wife. I don't even see other women." Sage had already managed to work his way halfway across the room with the mop.

"That's so sweet, Sage. You're both so lucky to have each other."

He smiled. "I agree. And as far as men finding Nanette attractive, I guess it must be—"

"Her tits," Marjorie finished.

The mop slipped out of Sage's hand and clattered to the floor.

Chapter 15

THE DOOR FLEW open with a bang and four people, three women and a man, entered the restaurant. Two other men in work clothes stood outside on the sidewalk. Lucky was sure this had to be the author's entourage. They were all dressed to kill in very expensive black outfits.

"Can I help you?" Lucky asked.

"Is this . . . is this the soup shop?" a tall blonde woman asked.

"Yes," Lucky responded.

She sniffed audibly. "I don't think this will do at all!"

"Excuse me?" Lucky asked.

Marjorie sat up straight at the counter and stared at the four strangers.

"I said," the blonde replied haughtily, "this just won't do. We were promised a large venue. Not a . . . soup restaurant."

"I see." Lucky sighed. "Well, you're certainly welcome to cancel the event, but we've closed early and Ms. Stone's assistant has signed a rental agreement for the evening."

Another woman dressed in a black cocktail dress with

platinum blonde hair began to laugh. "This is just *perfect*," she screamed.

"Hush, Sylvia," the portly man ordered. "Behave yourself." He stepped forward and extended a hand to Lucky. "I'm Derek Stone. I'm Hilary's son. And this is my . . ." He turned to the blonde with the shrill voice. "My wife, Sylvia."

"Lucky Jamieson." Lucky returned his handshake.

"At the risk of sounding rude, we *were* promised a very large space . . . and certainly not a restaurant. I don't know how appropriate this would be for what we have planned. Phoebe!" he shouted.

A thin woman, with dark hair pulled back tightly from her face, stepped forward. She also wore heels and a black pants suit, like the tall blonde woman. "Yes, Derek?"

"Did you know about this?" He waved his arm around the room then turned to Lucky. "Don't get me wrong, Miss . . ."

"Jamieson."

"Miss Jamieson, your restaurant is very quaint, but I would never have approved of holding this book signing in a soup shop. Did you book this, Phoebe?"

The woman's jaw clenched. "Yes, I did. And we were fortunate to get it. It was literally the only available place we could find."

"What happened to the meeting hall at the church?"

"Their roof has been leaking and they have construction going on there. It was impossible," she replied sharply. "This was the only other option."

Derek shook his head. "Ridiculous." He sighed. "Well, we'll just have to make the best of it. I'll try to explain to Mother."

"At least the flowers were delivered on time," the tall blonde remarked. A large manila envelope was tucked under her arm. She strode to the counter and examined the vases, then turned to Lucky. "Don't mind Derek. He likes to think he has a say in things."

Lucky glanced quickly at the short man. His face flushed a deep red. "I'll have you know . . ." he began.

"Oh, can it, Derek. Just stay out of our way tonight, okay? And can you make yourself useful? This was delivered to the office this morning. It's for your mother." She handed the large envelope to him. "Just make sure Hilary gets to see this as soon as possible." She turned to Lucky. "I'm Audra Klemack. I'm Ms. Stone's publicist." She didn't offer her hand.

"Very nice to meet you."

Audra spotted Sage, who hadn't said a word during their exchange. "You. You look like you work here. Help me get these vases placed around the room." She turned back to Lucky. "And let's turn off the bright lights and turn on some of these lamps. We want to create a little *atmosphere*, do you understand?"

Lucky bit her tongue. The sooner these people got what they wanted, the sooner they'd be out of her hair. "Completely."

"Well, hurry up then. We don't have much time." She heaved a big sigh. "Phoebe, get those two men busy hanging the banner outside, will you?"

Phoebe nodded and stepped out the door.

Lucky spoke. "Why don't you all leave your purses and laptops in the office. It's just down the hall through that door." She pointed.

"Good idea. Thanks," the blonde woman said. "Come on, everyone. Look sharp. The photographer and the crowds will be arriving any minute." Her eyes rested on Marjorie, who sat speechless on a stool at the counter. "Why don't you make yourself useful, dear, and start lining up chairs for people to sit in."

Marjorie's eyebrows rose to her hairline.

Lucky sighed. Why had she ever agreed to this?

Chapter 16

BY THE TIME the room was prepared—the lights dimmed, the photographer waiting and a long table stacked with books had been set up at the far end of the room—Derek Stone had disappeared and reappeared fifteen minutes later, escorting a glamorous, silver-haired woman also dressed all in black to the long table. A heavy necklace of sapphires and diamonds hung around her neck. Hilary Stone had arrived and must have entered through the back door. Lucky had peeked out the window and noticed that Broadway was now lined with cars, some drivers anxious and leaning on their horns. A crowd of perhaps fifty people milled around outside the Spoonful. She spotted more groups down the street also heading their way. She hoped the pastries she had ordered would last the evening.

To Marjorie's credit, she was more than willing to help out and Lucky was grateful for her presence. Marjorie had managed to find a moment to approach Hilary Stone and introduce herself. She gushed when Hilary autographed her book. So far, the author herself seemed the most down-to-earth person of the lot.

Before she knew it, the room was filled to capacity. It was standing room only and the line to get in stretched down the block. Lucky marveled at the turnout. Their restaurant was popular and busy, but had never hosted a crowd of this size. She and Sage manned the coffee and tea urns and discreetly moved around the room retrieving dirty cups and plates. The photographer snapped pictures while a smiling Hilary Stone chatted with her fans. Lucky had turned on the CD player and a soft jazz instrumental was playing. It was difficult to hear since the noise level had been rising steadily as more and more people squeezed in and milled about.

Derek Stone stood to the side, near his mother, very solicitous of her well-being. He stepped in front of the table and clinked a spoon against a glass to ask for quiet. "Thank you all for coming. Ms. Stone will speak very briefly about her upcoming work, and then we'll have a fifteen-minute session during which you may ask questions of her. After that, she will autograph her books until nine o'clock."

A few groans and grumbles were heard around the room. Someone called out, "What if we can't get to the top of the line by then?"

"I'm very sorry. Ms. Stone will do the best she can. When it's your turn, please step forward quickly. The faster the line moves, the more people will be able to get their books signed."

Sage paused the music and the room fell silent. The author spoke briefly about her protagonist and the research she had done. Many people questioned her about the sequel to her current book. She assured her fans that a sequel was in the works, although she couldn't reveal very much. She said she was still working hard at the moment and wasn't quite sure when the second book would be released.

Derek Stone, at a signal from his mother, stepped forward. "All right, everyone. If you haven't purchased *Murder Comes Calling*, please step over here," he said, indicating a side table where Phoebe, the author's personal assistant, sat. "You may make your purchase right there and Ms. Stone will now begin to sign." He glanced around the packed room and smiled. "Of course, if you already own a copy of *Murder*

Comes Calling, Ms. Stone will be happy to sign that as well. Thank you."

There was a general rush to the side table. Meg had placed herself close to the front table and managed to be the first in line. Lucky noticed she held two books in her hand. Meg's face was flushed and Lucky could see her speaking excitedly to Hilary Stone. The signing continued as the line shuffled forward. Fortunately, everyone was polite and patient. Lucky stood on tiptoes to get a better look at the author. Hilary Stone seemed completely free of stress and took her time chatting with each book buyer. She didn't seem to be in any hurry at all.

Sophie had slipped in through the back entrance and worked her way toward the coffee urn. She put an arm around Lucky's shoulder. "Sorry I'm late. I wanted to get here earlier. I'll give you guys a hand." She kissed Sage on the cheek.

"Thanks, Sophie. It's been a very interesting evening, to say the least."

Sophie glanced around the room. "Where did all these people come from? Oh, look, there's Susanna Edgerton. And I see Miriam too. I wonder if Nate will be here?"

"I doubt that," Sage answered. "He's investigating a real murder."

"Right," Sophie agreed. "Best not to talk about that tonight."

The three continued to man the coffee and tea urns. Each person approached for a cup of coffee or tea and a pastry once their books were signed, then searched for a seat. A steady buzz of conversation filled the room as fans lined up to reach the front table. Derek Stone stood guard behind his mother. At one point, he slipped around the room and reached Sage.

"Could you please fix a cup of tea with lemon for my mother?" he asked.

"Of course," Sage replied, deftly preparing the tea.

Derek waited, then returned to the front table and placed the teacup next to his mother. She smiled gratefully at him and took a sip in between signing books.

Sage moved closer to Lucky. "How long is this going to go on?"

Lucky shrugged. "Till nine."

He groaned. "What time is it now?"

Lucky checked her watch. "Close. It's eight thirty."

"They're racking up the sales, aren't they? How much are they charging for this book?"

"I'm not sure. I think I heard twenty-eight ninety-nine."

Sage whistled. "And they've sold hundreds so far."

Meg, her face flushed, pushed her way through the crowd. She held two copies of *Murder Comes Calling.* "This is for you, Lucky. It's autographed."

"For me?"

"Yes. You have to read it! I know you won't be able to put it down."

"Oh, Meg, you shouldn't have spent your money. I'll pay you back," Lucky replied.

"Oh, no. This is a present . . . from me. Kind of an apology. I know I've been a brat all week and I feel so bad I forced you to hire Nanette. I know she really annoys you."

"Well, thank you." Lucky reached over and hugged Meg. "You're a doll. That was so sweet and thoughtful of you."

Meg smiled. "It'll keep you awake at night, I warn you." She ducked back into the crowd.

Lucky glanced at the table where Phoebe sat. Hilary Stone's assistant seemed anxious. There were dark circles under her eyes. One of the workmen who had hung the banner outside the restaurant had been helping, lugging in cartons of books to be sold.

Lucky turned to Sage, "They've certainly compensated us generously for the use of our space, so I can't complain. This'll be over soon. All I want to do is go home and climb into a nice hot bubble bath. For some reason, this evening feels like ten times more work than one of our normal nights."

Sage nodded his agreement. "It's the energy in the room. All these weird personalities."

Lucky felt a presence near her and turned to see Audra

Klemack. "Amazing," she remarked to the publicist. "Her book must be fascinating."

Audra shrugged. "Well, darling, it helps if you're married to the publisher."

"Oh?"

Audra laughed mirthlessly. "Married to the publisher and bags of money to pay people like me."

Sylvia Stone, overdressed for the occasion in a slinky cocktail outfit and looking completely bored, waved across the room at her husband. Derek ignored her. Sylvia reached under her chair and retrieved a large black purse. She pulled a thin silver flask out of her purse and poured a generous amount of a dark brown liquid into her teacup.

Audra nodded her head, indicating Sylvia Stone. "My job would be a whole lot easier if I didn't have to contend with that emasculated doting excuse for a son and his tipsy wife."

Lucky, unsure how to respond to these revelations, decided to say nothing.

"Oh, well. It could always be worse," Audra sighed. "I suppose I could be someplace even farther away from Manhattan."

Chapter 17

DEREK STONE PULLED his sleeve back and checked his watch. "Sorry, folks. The evening is over." The line still stretched out to the sidewalk and down the block. A general groan went up from the crowd. "But if you would still like your book signed, please take a business card and our publicist will be happy to help you, won't you, Audra?" He smiled at Audra, the smile not reaching his eyes, and several heads turned to her.

Lucky heard Audra mutter under her breath but she smiled quickly and stepped forward. "That's right, folks. Please take a card. You can mail your copies of *Murder Comes Calling* to me, with a stamped self-addressed envelope, of course, and I'll see that they are autographed and returned to you.

There were general grumbles around the room but Derek stepped into the breach. "Please be considerate. Ms. Stone has been signing for almost three hours now and she is very tired. I'm sure you can all understand."

"That's a tough order, isn't it?" Lucky remarked to Audra. "Signing all those books that people mail to her."

"Oh, please," Audra sneered. "Phoebe can do her signature perfectly. They'll be none the wiser."

"Ah. I see."

"I better wake Sylvia up and drag her back to the B and B. Derek certainly won't and I'm sure you won't want to find her here in the morning."

No, Lucky thought, *I certainly wouldn't.*

The line broke up and people milled around the room for several more minutes, but once Derek had escorted his mother out of the room and down the corridor to the back door, everyone started drifting away. The two workmen who had arrived with the entourage took down the banner from the front of the restaurant and then came inside. They carried the few remaining cartons of books down the corridor and into a waiting van at the rear of the restaurant. When the last person had gone, Lucky locked the front door. Sophie and Sage rearranged the tables and chairs for the morning and Lucky loaded the dishwasher with all the cups and small dishes. The pastries had evaporated an hour before.

"What should we do with these flowers, Lucky?" Sage asked.

Lucky plopped into a chair. "I have no idea. Let's just move them around into the corners where they'll be out of the way. If they want their flowers, they'll have to send someone over to get them."

The phone in the kitchen began to ring. "I'll get it," Sage said. He hurried into the kitchen and grabbed it on the third ring. Lucky heard him exchange a few words with the caller. Then he returned to the front room.

"Who was that?" she asked.

"That," Sage replied, "was Audra Klemack. Hilary Stone would like some soups delivered to her room."

"What? You're kidding! Can't the Drake House fix her something?"

"Apparently not. She's heard that we have the best soups in town."

"Well, we do. But still. Why couldn't she have said something when she was here?"

Sage shrugged. "Why don't I fix something and run it over?"

"No, that's all right. I'll bring it down there. You two go home. I'm sure Sophie's tired too."

"Okay, thanks, Lucky. I won't ask twice."

She smiled. "Thanks for being here tonight. But I mean it. Go home. I'll take care of it."

Chapter 18

LUCKY PACKED A plastic container with two different half sandwiches and two different soups—the cream of asparagus and the carrot ginger soup, two of Sage's specials of the week along with two bowls marked with the Spoonful logo. Those choices would offer a variety. Barbara Drake had promised to cover the expenses, whatever it took to keep her celebrity guests happy.

Once the bin was securely packed, she tucked Meg's present into her purse and checked the locks on the front door. She carried the bin to the trunk of her car, emptied the trash bags in the Dumpster and locked the back door of the Spoonful. As tired as she was, she didn't regret sending Sage home. He had been through enough for the week, especially dealing with Meg's outbursts and Nanette's meddling, not to mention the attitude he had experienced at the hands of the Stone entourage.

She drove the few blocks to the edge of town and pulled into the drive of the Drake House, a yellow two-story colonial with white shutters, each shutter decorated with the cutout of a candlestick. This bed-and-breakfast was the only form of overnight accommodation in the village. Barbara Drake had inherited the house from her grandparents and, instead of promptly selling it to the highest bidder, had lovingly restored the charming home and created a business.

The front door swung open as she approached. Barbara, her hair pinned up in ringlets, looked exhausted, but she smiled and welcomed her in.

"Thanks so much, Lucky! I really appreciate this."

"No worries. It'll keep your famous guest happy."

Barbara shook her head. "What a bunch they are too! Demanding, arrogant. Hilary Stone, as prickly as she is, is the best of the lot."

"Really? Well, that's good to hear. They were all at the Spoonful tonight and there were mobs of people, but I didn't really have a chance to talk to her. She's well protected by her son and assistant and all."

"Come on in the kitchen and we'll put all this on a tray. I was hoping to get there tonight but I was just too busy," Barbara said, leading the way to the rear of the home. "And keep track of all this so I can compensate you."

Lucky pulled a stool up to the island and watched Barbara unpack the bin. "I packed two different half sandwiches and two soups. The soups should still be warm."

"I'll give 'em a blast in the microwave and have Ginny bring them up to her room. Oh!" Barbara exclaimed. "Wait. She's clearing the dining room."

"Don't worry about it," Lucky said. "I'll take the tray up to her. I can explain what I'm bringing her better anyway."

"You don't mind?" Barbara asked.

"No. Not at all. And then I'm heading home and soaking in a nice hot tub full of bubbles. It's been a day and a half."

Barbara laughed ruefully. "Same here. Most of our guests are no trouble at all, but I'll tell you, running a bed-and-breakfast is more work than even I could have imagined. I'd be lost without Ginny though. I don't know what I did before she came."

Lucky wondered what Barbara was leaving unsaid. "And your second-floor lot?"

Barbara took a deep breath. She placed two piping hot

bowls of soup on a large tray and laid the sandwiches in a cloth-covered wicker basket. Barbara shrugged her shoulders. "Well, the assistant, Phoebe, is the only one who's within normal limits, but that publicist from New York . . ." Barbara leaned over the island. "And the daughter-in-law . . ."

"Sylvia?"

"That's the one. What a nightmare she is. Frankly, I don't know how her husband puts up with her. And him . . . the poor thing, I think his mother had his you-know-whats removed at birth."

Lucky laughed in spite of herself. "That's rather the impression I had as well."

"Here you go," Barbara said, passing the tray to Lucky. "The Queen Bee is in the second room on the left."

Lucky nodded and climbed the stairs, carefully balancing the heavy tray. She placed it on a hallway table and knocked on the door.

"Come in," a voice said.

Lucky turned the knob. The door swung open as she picked up the tray. "Good evening," she said as she entered. "I've brought you two different soups and half sandwiches. I hope you like them. We have a fabulous chef at the By the Spoonful."

"Oh." The handsome silver-haired woman looked up from her dressing table. Without makeup, her age was more apparent and the lines around her eyes were obvious. Her sparkling necklace and earrings were strewn across the mirrored top of the vanity. "Thank you, that's very kind of you to bring it over to me. I didn't realize how hungry I was until the book signing was over."

Lucky thought her a very courteous woman, but something just under the surface promised a psyche of steel. *A very strong-willed woman*, Lucky mused, *in spite of her gracious manner.*

A gentle tap came on the slightly open door. Derek Stone peeked into his mother's bedroom. "Mother? Are you all right?" He stepped into the room and froze when he saw Lucky. "What are *you* doing here?" he demanded.

Lucky opened her mouth to respond, but before she could reply, Hilary Stone cut in, "Don't be an idiot, Derek. I asked for her. Now go back to your room and keep that wife of yours under control . . . if you can," she replied icily.

Derek's soft face blushed a bright red and he turned and left, shutting the door quietly behind him.

"Please excuse my son. He tries to control every aspect of my life. I'd never travel with him, but I do need his help occasionally, as unpleasant as the whole experience is," Hilary said dismissively.

Lucky could think of no appropriate response to make. It always amazed her when strangers aired their dirty family linen. "Well, enjoy the soups. They really are wonderful. Barbara or Ginny will be back to pick up your tray in a short while."

Ms. Stone nodded dismissively. Lucky left the room without another word. When she reached the top of the stairway, she breathed a sigh of relief. She hadn't realized she had been holding her breath.

Chapter 19

LUCKY CLIMBED OUT of the bathtub and pulled the plug from the drain. The sudsy water gurgled and swirled as the tub emptied. Wrapping a large bath towel around herself, she padded to the bedroom, leaving damp footprints on the wood floor. She slipped on a nightie and a terry cloth robe, so grateful to be in her small apartment and away from the annoyances and crowds of the day. She had a new appreciation for popular writers after watching Hilary Stone sign her name for hours and smile at every fan. What stamina the woman had!

Meg's gift sat on the kitchen table. Curiosity got the better of her. She picked it up and carried it to the living room. Snuggling on the sofa near the floor lamp, she cracked it open. The dedication page read, "*To Lucky . . . Hilary Stone.*" Lucky appreciated the thought behind the gift but felt guilty that Meg had spent her hard-earned money. She turned the page and began to read:

Rebecca Mayfield was lost in thought as she sat on the subway bench waiting for her train to arrive. The murderer had targeted women alone at night, in dark alleys and city streets. Each victim had complained of mysterious phone calls for three consecutive days before their deaths. All young women in the prime of their lives. What sort of monster would violate the innocent? *she thought. She knew she was onto something, but her editor had threatened to pull the story unless she came up with something solid, something the police hadn't yet discovered.*

The bench began to vibrate beneath her. She heard the roar of the incoming train. Gathering her purse, she stood and approached the edge of the platform. She glanced down. Her heart almost stopped. On the tracks below lay another victim of the killer, a thin plastic cord wrapped around her neck. Rebecca's screams were drowned by the roaring sound. She couldn't possibly halt the train in time. She covered her eyes as the brakes began to squeal.

Lucky heard a firm knock at her door and nearly jumped out of her skin. She took a deep breath and hurried down the hall. "Who is it?" she called out. Only Sophie or Elias would ever come to her door unannounced this late in the evening.

"House call," Elias replied.

Lucky laughed and opened the door. "I didn't expect you."

"What have you been up to?"

"Oh, I was just starting to read *Murder Comes Calling*. Meg bought me a copy."

"Not you too! Are you turning into a crazed fan?"

"I hope not. But it did make me jump when I heard you knock."

He smiled and enveloped her in a hug. "I just got back from the hospital in Lincoln Falls and didn't want to spend the night alone." He pulled back to take a better look at her. "You're all pink."

"I just got out of the tub."

"Hmmm, I don't know about that. It might be caused by a rare disease. I think you need a doctor's attention—stat." He grinned from ear to ear.

"I certainly could use some attention and some tender loving care, but how 'bout a glass of wine first."

"I can manage that," he replied, following Lucky back to the kitchen. She pulled two wineglasses from the cupboard and a bottle of white wine from the refrigerator.

"You can do the honors," she said, handing him a wine cork remover. "I'm terrible at this."

Elias deftly released the cork. "What is this?"

"Something Sage recommended. Should be good."

Elias poured a small amount into one of the wineglasses and held the glass to his nose. "Mmmm, Sage has good taste." He poured some into Lucky's glass and more into his own. "How was your day? Oh, I just remembered . . . you had the book signing tonight! How did it go?"

"Fine, I think. It was a bit stressful dealing with all the personalities. They're quite a bunch, but Hilary Stone seems like an interesting woman and she certainly has her fans. The street was packed with people. It went on for hours and unfortunately a lot of them weren't able to get their books signed after waiting in line for a long time."

"That's too bad."

"But . . . I have to hand it to her. She talked for a few minutes and then people asked questions, so she kept up the signing for close to two and a half hours."

"Commendable." Elias reached across the table and grasped her hand. "You have a funny look on your face. What's wrong?"

"Oh." Lucky shrugged her shoulders. "Nothing."

"Not likely. What is it?"

"It's Jack. I'm concerned about him."

"What's going on?"

"This woman . . . this Nanette. It's revolting, Elias. She flirts with him and rubs his arm, and every time I turn around, she's at the cash register with Jack for any excuse whatsoever."

"Look, maybe she just likes him. Jack is very likable."

"Of course he is, but he is completely smitten with this woman. He watches her all day long with this adoring look in his eye. And she's got to be ages younger. I love Jack but I find it hard to believe she's really attracted to him. I'm just worried that she has some other agenda. And then, she's sticking her nose in where it doesn't belong and telling Sage to change his recipes."

Elias coughed as a sip of wine went down his throat the wrong way. "Whaaa? Telling Sage how to cook?"

"Yes!" Lucky exclaimed. "Can you believe that! I caught her telling him he should change his recipes because they're boring. Unbelievable! The latest is she's decided the aprons should be changed. The ones my mother designed. Over my dead body. And she's got Jack to agree with her."

"I can see why you're upset. I don't know what to say . . . maybe give her a little time to settle in and learn how things really work at the Spoonful."

"I guess. I'm really trying hard to be patient. I can't afford to lose Meg."

"Speaking of patient . . . how 'bout that doctor's care I mentioned?" He smiled as he pulled her toward him and held her close. "You *are* very pink. The doctor is concerned."

Chapter 20

BARRY SANDERS APPROACHED his friend's house. He had walked down the hill from his own home on Crestline after spending the last day or so concerned about Hank. He stood, staring at the darkened house and the empty driveway. Wherever Hank had gone, he hadn't bothered to inform anyone, not even his best friend. And Barry had no doubt that he was Hank's best friend. He knew it was hard for other people to understand, but this behavior was so out of character for Hank and so out of the normal routine the two men had kept up in retirement.

Barry admired Hank greatly, his education, his work experience as a newspaper writer. Barry, on the other hand, was a barely educated electrician in his working life, yet he had done well financially and was able to enjoy his retirement. But he had to admit there were things about Hank that he had never dared approach. Some dark corner of his previous life that Hank would never talk about. Barry wasn't sure exactly what it was, or what it involved. He suspected something might have gone wrong in his career, something he might still be bitter about. But Hank had never offered to explain further and Barry was too polite to pry. Perhaps he had been dismissed from his job, or some shadow or ill luck had befallen him. Perhaps he had been impolitic and stepped on the wrong toes. Barry had no idea what it was exactly, but he could sense it. There was always some reticence when Hank would talk about his earlier life. Ultimately every conversation would end with Hank remarking that it was all water under the bridge.

What if Hank's car was in the shop and he hadn't gone out of town? What if Hank were really sick and couldn't reach a telephone? Maybe he should just check things out. Barry walked softly down the driveway and climbed the front steps. He peered through the glass of the door. The house was completely dark. If Hank were home, certainly the lamp in his living room would be lit. He pretty much left it burning day and night anyway, whether he was home or not. The living room itself didn't get much direct light on this side of the house and Hank never liked the dark. Barry rang the bell and heard it chime inside. No response. He sighed and retraced his steps, doing his best, in spite of his short stature, to peek into the side windows. He couldn't see very much. He pulled a flashlight out of his back pocket and pressed it against the glass. Nothing looked amiss. Neat as always. Next he peered into the back window of the kitchen. Not a cup or a spoon out of place. It was as if Hank had carefully put every loose item away, climbed in his car and driven off.

But to where? Barry wondered.

GINNY TAPPED LIGHTLY on the door to the suite. "Ms. Stone?" She waited, but heard no response. She knocked louder. Still no answer. She sighed and checked her watch. Ten fifty-five. She was due to go home in five more minutes. Twenty minutes earlier, she had approached the door but had heard raised voices. It sounded like their guest was arguing with someone—a man? Her son? She had thought better of knocking and finally decided to come back later. But now it *was* later. It was almost eleven o'clock. She was exhausted. It had been a very long day, and if it weren't for Hilary Stone and all the people who had come to town with the author, she would have been free to go home two hours ago. She decided to take a chance.

Ginny tapped one more time on the door and cracked it open. The room appeared to be empty. *Good*, she thought. She hurried to the table and loaded the empty dishes and used napkins on the tray. She turned back to the door and halted in her tracks. A stockinged foot peeked out from under the far side of the bed. Ginny forced herself to approach. Hilary Stone lay on the floor, between the bed and the wall, fully clothed, except for one shoe, a telephone cord wrapped around her neck. Her tongue, swollen and blue, protruded from her mouth. Ginny felt the tray slip from her fingers. She began to scream.

Chapter 21

LUCKY SNUGGLED INTO her heavy cardigan and turned the key in the ignition. She'd just have time to retrieve the dishes from the Drake House and get back to the Spoonful before opening. She rolled down the window and breathed deeply as she drove down Broadway. The morning air was cool but it promised to be a lush spring day. The storms and ice of winter had finally ended and soon everything would be in bloom. Forsythia bushes were everywhere now, brilliant sprays of bright yellow, but soon the lilacs would bloom. She smiled, thinking of Sophie's wedding last year. Sophie had carried lilacs and lavender. Lucky sighed, recalling what a happy day that had been.

There were several cars in the distance. She recognized the coroner's van from Lincoln Falls. She slowed and hit the brakes. Nate's cruiser was in the drive and one of the cars was Elias's silver sedan. Something was very wrong. Elias had left her apartment early that morning, before dawn. Had Nate called him to come to the Drake House? She pulled to the opposite side of the road and parked. What could have possibly happened since she had been here the night before?

She hurried across the road and up the path to the front door. The door swung open before she reached it. Barbara had seen her approaching.

"Oh, Lucky!" she cried.

"What's going on?"

"It's so terrible." Barbara burst into tears. "It's Hilary Stone. She's dead. She's been murdered."

Lucky gasped. "How? I mean, when did this happen?" The woman had been fine the night before when she had delivered the food.

"We don't know. We've been up all night. Ginny found her just before she was due to go off duty. She went in to get the dishes and things to wash them for you and found her. Ginny's a wreck."

Barbara fell into her arms, more for support than affection. Lucky wrapped her arms around Barbara's thin shoulders. Ginny appeared in the doorway to the dining room, her face a ghostly white. It was obvious neither woman had slept a wink all night.

"Come on, you need to sit down. Better yet, you need to lie down. I can stay for a while to help out. They can cover for me for a bit at the restaurant."

Ginny stepped forward. "I can help too, Barbara."

"I appreciate that, dear. But you should go home as soon as Nate releases you. He may want to talk to you again, I'm sure, but after that, go home and rest. Besides, Ralph and Dolores will be here any minute." Barbara referred to the husband-and-wife team, the Partridges, who cooked and served food for the bed-and-breakfast.

Ginny nodded. "Okay. I'll be back this afternoon. I just hope I'll be able to sleep." She turned away and headed for the rear of the house.

Lucky heard footsteps on the landing above her and the grunts of men struggling with a gurney. "Let's go in the kitchen," she said to Barbara, hoping the woman would not have to deal with the sight of a body being removed from her premises.

Barbara turned and saw the burden being carried down

her winding staircase. "Oh!" she exclaimed, her hand flying to her mouth.

"Come on." Lucky led her gently toward the entryway to the kitchen. Barbara allowed herself to be led to a chair. "Sit down and I'll fix you some tea."

"Make that coffee, Lucky. I can't sleep now. All my guests are in an uproar and they're confined to their rooms for the time being. I know there'll be an exodus and I can't blame them," she sobbed. "Who would want to stay in a place where there's been a murder?" Barbara rubbed her temples. "I need some aspirin."

Lucky opened a cabinet to search for a coffee mug. A fresh pot of brewed coffee sat on the machine. She pulled down a mug and filled it.

"Thanks," Barbara replied. "Could you be a dear and get me a glass of water. The aspirin is in that last cabinet on your left."

"Sure," Lucky replied, fulfilling Barbara's request.

"I can't believe this is happening. Why did that woman have to come to Snowflake and get herself murdered? And why here? At my bed-and-breakfast?" Barbara moaned.

"I don't know," Lucky sighed. "But stay here out of the way. I'll see if I can find that tray . . ."

"Everything's on the floor in the hallway right now. I'm afraid Ginny dropped the tray when she discovered the body." Barbara looked up ruefully. "One of the bowls broke. I'm sorry, I'll pay you for them."

"Don't be silly. Don't worry about it."

"They told me they dusted everything for fingerprints. I don't know what they think they can find. Everyone's been in and out of her room for the last few days anyway."

Lucky slipped out of the kitchen and walked quietly up the stairs. She looked up. Elias was coming down the stairs. They met on the landing. He put an arm around her shoulders and kissed her lightly. "What are you doing here?"

"I came back to get the dishes I delivered last night."

"After the book signing?"

Lucky nodded. "Can you tell me what happened?"

"Strangled, as far as I can tell. They'll have a full autopsy done over at Lincoln Falls. They'll make sure that's what happened."

Nate's heavy tread hit the stairway. "Lucky! What are you doing here?"

"I was just telling Elias. I came over to pick up my dishes before I went to the Spoonful."

"Ah." Nate sighed. "We saw the tray. What time were you here?"

"Um, well, it must have been about nine thirty, maybe nine forty-five. Her publicist called the restaurant. Ms. Stone decided she was hungry and only the Spoonful's food would do."

"That was nice of you, especially after hosting the book signing."

Lucky shrugged. "The answer would have been no if it had been any other situation. I really just did it for Barbara's sake."

Elias squeezed Lucky's shoulder. "I need to get going. I'll call you later." Lucky nodded in response as Elias bounded down the stairway.

"Excuse me." It was Derek Stone who spoke. He stood at the top of the stairway. His face was a ghastly gray and his eyes were red-rimmed and swollen.

"Yes." Nate turned to him.

"Where are they taking my mother?"

Nate climbed the stairs and rested his hand on the man's shoulder. "I'm very sorry for your loss." Derek remained silent, staring at Nate. "We're transporting her to Lincoln Falls, where there'll be a complete examination. I'll need everyone to remain here for a few days, but I'll let you know when you can make arrangements."

Derek's chest heaved. He looked as if he was about to burst into tears again.

"I'll be asking more questions later, but can you tell me when you last saw your mother alive?"

Derek's lip quivered. "Last night. I . . . I just popped in to say good night."

"And what time was that?"

"I don't know exactly. Maybe ten-ish, I guess. I was very tired and just wanted to get to sleep. Mother was getting ready for bed too. There was a tray on the desk. I guess she had had a bite to eat." He glanced at Lucky. "This lady had delivered it. Mother hadn't been hungry before the book event last night."

"How long were you with her?"

Derek shook his head, looking confused. "Not long. She asked me to help her with the clasp on her necklace. And then we said good night."

"Some of the guests claim they heard raised voices—they said it sounded like a man's voice. An argument. Did you hear anything like that?"

Derek looked mystified. "No. I didn't. Are you saying someone broke into my mother's room and . . ." He trailed off. "I didn't hear anything. Our room is at the end of the hallway. Phoebe, her assistant, is in the room next to her."

"I see," Nate replied. "I'll be talking to everyone again. Why don't you try to get some rest now."

"Derek!" A booming voice reached them from the downstairs lobby. Derek jumped involuntarily.

Lucky glanced down to where a distinguished-looking man with silver hair stood in the doorway of the Drake House. He spotted the group on the landing and strode up the stairs.

"Dad!" Derek said.

"I came as soon as I heard. Who's in charge here?" he demanded of Nate.

"I am," Nate replied. "Nate Edgerton. Chief of police. And you are?"

"Derek Stone, *Senior*." He reached out and forcefully shook Nate's hand.

"Why don't we go upstairs where we can talk privately," Nate requested.

"Glad to. This is just terrible news." He charged past Nate, patting his son on the shoulder. "Keep it together, Derek," he muttered.

Derek nodded and turned away, stumbling slightly as he walked down the hall. He held a hand to the wall as if to orient himself.

"Nate," Lucky said. "I'm sorry to barge in like this. I'll just pick up the tray and what's left of the dishes and get back to the restaurant."

"You do that. We're done with those. Tell Jack I'll stop in later." He turned away and climbed the stairs. The two men entered the sitting room and closed the door behind them.

Lucky retrieved the tray from the hallway table. She returned downstairs. When she reached the kitchen, Ralph and Dolores were already there, bustling about. They seemed to have breakfast well in hand. "Do you need any help, you two?" Lucky asked.

"Oh, no," Dolores replied. "We'll take care of everything." She turned to her employer. "Don't worry about a thing." Dolores was a plump, cheerful woman with a knot of gray hair pulled up on her head. She took the tray from Lucky's hands and quickly rinsed off the undamaged bowl. She dried it and slipped it into a paper bag with last night's plastic containers. "Here you go, dear." She shook her head and turned back to the stove. "This is a terrible thing to happen," she declared, slamming a heavy cast iron skillet on the stove. "Why couldn't these people stay where they belong?"

Chapter 22

"HOW DID YOU find out?" Marjorie asked breathlessly.

Lucky carried the sisters' cups of hot tea to the counter. "Well, I rushed over there early this morning to pick up my containers and dishes. Nate had been there all night and everyone was still running around. Otherwise, I wouldn't have known."

"Why were your dishes there?" Cecily asked.

"Last night after the book signing, they called and asked if I'd bring over some soups for Ms. Stone. She had heard how good our chef was."

"I just can't believe it. I was just chatting with her last night when she signed my book and now she's gone! And what about the next book she was working on? I suppose that will never happen now," Marjorie groaned.

Meg slipped behind the counter and joined the conversation. "You know, it might be finished already. Authors generally have their books ready way ahead of time. Her next book could be done and the publisher might still release it. I hope so anyway." Meg had the good grace to blush. "I mean . . . I'm sorry she's dead and all, but . . ." Meg looked at Lucky. "Did Nate tell you anything? Do you know how she was killed?"

Marjorie listened wide-eyed. Cecily groaned in response.

Lucky shivered. She wasn't about to pass on what Elias had told her on the landing. She shook her head. "Nate didn't tell me anything." At least that wasn't a lie, she thought. "I'm sure we'll find out soon enough."

"You don't suppose she was strangled with a telephone cord?" Meg asked. She turned to Marjorie, "Like in *Murder Comes Calling*?"

"That's right!" Marjorie exclaimed. "Oh, do you think Hilary Stone was killed by the same method?"

"Wouldn't that be exciting?" Meg's face was flushed.

"Hey, you two," Lucky interjected. "Stop that. This isn't a book. This is a real murder. That poor woman is dead."

Meg's face fell. "I'm sorry. You're right. I just get so excited about mysteries."

"Don't feel bad, Meg," Marjorie said. "I do too. Too easy to forget this is real life. But . . ." She smiled impishly. "In *Murder Comes Calling*, the culprit is . . ." She glanced around. "I don't want to tell you a spoiler."

Cecily spoke up. "We don't really care, Marjorie. I'm sure I'll never read it."

"Well," Marjorie huffed, "you just might learn something if you did."

"About what?" Cecily replied snarkily.

"About decomposition and time of death and how to tell strangulation from suffocation and all that."

"I'm sure that would come in quite handy in my world," Cecily remarked, catching Lucky's eye.

"As I was saying . . ." Marjorie drew herself up straighter. "Since no one other than Meg and myself have read *Murder Comes Calling*, much less *cares*"—she shot a glance at her sister—"the suspect was her ex-husband." Marjorie's brow furrowed. "Although he was innocent in the end. The real killer was the estranged daughter who had changed her name. That's why the police couldn't find her."

"Ah," Lucky remarked. "Sounds like an interesting story," she replied diplomatically.

"Well, I'm glad there's at least one person here with an open mind." She cast a dark look at her sister.

The bell at the front door jingled. Horace stepped inside, leading Cicero on his leash.

"Hello, Horace," Cecily called out. "Come and join us. Maybe we can talk about something other than bodily decomposition."

Marjorie closed her eyes in annoyance.

"Hello, ladies." He sat on the stool next to Cecily. "Am I correct in thinking you are all chatting about the demise of Ms. Hilary Stone?"

"That's right," Meg said. "How did you hear, Horace?"

"Oh, my! Three people stopped me as I walked over from the Village Green. It seems it's all anyone can talk about." He shook his head, "It's driven the other murder out of everyone's minds. Terrible thing to happen in our village of all places."

Lucky smiled at Horace's reference to "our" village. Horace no longer thought of himself as an outsider. He had been living in her parents' home for more than two years now, still working on his book about the Revolutionary War years in Vermont. She was positive Horace would never want to leave Snowflake.

A few more customers arrived. They looked vaguely familiar. Lucky thought perhaps they had attended the book-signing event the evening before. Meg pulled her order pad out of her apron and headed for their table. The bell jingled once more. Barry stepped inside and looked around the room. He was alone. He approached the counter.

"Good morning, Barry," Horace said.

"Uh . . ." Barry seemed distracted. "Lucky, is your grandfather here?"

"Yes."

"Could I talk to him for a minute?"

"Sure, grab a seat. I'll tell him you're here." Jack, she knew, was in the office counting the cash register receipts from the night before. With the book signing and all, he hadn't been able to follow his usual routine. She glanced over the counter to make sure everyone was set and then hurried down the hall. She pushed the door open. In the office, piles of cash were sitting in stacks on top of the desk. Jack was seated in her father's worn leather chair behind the desk with a pen and a pad of paper in his hand while Nanette was counting the stacks of bills.

Lucky's immediate reaction was one of alarm. Why was Nanette here? Only she and Jack were allowed to handle the restaurant receipts. "Nanette! What are you doing?"

Nanette looked up and smiled widely. "Ah was just helpin' Jack. He seemed to have so much to do."

"Hmm. Well, maybe you could give Meg a hand." *Doing the job you were hired to do*, she thought, but didn't say it. "She's getting busy out there."

"Happy to," Nanette replied sharply, replacing the cash on the desk. "I can help you anytime, Jack. You just let me know." Nanette wiggled her shoulders as she stood and passed by Lucky without a word.

Lucky sat in the chair that Nanette had vacated. "Jack?" Her grandfather looked up. "Look, I don't mean to criticize, but I don't really feel comfortable having Nanette in the office or her counting the register."

Jack looked up at her. "She was just trying to be helpful," he replied.

Lucky decided to bite her tongue. "I realize that, Jack, but we don't know her at all. She just walked in off the street. I think we have to be careful until we know we can trust her."

"Listen, my girl, she's a very nice woman." He smiled. "Don't you think you're being a little harsh with her?"

Lucky took a deep breath. "No, actually, I don't. And that reminds me, she was supposed to bring in her driver's license and social security card. I'll have to remind her."

"Oh, she told me about that. She just moved and she's having a little trouble finding all her papers."

"Oh really?" Lucky replied, but the sarcasm was lost on Jack. Once again, Lucky's suspicions were aroused. Why was Nanette so focused on a man decades older? It was obvious Jack was smitten with this woman. Lucky worried he was being played for a fool and that he'd be terribly hurt. "I almost forgot why I came in. Barry's out front. He says he needs to talk to you."

"Okay." Jack replied, bundling the stacks of cash with rubber bands. "Tell him to come on in. I'll just lock this in the drawer until I can get to the bank."

Lucky once again thought it was high time the restaurant had some sort of safe, preferably a hidden one. There were too many days when cash piled up and neither she nor Jack could get to the bank on a daily basis. "Thanks, Jack." Lucky hesitated in the doorway and turned back. "Jack. I love you very much. I only have your best interests at heart. You know that, don't you?"

Jack looked up, surprised. "Of course I do, my girl. I never doubt that for a second."

"Just please be careful who you trust."

WHEN LUCKY RETURNED to the counter, Marjorie and Cecily had already left to open their shop. Meg was busy with a new table and Nanette was taking orders from another group.

Horace leaned across the counter. "Barry looked upset, didn't he? Is everything all right?"

Lucky shrugged. "I don't know. I know he and Hank always come in together. He mentioned Hank wasn't feeling well but that was a few days ago. I hope nothing's really wrong." Lucky swept away a used coffee cup. "What can I get you, Horace?"

Horace's face brightened. "I really want to try that new chicken almond soup that Sage came up with. Maybe with some French bread if you have that?"

"Sure. Coming right up."

A few minutes later, Barry pushed through the swinging door from the corridor. He walked through the restaurant and exited by the front door without a word. Jack returned to the front room and took the stool next to Horace while Meg covered the cash register.

Horace turned to watch Barry's retreat, then turned back to Jack. "Is something wrong?" he asked.

"Ah, Barry's worried about Hank. He's been calling, but Hank hasn't picked up. I told him not to worry, maybe Hank had to do an errand in Lincoln Falls or something. But Barry swears Hank would have mentioned it, or at least called him. Then he was telling me he went by the house late last night just to check on him, make sure Hank wasn't sick or anything, but he still wasn't back, and his car's still gone."

"That is odd," Horace remarked. "Doesn't sound like Hank at all. He knows Barry meets him every morning and comes down to the Spoonful. You'd think he would've mentioned something to his friend if he had to go out of town."

"You'd think so, wouldn't you?" Jack agreed. He checked his watch. "I better get busy. It's just gone four bells." He hurried over to the cash register to relieve Meg.

Lucky filled coffee cups for two new arrivals, then took their orders and placed the slips on the hatch. She returned to Horace's spot. "You have a funny look on your face, Horace," she remarked.

"How long has Hank been missing in action?" he asked.

"Since . . ." Lucky hesitated. "Well, what day is this? Thursday? I guess it was Monday that Barry first mentioned Hank wasn't feeling well. But Barry did talk to him on the phone that first day. Why do you ask?"

Horace sighed. "That is strange. I didn't want to say anything in front of Jack or anyone, but I saw Hank last night when I drove into town to take Cicero for a walk."

"Where did you see him?" Lucky asked.

"He was just leaving the Drake House."

"Last night? What time?"

"Oh, it was late. It must have been about . . . after ten o'clock."

"The night of the murder?" A chill ran up Lucky's spine. What could Hank possibly have been doing at the Drake House?

Chapter 23

NATE REGARDED THE tall man carefully. “I’m very sorry for your loss, Mr. Stone.”

Derek Stone nodded and wiped his forehead. “Thank you. This is a terrible shock. Who would have wanted to hurt poor Hilary?”

“Can you tell me your whereabouts last evening, Mr. Stone?” Nate flipped open his notebook.

Stone cleared his throat. “I was at a dinner in Manhattan all evening. A retirement dinner.”

“And what time was that?”

“It . . . uh, well, we gathered for cocktails at six thirty. And the dinner began around eight. I left about ten thirty, almost eleven, and my driver took me home. There was a phone message from my son when I arrived.”

“I see.” Nate jotted a few lines in the notebook. “And you’ll be able to give me the names of some people who can vouch for you?”

Stone looked up quickly. He drew himself up in the chair. “What are you implying? That I . . . that I had something to do with Hilary’s death?”

Nate responded patiently, "This is a murder investigation, Mr. Stone. Everyone's whereabouts need to be verified." Nate realized that if Stone's story checked out, he could eliminate the man from any suspicion.

Stone sighed heavily. "Yes, yes. You're right. I can give you several names."

"That's good." Nate stared at the man for a moment. "How was your marriage?"

"What? My marriage?" Nate waited. "We . . . uh, we, Hilary and I . . .we've been on good terms. We live rather separate lives, really. Some people may not see us as close, but we get along. We had no problems."

"Can you tell me the terms of your wife's estate?"

"All of Hilary's assets will go to Derek. That's what we decided. In the event of my death, my estate would be . . . would have been divided equally between Hilary and my son, except for the business. Hilary would have inherited that." He sighed. "I just can't . . ." He trailed off. "This shouldn't have happened. I feel just terrible. This wouldn't have happened if I hadn't pressured her for a sequel to *Murder Comes Calling*. She never would have been here . . ."

"We don't know that, Mr. Stone. We won't know that until this crime is solved."

"There's something else," he hesitated. "I suppose I should mention it."

"Oh?" Nate's ears perked up.

"Hilary had spoken to me about changing the terms of her will. She, well, we both were, very upset about Derek's marriage. I don't know if she ever got around to it. But I think she was talking to our attorney about setting up her trust in a way that Sylvia, Derek's wife, would not have access to any of the funds. We wanted Derek to inherit but hoped to protect his assets in some way. But again, I don't know if Hilary had actually done that."

"I see." *Well, that's interesting,* Nate thought to himself. "Please make sure you leave your attorney's contact information with me. How long are you staying?"

"I'll visit with my son and then I will probably go back

to the city later today. That's if you have no objection," Stone answered. "I doubt there's anything more I can do here now."

"Please leave a list of contacts who can verify your movements with my deputy before you go."

"I will." Stone stood and, heaving a great sigh, left the room.

Chapter 24

NATE STOOD IN the center of the room recently occupied by Hilary Stone. Something was bothering him. It was just at the edge of his consciousness but he couldn't grasp it, he thought, the same way you walk into a room to retrieve something, but by the time you arrive, you've forgotten what it was you wanted. He couldn't quite put his finger on what was unsettling him. He turned in a circle and carefully surveyed everything again. What was he missing? All personal items had been left untouched in the room. A list had been carefully made of each item. Nothing seemed amiss. The only signs of a struggle were disturbed bedclothes and a pair of crushed eyeglasses on the floor next to the woman's body. She must have attempted to fight, to reach out for help, but could only grasp the bedspread.

As if she had just stepped to the side of her bed, about to pull down the covers, when she had been attacked. The phone and its cord had been right there, next to her on the nightstand. Premeditated? Or was it a case that the murder weapon had been at hand and this was done in a fit of rage? An impulse killing? The woman was average height, but seeing her body,

Nate wouldn't have thought her to have been a particularly strong woman. If she had turned her back and someone slipped the cord around her neck, it had to be someone she had trusted. Someone known to her and definitely not a stranger.

Idly, he opened and closed each of the bureau drawers. He knelt down and checked under the bed. He lightly touched each of the bottles and cosmetics in the bathroom. Nothing seemed out of place or unusual. A stack of books sat on the desk. He picked one up and leafed through it. On the back cover was a photo of the dead woman. Hilary Stone's hair was artfully arranged. She wore an attractive pair of glasses in pastel frames. Nate felt a thrill run through him. Eyeglasses.

He returned to the side of the bed and picked up the broken eyeglasses with a tissue, grasping the thin metal frame. Pince-nez glasses. He had assumed this pair belonged to the murdered woman. He held one lens up to his eye. Very strong. He opened the purse on the bureau and found another pair that had definitely belonged to the murdered woman. These were framed in a light-colored plastic like the photo on the book cover. He tested them. Only slight magnification. Readers. These twisted eyeglasses belonged to someone else.

A tap came on the door to the bedroom. "Nate?" Barbara Drake stood in the doorway. "Is it okay to come in?"

"Yes, it's fine. I'm just about done here." He held up the twisted eyeglasses. "Do you recognize these?"

"No. Sorry. I know Ms. Stone wore glasses but I don't remember her wearing anything like those."

"More like these?" Nate asked, holding up the plastic-framed glasses.

"Yes, those were hers. I saw her wearing them."

"Just as I thought," Nate replied. "While I have you here, have you noticed anything unusual since these guests arrived?"

"Well, they're a pretty unusual bunch, but no. Nothing I can think of."

"Anyone strange hanging around that you might have noticed? Did anyone try to come to see Ms. Stone?"

Barbara began to shake her head. "No. I don't think . . . wait, yes, there was someone, a woman."

"She came here?"

"Yes, very polite. She asked to speak to Ms. Stone."

"Did she? When was this?"

"Uh, it was a few days ago. Sunday morning, I think. I thought I saw Phoebe stop and speak to her, but I'm not really positive. I did buzz Mr. Stone in his room and he came down to talk to her. He's been very adamant about not having his mother disturbed by anyone."

"Did she leave her name by any chance?"

Barbara shook her head. "No. I don't think so. At least not with me."

"What did she look like?"

"Oh . . ." Barbara hesitated. "Average. I really didn't pay much attention. Just got a quick look. Well groomed, about my height, attractive, short brown hair as I recall. I left her to wait for Derek to come down and went back to the kitchen. You'll have to ask him."

Nate reached inside his jacket and pulled out a photo. "Is this the woman?"

Barbara stared at the photo. "Oh!" She raised a hand to her mouth. "Is this the woman you found in the woods?"

Nate nodded. "Was this her?"

Barbara stared at the photo for a few more moments. "I . . . it could be, Nate. I'm not sure. I didn't pay much attention and this picture is . . . horrible. It could be, but I can't swear to it."

"Okay, that's fine, Barbara. If you remember anything else, will you call me?" Barbara nodded. Her face looked pale. She left the room without another word.

PHOEBE HOLLISTER SAT quietly in the chair, her hands clasped tightly together on her lap. Her eyes were red-rimmed and her face swollen. She had been crying for a long time. Nate had taken over the common suite on the second floor to question the Stone entourage and the rest of the guests at the Drake House.

"How long did you work for Ms. Stone, Phoebe?"

"Not long, only about a month."

"Really? Where did you work before?"

"Oh. I see what you mean. I worked for Mr. Stone at the publishing house, Hilary's . . . Ms. Stone's husband. I started there a couple of months ago, and when this trip was arranged, Mr. Stone asked me if I would like to be her assistant on the road. Sort of a temporary arrangement."

"And how did you like working for her?"

"She was fine. She could be very fussy sometimes, but she was never unkind to me. The hard part has been . . ." She trailed off.

"What's been the hard part?"

"Oh." She shrugged. "Just dealing with everyone else. Audra's okay, but sometimes Derek, Ms. Stone's son, and his wife could be difficult. It's just been a juggling job taking care of limousines and travel arrangements and such, but it's also been a nice change in routine for me."

"And how did you come to work for Lexington Avenue Publishing?"

"A friend told me about a possible opening, and I just applied. I had been doing temporary work in the city and I was looking for a permanent spot. It was good timing." Phoebe's jaw clenched and her hands gripped each other. Nate felt he was going out of his way to make her comfortable with his questions, but she seemed to grow more uncomfortable the more he questioned her.

"Can you tell me everything you did and saw last night?"

"There was nothing remarkable," she replied curtly. "The book signing ended promptly at nine o'clock. I was grateful for that. It had been a long day. We came back here together, Ms. Stone and I. Derek drove us back. Hilary said she was a bit hungry and she wanted something light to eat but the kitchen downstairs was closed. Someone had mentioned the chef at the Spoonful and she wanted me to order something from there."

"How did you arrange that?"

Phoebe sighed in annoyance. "I told all this to your deputy. I really don't see why you can't talk to him."

Nate struggled to keep his voice level. "I realize that. But sometimes going over your recollections can bring new things to light." He repeated his question. "How did you arrange for the food to be delivered?"

Phoebe closed her eyes for a long second and took a deep breath. "I was afraid the restaurant would be closed. I went downstairs to talk to Mrs. Drake, the owner. She gave me the number. I asked Audra if she wanted anything. She did not, but she called the restaurant and they said they'd take care of it." All this was recited in a robotic voice.

"And then?"

"Then?" Phoebe pursed her lips.

"Yes. What did you do after that?"

She sighed again, a look of anger crossing her face. "I tapped on Hilary's door to let her know someone would be bringing up food for her. I asked her if there was anything else she needed. There wasn't. That was it. Hilary said she was fine, so I went back to my room and got ready for bed."

"And what time was that?"

"I guess it must have been around . . . nine thirty or a little after. I didn't really pay attention."

"Some of the guests heard loud voices on the second floor a little after that time. Did you hear anything?"

Phoebe nodded. "I did. I heard a man's voice. It sounded like an argument."

"Did you come out of your room?"

"No," Phoebe snapped back. "I certainly did not."

"Why not?" Nate asked mildly. "Weren't you concerned?"

"I assumed it was Derek and his wife. Sometimes they argue and get quite loud. I wasn't about to interfere or step into that. So I stayed put." Phoebe's brow furrowed. "Are you saying that . . . that I should have checked on her?"

"I'm not saying that. Besides, you couldn't possibly have known. And you might be right. It could just have been Mr. Stone and his wife." Nate scribbled on the pad in front of him. "They argue a lot?"

"Who?"

"Mr. Stone and his wife?"

"I don't know if you'd call it arguing. That would take two people. Mostly it's just Sylvia yelling at him." She continued to twist her fingers nervously.

"I see." Nate flicked his ballpoint pen closed. "Okay, Phoebe. That's all for now."

"Do you know when can we get back to New York?"

"In a few days. I'm sorry. I'm just asking everyone to stay just in case I have more questions. I'll let you know."

Phoebe nodded. She rose and walked to the door, then hesitated and turned back.

"Yes?" Nate looked up.

"I just wanted to say that . . . whoever did this, you won't have to look very far for motives." She slipped out the door and shut it quietly behind her.

Nate stared at her retreating figure.

Chapter 25

LUCKY LOOKED UP as Jack pushed open the door of the office and entered.

"Got a minute?" he asked.

"Sure." Lucky pushed the stack of bills to the side. The old leather desk chair creaked as she sat back.

"Uh . . ." Jack hesitated. "What did you think about Nanette's idea, my girl?"

Lucky had to focus to recall what Jack was talking about. "I'm sorry, Jack, I don't—"

"Her idea about changing the design of the aprons and all," he said as he sat in the chair on the other side of the desk.

"Oh." Lucky hesitated. "That. Um . . ." She wasn't sure how to broach the subject. "Do you really want to know how I feel?"

"Well, of course I do, my girl."

Lucky looked across the desk at her grandfather. She mentally counted to three to soften what she was about to say. "I really love the aprons the way they are. And I love my dad's sign in the window. Every time I pull an apron out of the closet, I think about Mom, and every time I see the neon sign in the window, I remember my dad. So, to answer your question, the last thing I want to do is let go of those little symbols of their being here."

Jack nodded. "I understand. It's just that Nanette seems to have a good eye for these things and she's worked in a lot of places, she's told me, so—"

"Frankly, Jack. She's really put my back up."

"What are you sayin'?"

"She still hasn't given me any identification, a driver's license, social security card, something. In fact, if she doesn't provide it very soon, I'm going to have to pay her for her time and let her go."

"What?" Jack almost shouted.

"I'm going to have to let her go. I can't have someone working here who can't provide valid tax identification. It's against the law and we don't need that kind of trouble."

"I'll have a talk with her."

"It's not just that. It's everything about her. She's argued with Sage and told him his recipes needed improvement, which is just ridiculous. She's been here three seconds and already she's trying to change things and offer opinions about things that don't concern her. She spends more time hanging around you at the cash register than she does waiting on tables."

"Well, I like her company. It's partly my fault. I've encouraged her to chat with me."

"Don't you think she's being a little too friendly? A little inappropriate?"

"What do you mean?" Jack asked in a shocked voice.

Lucky took a deep breath. "Jack! I've seen her put her arm around you. She rubs your shoulder . . ."

"She likes me. What's wrong with that? You think 'cause I'm an old man, no woman would be attracted to me, is that what you mean?" Jack's voice rose.

"No. That's unfair, Jack. That's not what I mean."

"Look, you just don't like her. She told me she's had trouble like that where she's worked before. It's just women that don't like her and take it out on her. Just jealousy."

"Oh"—Lucky could feel her temper rising—"a regular martyr, now, is she?"

Jack's jaw clamped shut. "Well, if you're gonna take that attitude, there's no use talking to you."

"I'll just bet she's had trouble every place she worked. I can certainly see why," Lucky retorted.

"You know what? You're every bit as stubborn and pig-headed as your father, you know that?"

"Probably I am. But the next time she's hanging around your neck at the cash register, please ask her to produce some real identification, will you?"

Jack face darkened. "This is my business too, my girl. I know your parents left it to you, but I'm part owner and I've got a say in what goes on here." Jack stood and stormed to the door, slamming it behind him.

Lucky sat staring at the door her grandfather had just stomped out of. *Why is this happening?* she thought. Arguing with Jack, a man she loved with all her heart? She shook her head. This was out of control. Nanette had to go. Something was not right about that woman. But first she needed someone to replace her. She couldn't risk Meg's quitting.

Lucky heard a tap on the door. "What?" she shouted.

The door cracked open and Sophie peeked around the doorway. "Uh-oh. What's wrong?"

"Nothing!"

"Oh, right. Your face is beet red and your breathing's shallow. What's going on? I thought I heard Jack yelling."

Lucky heaved a sigh. "You did."

"I've never seen him get upset . . . much less argue with you."

"I know. I feel bad. I was kind of sarcastic to him. I should have been gentler. I tried, I really did. We were arguing about Nanette."

"Oh." A wealth of opinion was in the one word that Sophie uttered.

"What's your impression of her?"

"Well, she's managed to get Sage in an uproar. You know

how he is about his kitchen. He couldn't stop complaining the other night."

"That's what I mean. I told Jack what I thought of her hanging around the cash register and sticking her nose in where it doesn't belong."

"What was his reaction?"

"He defended her!" Lucky almost shouted. "Can you believe that? The woman still hasn't given me any proper identification. And now she's on about how we should change the aprons and the neon sign and all that."

"What does Jack say?"

"He thinks she has good ideas!"

"This woman has a colossal nerve. How long has she worked here? A few days maybe?"

Lucky shook her head. "She's making me crazy. And there's no way in hell the aprons or the sign are changing. No way. Over my dead body."

"Be careful what you say," Sophie warned. "Besides, it's your business. What do you care what she thinks?"

"Oh, Sophie." Lucky leaned back in the chair. "It's really Jack's too. I can't deny that. He started it with my parents. He's part of it. Just because they left it to me. If I had decided not to come back, I don't think Jack could have or would have kept it running, but he's still part owner, ethically at least. Besides, even if he weren't, I don't want to hurt his feelings or argue with him. I feel really bad that I got him upset. It's just not how I want my working days to be. Jack and I are really close. I love him to pieces. If he walked out, I'd never forgive myself. I don't know how I'd feel."

Sophie plopped heavily into the chair that Jack had vacated. "That woman is a snake."

Chapter 26

MEG WIPED OFF the last of the tables and straightened the chairs. She lifted the basin of dirty dishes from the counter and carried it into the kitchen. Lucky shot a glance at Jack, who sat at the cash register counting the day's earnings. There had been an uncomfortable silence between them all day. At one point, Lucky spotted Nanette at the register with her arm around Jack's shoulder, leaning against him. When Nanette noticed Lucky watching, Nanette shot her a scathing look and moved away. Lucky breathed a sigh of relief when the woman finally left for the day. She finished cleaning up the counter and stepped into the kitchen, where Sage was helping Meg load the dishwasher.

"Anything else you need tonight, Lucky?" Sage asked.

"No. I'm fine, thanks. You two go ahead and take off."

Meg straightened and turned to her, "I'm sorry," she said, wiping her hands on a towel.

Lucky raised her eyebrows. "About what?"

"I know you can't stand Nanette. And I know you hired her because of me. I feel really bad to have pressured you, Lucky."

"Don't feel bad, please, Meg. You were absolutely right. It's been way too much work for you. I just wish I hadn't been so hasty, but she sort of bulldozed her way in."

"Well, I'm with Lucky," Sage offered. "That woman better not come into my kitchen again and try to tell me how to cook."

Lucky laughed. "It's ridiculous, I know. But I think after I spoke to her . . . I came down on her pretty hard. I don't think she'll go near you again." Lucky hesitated. "I just wish I had chatted with Miriam Leonard sooner."

"Janie's mom? What do you mean?" Meg asked.

"I think Miriam's kind of lonely now with Janie at school. She mentioned she was thinking of getting a job somewhere in town. I don't know if she'd consider working here, at least part-time, but I'd love to have her."

"That would be great," Meg agreed.

"Well, we'll see what happens. It's early days yet," Lucky replied. She decided to give Nanette an ultimatum first thing in the morning. Twenty-four hours to produce valid identification and a social security card. No matter what Jack said, she had no choice. She glanced out at the front room and saw that Jack was sitting at his table by the front window. "You two go ahead. I'll take care of loose ends."

"Okay," Sage agreed. "I won't argue. I'll take the trash out to the Dumpster though." He hefted a large garbage bag over his shoulder and headed for the corridor.

"Good night." Meg waved as she left.

Lucky steeled herself. There couldn't be a better time to talk to Jack and try to mend her fences. She returned to the front room and sat at Jack's table.

"I'm sorry, Jack."

Her grandfather looked up. "About what?"

"I don't want to argue with you. I love you and I've felt awful all day."

He reached across the table and grasped her hand. "Nothing to worry about, my girl. I'm sorry if I got a little bit upset. You're right to insist on identification and proof and all that stuff the government wants. I guess my head's been turned a little. I'm an old man and I get lonely sometimes and it's nice to get female attention. Everybody likes attention."

"As long as that's all Nanette wants. She just really rubs me the wrong way. I don't know why. Some of the things she's neglected to tell me and . . . it's just . . ."

"Don't worry your head," Jack replied. "She's probably just humoring an old man. She's—" A tap on the door interrupted Jack's thoughts.

They both looked up to see Nate standing outside the front door. Lucky hurried over and unlocked it for him.

"Thanks, Lucky," he said as he entered.

"Something from the kitchen, Nate?"

"Nah. But I'd love a beer. Susanna called and she's got something in the oven for me. I just wanted to stop in and decompress. I don't like to bring my job home with me." Nate sat at the small round table with Jack. Lucky hurried to the refrigerator in the kitchen and grabbed a beer for Nate. She returned to the table with the bottle, a napkin and a chilled glass.

Jack asked, "How's the investigation going?"

"I'm making some progress. Dr. Cranleigh, our murder victim, arranged for some time off, but nobody seems to know why. They assumed it might be family issues. But here's the strange thing. She doesn't appear to have any family. She has an apartment in Bournmouth. Quiet woman, quiet life, devoted to her patients from all accounts. A few friends at work. No husband or boyfriend that anyone knew about." Nate took a sip of his beer. "I told you we found her car on a dirt road about a quarter of a mile away. The question is, why was she taking a leave right now? No one seems to have a good answer. There must have been a reason and it could be the reason she was killed. She doesn't seem like the kind of person who'd be vulnerable to a random attack."

"Why do you say that?" Lucky asked.

"Well, she strikes me as a careful woman. Her apartment was neat as a pin. All her papers were organized. Nothing to indicate personal problems or why she would have taken off like that. Not the type to pick up hitchhikers. And most importantly, nothing mechanically wrong with her car. If she had had problems on the road, car breaking down, flat tire, I could understand how the wrong person might stop to help, but the mechanics couldn't find anything wrong with it. She might have driven to the pond and got out to look at the scenery. Either she didn't make it or she was somehow lured back into the woods. Personally, I think her car was deliberately moved to stall identification."

Lucky shuddered. "Horrible."

"I agree. Murder always is," Nate remarked.

"Any progress with your other case?" Jack asked.

Nate shook his head. "That bunch. Gives me a headache just thinkin' about them. They all claim this lady, Hilary Stone, was fine when they said good night. Nobody admits going back into her room. Her assistant claims she heard an argument, a man's voice, around nine forty-five, but the publicist, Audra, and a few people downstairs, heard an argument later, around ten. An argument with a man. They all assumed it was Derek and his wife going at it. That's why they didn't bother to go see what was happening. That wife is quite a harpy too. Ginny, the maid, also claims she heard raised voices later around ten thirty when she went up to get the tray. She listened at the doorway, but she couldn't tell who Ms. Stone was arguing with. She couldn't even identify for sure if it was a man or a woman."

"So people heard an argument around nine forty-five or ten o'clock, but the maid heard one at ten thirty?"

"Yup."

"Could someone have been with her that whole time and the argument just escalated? Or were there two different people in her room that night?"

"Good question. I'd tend to doubt the maid, but she's adamant about the time because she was just waiting to go home at eleven. I'm still trying to pin everybody's timeline down, assuming they're not lying to me." Nate looked across the table. "What do you think, Jack?"

"I think it's a damn shame we've had another murder . . . two murders . . . in our village again."

"And it's way too much of a coincidence both these women were strangled, likely with the same device." Nate took a last sip of his beer. "Susanna's told me all about *Murder Comes Calling* . . ." He looked from Lucky to Nate. "Have either of you read it?"

"No, but Meg told me the murder weapon in Hilary's book is a telephone cord," Lucky said. "There must be a connection between these two women."

Nate nodded. "Has to be. I just haven't found it yet. I do plan to keep looking." Nate rose from his chair. "Well, good night, you two. I'll be on my way. Thanks again for the beer." Nate walked to the front door, then turned back to them. "By the way, either of you seen Hank Northcross lately?"

"No, I haven't, come to think of it." Jack said.

Lucky shook her head negatively. "I know Barry hasn't been able to find him." She wondered why Nate was asking. Should she mention that Horace had seen Hank leaving the Drake House? Some instinct made her hesitate.

"If you do see him, would you let me know? I've been looking all over for him." Nate held up a hand to say good night and closed the door behind him.

Jack looked at Lucky, "Why do you think Nate's looking for Hank?"

"I don't know. Barry's been worried about him and maybe he's been talking to Nate about it. But here's the thing . . . Horace told me he saw Hank the night of the murder."

"Where?"

"Leaving the Drake House."

Jack's brow furrowed. "What would he be doing there?"

"That's a good question."

"You think Hank not being around has something to do with Nate's investigation?" Jack asked.

"I certainly hope not," Lucky answered, but she couldn't escape the feeling that Hank's disappearance was too much of a coincidence.

Chapter 27

AS SOON AS Jack left for home, Lucky turned off the neon sign in the front window and checked the kitchen to make sure the dishwasher had finished its cycle. She tied the sleeves of her sweater around her neck and slung her purse over her shoulder. She stepped out the back door, locked it and wiggled the handle to make sure the lock was secure.

A wave of loneliness swept over her. She wished Elias were home tonight. She could ask him to stop by, and they could make popcorn and watch a movie. But he was in Lincoln Falls for the night, checking a post-op patient, and had early rounds to do in the morning.

The night was still and clear, only a hint of the warmth to come. The smell of freshly tilled earth from the Victory Garden on the next block filled the air. She unlocked her car door and tossed her purse on the passenger seat. Something shifted in the atmosphere. The hairs on the back of her neck stood at attention. A heavy hand fell on her shoulder.

"Lucky."

She screamed involuntarily and spun around.

"Barry!" She breathed a sigh of relief. "You scared me half to death. What are you doing here?"

"I've just been out walking." He shoved his hands in his jacket pockets. "Don't know what to do with myself. I'm worried sick."

"No word from Hank?"

"Nope." Barry shook his head.

"And you've talked to Nate?" she asked.

"Yes. Of course. Nothing he can do. Hank's car hasn't been seen anywhere. No report of an accident. No hospital admissions."

"I know you're worried about him. But it sounds like you've done everything you possibly can." She thought of Nate's visit earlier that evening. "Nate did ask us if we had heard from Hank or seen him."

"I'm sure he did. He wants to question Hank. He told me himself."

"Question him? Why?"

"People saw him at the Drake House that night . . . the night of the murder."

"Ah," Lucky replied. No surprise there. Sooner or later the news would get to Nate. She was relieved she needn't feel guilty about not mentioning the sighting to Nate. Probably more people than just Horace had seen Hank that evening.

"What I'm wondering, Lucky . . ." Barry trailed off. Lucky waited patiently. "I'm wondering if you'd help me. Help me find Hank."

Lucky felt confused. "Barry . . . I'd be glad to help you, but I don't know what I could possibly do."

"I've asked Jack but he seems preoccupied lately. And I'm asking you because you've helped so many people. You saved Sage from a jail sentence and you rescued Janie from that criminal. I've given it some thought and I finally realized that you're the best person to ask for help."

"I . . . I don't know what to say, Barry. I don't have any special skills. I'll help you any way I can but I wouldn't know where to begin."

"I have some ideas." Lucky waited. "I wouldn't suggest this normally, but I have an emergency key to Hank's house. He gave it to me years ago. We gave each other keys to both our houses. I mean, we're getting older, you never know when we might have a medical emergency or something, that's why we did that. I'd never use it otherwise, but I guess I'm hoping there's a letter or a call on the phone machine or *something* that could tell us where he's gone or what's going on with him."

"I don't know, Barry." Lucky shook her head. "I hate the idea of prying into his personal life."

"I do too, Lucky. But he's my best buddy. After my wife died . . . well, we've been good friends since we both retired and ended up here in Snowflake. I know Hank. Nate doesn't quite believe me, but I know Hank wouldn't just take off without a word unless something was really wrong. And I certainly don't believe he had anything to do with that woman's murder at the Drake House."

"I agree with you there. You want me to go with you?"

"Yes. I do. Maybe you'll see something I wouldn't. I don't want to do this alone."

"Okay. When?"

"How 'bout now?"

"Now?" Lucky squeaked. All she wanted to do was go home and put her feet up and relax.

Barry nodded.

"Okay," she agreed. "No time like the present. Hop in," she said, indicating the passenger door.

LUCKY SHIVERED IN the chill night air, waiting for Barry to fiddle through a large key ring searching for the correct one. From the exterior, the house was completely dark, no light at the front, no light emanating from the interior. Finally, Barry uttered an exclamation and they heard the lock click. Barry entered first and held the door open for Lucky. She stepped inside. In the complete dark her nose twitched. The house had an abandoned feel, as if a thin layer of dust lay over everything, even though Hank had only been gone a few days. No odor of meals being recently cooked, a complete lack of warmth.

Barry reached over and flicked on the hallway lamp. Ghostly shadows played against the walls, fingers of light tickling the edges of the room.

"Where do we start?" Lucky asked, having an overwhelming sense of doing something she should definitely not be doing.

Barry, as if reading her mind, said, "Don't feel bad. This is the reason Hank gave me a key. In case he was ever sick or in case anything ever happened to him. Otherwise, I'd never intrude in his house myself." Barry moved forward into the living room, his shadow stretching and fading into the darkness. He found another lamp and turned it on.

Lucky stepped through the archway into the small front room of Hank's cottage. The walls were lined with books, floor to ceiling. Two large comfortable-looking chairs upholstered in a plaid fabric stood next to the fireplace, an ottoman between them. A heavy oak credenza was against the opposite wall, with square drawers that looked as if they might be used to hold files. A wooden desk took up the corner of the room. Its top was completely neat, everything in place. A small wicker basket on top of the desk held recent mail. Hank's living room was a comfortable masculine den. She could visualize him at night, sitting by a fire and reading. She turned in a circle, surveying the bookshelves. "This is amazing. Hank might have more books here than the Snowflake library."

"I know. And he's donated tons to the library too. Hank's a very well-read guy. He's smart, educated. Not like me. I'm just a retired electrician, never was much of a reader, but Hank's loaned me lots of books, now that I have so much time on my hands."

"I guess if he earned his living writing, he'd be a great reader. Until you told me about his prior life, I never knew what he did."

"Well?" Barry looked at her earnestly. "Where should we start?"

Lucky dropped her purse on one of the large chairs and draped her sweater over it. "Why don't you check the mailbox? I'll see where Hank might be keeping recent correspondence and I'll check the messages on his answering machine. Let's start with the obvious."

Barry hurried back to the front door. Lucky heard the metal clang of the mailbox. He returned carrying a stack of envelopes.

Lucky sat at the desk chair and took the stack of envelopes from Barry's hands. Several flyers, some junk mail advertisements and two bills. "Nothing out of the ordinary here." She reached across for the wicker basket and flipped through its contents. A dental bill to be paid, a flyer from Guy's Auto Shop offering a discount for oil changes. That was all. She placed all the mail in the basket then methodically went through each drawer of the desk.

"What can I do, Lucky?" Barry asked.

"Maybe open that big credenza and see what's inside. Looks like it might hold files." She turned back to the desk. Every drawer was neatly organized—pens, notepads, paper clips, a box of staples, stationery in the bottom drawer. She rummaged through the contents of each drawer and returned every item neatly. Then she knelt on the floor and pulled one drawer after another out all the way, feeling underneath to see if anything might be hidden there.

"Barry?"

"Yup." Barry was kneeling on the floor by the oak credenza.

"Does Hank have any family that you know of?"

"No. He had a sister but she died years ago. He mentioned once she was the last of his family."

Lucky checked the back of the desk to make sure nothing was taped there. She sighed. Absolutely nothing to indicate what had been going on recently in Hank's life. She closed all the drawers, lifted the desk blotter from its frame, checked underneath and then straightened the top items carefully. Hank would know someone had been here, but nothing would be disturbed.

The phone and answering machine sat at the far corner of the desk. She pressed the button. A disembodied voice announced five messages. Lucky listened to each one. Three were from Barry, one from Hank's dental office and a third from a bookstore in Lincoln Falls to tell him his order had come in.

"Anything?" Barry asked. He was now sitting cross-legged on the floor flicking through a stack of files he had lifted from a file drawer.

"Absolutely nothing. Completely ordinary. I could take lessons in neatness from Hank though." She stood and moved to the oak credenza. "I'll give you a hand with this . . ." She hesitated.

Barry looked up. "What is it?"

"I . . ." Lucky took a step backward. "Something," she said. "Over here. Something sparkled." She moved to a darkened corner next to the fireplace, sure she had seen something.

Barry clambered to his feet and moved to the other side of the room. "This will give you some light." He turned on a floor lamp on the other side of the desk.

"Look," Lucky said, pointing to the floor. "It looks like a few tiny pieces of broken glass."

"You're right," Barry said, peering down at the floor. "Something broke and Hank must have missed this when he cleaned up."

"Let's see if we can figure out what was broken." She walked down the short hallway to the kitchen. She flicked on the overhead light and opened the doors to the cabinet under the sink, where a small plastic garbage can rested. Barry peered over her shoulder as she pulled it out. She grabbed a paper towel from a roll next to the sink and gingerly removed an empty milk container and a paper plate. She placed the discarded items in the sink and peered into the plastic bin.

"What's that?" Barry asked.

With two fingers, Lucky pulled out a small wooden picture frame that had separated into two pieces. There was more broken glass at the bottom of the bin. She reached in and lifted out the largest piece of glass. Stuck to it was the soggy remnant of a photograph. "Take a look at this." She gently pulled the photograph away from the glass shard and held it up.

Barry slipped on his glasses and took it from her hand. "It's Hank!"

"You're sure?"

"Yes. Much younger, but it's him. It looks like . . ." He trailed off.

"A wedding picture," Lucky finished.

Barry stared at the photograph in his hand for several moments. He barely seemed to breathe. He looked questioningly at Lucky. "Hank never told me he had been married . . . was married." He shook his head. "I don't know what to think."

"Maybe it was something he just didn't want to talk about," Lucky replied. "Can I see that for a second?"

Barry handed back the photograph. His expression was one of hurt. "That could be. But we are good friends, Lucky. Really, we are. I wouldn't have pried. It just seemed strange that we've talked about our lives and the things we've done. You'd think he might have mentioned it at least once."

Lucky stared at the photograph and a shiver went up her spine. "Do you recognize this woman?"

"You mean the woman in the picture?" Barry shook his head. "No one I know."

"I'd bet my last dollar this is Hilary Stone."

Chapter 28

BARRY SNATCHED THE photo from Lucky's hand. "The mystery writer? The one who was just murdered at the Drake House?"

"Yes." Lucky nodded. "I'm positive that's her. She's much younger in this photograph, but she still looks pretty much the same. You didn't see her at the book signing?"

"No. I didn't go. Not my thing," he answered. "What do you know? Hank was married to a famous mystery writer!" He handed the photo back to Lucky.

"Well, I doubt she was famous then. This was taken a long time ago, judging by her hairstyle and Hank's suit. She didn't publish her book until late last year. And come to think of it, her publicist Audra mentioned that she's married to the head of the publishing house."

"She and Hank must be divorced then. Do you know anything else about her?"

"No. Just that she has a son . . . Derek." Lucky hesitated, but finally replaced the photo in the trash along with the rest of the items from the kitchen sink.

"How old is he?" Barry asked.

"Hard to say. Not very old, but he's a little overweight so I think he looks older than he is. Maybe he's thirty-ish, early thirties."

Barry's face shifted. "You don't think he could be Hank's son, do you?"

Lucky shrugged. "I have no idea." She thought a moment. "Hank's in his late sixties. I guess it's possible."

"Well, that is really strange," Barry remarked, "if he had a *son* and never mentioned it. Just goes to show you what you don't know about people you think you know well."

"This might be the reason Hank's left town. It's too much of a coincidence that these people show up and Hank takes off. Let's keep searching though. He might have kept documents, maybe a photo album. How far did you get with those files in the credenza?"

"Not far. Let's go through that stuff together. I'll bet Hank saw the newspapers and realized his ex-wife was coming to town. Maybe he just wanted to avoid her. Maybe it freaked him out."

Lucky followed Barry back to the living room. "I didn't want to say anything before, but now that you know, Horace mentioned to me that he had seen Hank the night of the murder. Horace was out walking Cicero and saw Hank leaving the Drake House."

Barry looked crestfallen. "I don't know what to think. If he had something on his mind, why couldn't he have come and talked to me? I blab all the time. He knows everything about my life. Not that there's that much to tell but I don't have any secrets."

"To each his own, I guess. Come on, it's late, let's get busy. Maybe we'll turn something up."

Lucky started at the top drawer at one end of the credenza. She patiently went through each file; all were neatly labeled. Tax returns, household bills, bank statements. All current and nothing unusual. "Well, Hank's nothing if not neat. I'll give him that."

Barry sat back on the floor. He held a folder in his hand. "I think I've got something, Lucky."

"What is it?" She scooted across the carpet on her knees and looked over Barry's shoulder. He held a file labeled simply HILARY.

Barry turned over the pages one by one. "It's a marriage license and divorce paperwork. Interesting. Look at this." Barry pointed to the front page of the divorce petition.

"No children," Lucky answered. "Well, that solves the mystery of Derek. He's not Hank's son." She took the folder from Barry's hands. "Her name here is Hilary Means. Must be her maiden name. And it looks like they were married a little less than five years. Hank was the one to file for divorce."

"Doesn't sound like a match made in heaven to me," Barry stated flatly.

Lucky agreed. "And I'll bet Hank must have been thrown for a loop when Hilary Stone, or whatever her name is now, turned up in Snowflake."

"What are you sayin', Lucky? That Hank might have had a motive to kill his ex-wife?"

"No," Lucky hastened to assure him. "That's not what I meant. I just meant maybe Hank could have still had feelings for her. You never know. Or maybe . . . especially if he never talked about the fact that he was once married, he was very sensitive on the subject. And then, for her name to be all over the newspapers and with her planning to live here, it might all have been too much for him."

Barry looked at her questioningly. "What do you mean . . . live here?"

"Oh, I happen to know this only because Eleanor Jensen told me. Hank might not have known. Ms. Stone was looking for a home to buy. She wanted to get away from the hustle and bustle of New York and find a quiet place to work on her next book."

"Whew," Barry whistled. "I can see why that would be a bit much. Too close for comfort." Barry sat heavily in one of the armchairs by the fire and heaved a sigh. "I can't get over it. That Hank wouldn't want to talk to me. It hurts, you know."

Lucky patted his shoulder. "I'm sure it does. But I'm sure he had some very good reasons for wanting his past to remain private. We'll find him. I'll have a quick look in the bedroom and bath and then what do you say we lock up and head home?"

"I guess that's all we can do. Except . . ."

"What?" Lucky asked, slipping on her sweater.

"I'm taking this." Barry rose and walked over to the corner desk. He picked up a small, old-fashioned Rolodex. "Tomorrow I'll go through this and call everyone in here that might have a clue where Hank is, or where he might have gone."

"What will you say if someone asks why you're calling?"

"Well, anyone who's on one of these cards knows Hank. I'll make something up. I don't know. But it's the only thing I can think of doing."

"Well, it's a plan. I wish I could think of something better, but I don't have any good ideas." Lucky, feeling like an intruder, quickly checked Hank's bedroom, bedside table, kitchen and medicine cabinet. Nothing looked remarkable, and like the rest of the house, everything was in its place. She returned to the hallway and waited while Barry turned off the lights in the living room. They headed for the front door. "Maybe we'll find some inspiration tomorrow," she said.

Barry was silent as he turned off the hallway light and locked Hank's front door behind him.

Chapter 29

SOPHIE SWIVELED ON her stool, watching Nanette as the woman made her rounds from table to table. She turned back to Lucky with a catlike smile. "I gotta say, she really knows how to work the room."

Lucky raised one eyebrow. "Tell me about it. There's not a man in the place that isn't checking her out."

"And speaking of men . . ." Sophie nodded her head toward the front door as Elias entered. He caught Lucky's eye from across the room and smiled widely.

Elias slid onto a stool at the counter next to Sophie and reached across to squeeze Lucky's hand. "How's it going?" he asked.

"Oh, fine." Lucky smiled in return, a flush creeping up her cheeks. Elias always had this effect on her. She didn't mind the warm feeling that suffused her when he walked into a room but could never seem to conquer the blush that she knew always hit her cheeks.

"We were just discussing the male attention being paid to the new waitress," Sophie leaned over to whisper to Elias.

"Ah, yes. I've been hearing about her." He turned on his

stool to survey the restaurant and discreetly caught a glimpse of the infamous Nanette. He turned back and smiled at Lucky. "She still driving you crazy?"

"Absolutely." Lucky sighed. "But what can I get you this morning?"

"A bagel would be great with some cream cheese and a coffee. I don't have much time. I'm just back from Lincoln Falls and I'm due at the Clinic in half an hour."

"Just take a second," Lucky replied. She popped a bagel in the toaster and poured a mug of coffee for Elias.

"So what do you think, Elias?" Sophie asked.

He took a sip of coffee. "About what?" He raised his eyebrows.

"Nanette, of course! The new waitress," Sophie replied in exasperation.

"Oh, hmm, well, I can see why she'd appeal to certain tastes." He held up his hands in surrender as Lucky placed his order on the placemat. "Not me. Don't look at me."

Lucky laughed. "Stop giving Elias a bad time," she said to her friend.

"Okay, I'll be good." Sophie smirked. "I'm taking off now, but I'll be back later to meet Sage. Let me know if I can help out, okay?"

"I think we'll be all right. As much as I hate to admit it, our new hire is a good waitress. She is very competent. And that reminds me. I've got to pin her down about producing her identification."

"You're kidding!" Sophie exclaimed.

"No. I'm not. That's what started the argument between me and Jack. In fact, I could use your help for a couple of minutes right now."

"Sure. What do you need?"

"Can you take over the counter for a minute. I need to have another word with her."

"Hey, Lucky," Elias asked. "Before you disappear, how about going out to a nice dinner this weekend?"

"Oh, I'd love to. Did you say 'out'?"

"Yes. I was thinking why don't we go someplace special—maybe the Mont Blanc at the Resort?"

"Wow! Okay. Is this a special event?"

"No. Not really. I just thought it would be great to not inflict my cooking on you another night."

Lucky laughed, "Your cooking is wonderful and that sounds fantastic. I'll be back in just a minute." She ducked under the counter hatch and walked over to Nanette.

"Nanette, can you come into the office for a minute?"

"Well, I've got a bunch of orders right now."

"Just leave them on the hatch for Sage. This will only take a second."

"All right," Nanette answered sulkily.

Lucky walked down the corridor to the office and held the door open for Nanette. "Please come in."

Nanette walked in without a word.

"Look, Nanette. You're a very good waitress, but I'm sorry, I have to put my foot down. Either you bring in your identification so I can make a copy or don't bother to come back tomorrow."

"You can't mean that!" she cried out.

"I'm sorry, but I do. I can't run a business this way. I can't have employees who are off the books. You have twenty-four hours."

"You are such a hard-hearted woman. I can't believe you'd treat me like this."

"I—"

"Ah'm gonna have a talk with Jack. I told him I've just moved and I can't find my identification. I know it's in a box somewhere, and I'll find it."

"You expect me to believe you're driving around with no driver's license in your possession? That alone is against the law."

Nanette's eyes filled with tears. "I'm gonna have to talk to Jack. He said I had all the time in the world and not to worry about it."

"Don't bother talking to Jack. I'm the one who runs this

restaurant and makes the decisions. It's me you have to answer to." Lucky wasn't sure where her resolve was coming from but this was something she just had to deal with.

Nanette stifled a sob and ran down the corridor, her heels clacking against the wooden floor. Lucky was sure she'd be in Jack's ear at the cash register in one second. She didn't relish another argument with Jack, but she had to pin this woman down. Her story was utter nonsense.

She returned to the counter, and sure enough, Nanette was at the cash register, tears streaming down her face, whispering in Jack's ear. He patted her hand and did his best to make change for a departing customer while trying to reassure her that he'd try to straighten things out. Lucky glared across the room at her.

Sophie ducked under the hatch and slung her purse over her shoulder. "Everything all right?" she asked, glancing at Lucky's face. "Your face is bright red."

"I do think there's gonna be fireworks soon. But I'm fine. You go on. Nothing to worry about."

Sophie nodded and waved good-bye to Elias. He rose from his stool and said, "I have to run too. Sorry. I'll call you later, Lucky."

"Oh. Okay. Bye, you two," she said to Elias's retreating back.

ELIAS REACHED THE sidewalk and spotted Sophie heading toward Chestnut Street. He hurried to catch up. "Hey, Sophie."

Sophie turned. "Elias! Thought you were going back to the Clinic?"

"I am. But I just wanted to catch you alone for a minute."

Sophie waited. She couldn't imagine what Elias could possibly want to talk to her about.

He reached into his jacket pocket and retrieved a small box. "I don't mean to put you on the spot, but I need a woman's opinion."

Sophie grinned from ear to ear. "Is that what I think it is?"

Elias took a deep breath. "It was my mother's. I think it's really lovely, but it's old-fashioned and I'm not sure if Lucky will like it. Tell me what you think. If you think it won't do, I'll get something more modern."

Sophie clicked open the small jewel box. The square-cut diamond sat within a border of tiny diamonds. The sides of the band were set off with more sparkling stones on each side of the main gem. "Oh. It's gorgeous, Elias! She'll love this. I know she will."

"You're sure. She won't think I should be buying her a new ring?"

Sophie tilted her head to one side. "Elias. Please. This is Lucky. She'd be thrilled if you gave her a Captain America decoder ring from a cereal box. You know her better than that. She'll be blown away. She'll probably be afraid to wear it."

He breathed a sigh of relief. "I'm so nervous about this. I don't know why, but I am."

"That's what the special dinner date at the Mont Blanc is about?"

"Yes." He nodded.

"Well, I'm thrilled and it's about time you popped the question. I thought you were never gonna get around to it."

Elias's face fell. "I would have done this a long time ago, but we've had our ups and downs. I'm sure you know all that. I thought for a while that it was over between us. I just wanted to make sure we were still on an even keel."

Sophie nudged him with her elbow. "I'm just teasing you. Don't be so sensitive."

"Okay. Okay. You're right. I'm just a little touchy right now. Please don't say anything about this, all right? Not even to Sage?"

"What?" Sophie squeaked. "I can't tell Sage?"

"Well, okay, you can tell Sage, but he's got to keep his mouth shut. I really want this to be a surprise."

"I promise." She reached up and gave Elias a hug. "Good luck. I can't wait to hear all about it."

"Thanks, Sophie. Sorry, I gotta run." Elias turned and hurried down Broadway in the direction of the Snowflake Clinic.

Sophie watched him until he turned the corner. She smiled to herself. Now she could be a bridesmaid and pay Lucky back for all the work she had done for her own wedding.

JACK SHOT LUCKY a look that seemed to be pleading with her. Lucky shook her head ever so slightly. She knew Jack agreed they couldn't possibly have employees who weren't on the books. Nanette had calmed down somewhat but she was definitely sulking. It didn't matter. This was ridiculous and couldn't possibly go on. If Nanette couldn't provide identification, she would have to be let go. Even if Meg pitched a fit and walked out. They couldn't risk breaking the law or getting the business into any kind of trouble.

The worst of the morning rush seemed to be ending. Lucky was considering taking a break in the kitchen with Sage when the front door flew open, the glass panes rattling in their frames. Flo Sullivan paused on the threshold. Her halo of psychedelic orange hair stood out from her head. She was dressed in flowing pants and a top in a red, orange and yellow floral design. *We'll all need sunglasses*, Lucky thought to herself. Jack, panicking, half rose from his stool. Flo ignored him and headed straight for the counter. She stood with her hands on her hips. "Is it true?" she demanded of Lucky.

"Is what true, Flo?"

"Is it true you've hired another waitress?" Flo demanded shrilly. Several heads turned to stare. Jack's complexion had blanched.

Lucky nodded, wishing she had spent the day in bed with the covers over her head.

"Yes, we have, Flo."

"Who? That's what I want to know. Who is this woman?"

She spun around and spotted Nanette. "Is that her?" Flo shouted, pointing a finger at Nanette. Nanette stopped in her tracks. The room became silent as death. "Why didn't you call me first, Lucky? You know I can come back at any time! Jack!" Flo turned in his direction. "Why'd you go and hire this cheap hussy?"

"Who you callin' cheap, you scrawny scag?" Nanette's voice was even louder.

"I tell it like I see it," Flo retorted.

"Why you . . ." Nanette flew across the room and, reaching out, grabbed a handful of Flo's orange hair.

Flo flailed against Nanette's attack in vain. "Help!" Flo screamed. "Help!"

"Hey, stop!" Lucky shouted. She ducked under the counter and wrestled Nanette away from Flo. Nanette's body was solid muscle. She could barely hold on to the woman. Out of the corner of her eye she saw Sage fly through the kitchen door and insert himself between the two women.

"Stop that! That's enough," Lucky shouted. She grabbed Nanette's arm. "In the office, you."

"I'm not puttin' up with this kind of treatment," Nanette bawled. "I'm going home." She flung her order pad on the floor and charged through the swinging door to the corridor.

"Good. That's a good idea," Lucky replied to Nanette's retreating back. "And Flo, I think you should leave now. You've caused enough trouble."

Flo patted her head. "Told you. She's a cheap hussy." This last remark was directed at Jack, who was scrambling to follow Nanette down the corridor. Flo stuck her nose in the air and marched out of the Spoonful. Her exit was followed by a burst of applause from a group at the large round table in the center of the room. It was joined by others who clapped at the performance.

"You okay?" Sage asked.

Lucky nodded. She turned around to face the room, "Excitement's over, everyone. Sorry about the disturbance." Someone from the rear of the room shouted, "Best show in town, Lucky."

Lucky looked at Sage and heaved a sigh, "Why don't you just shoot me?" She picked up Nanette's order pad from the floor and handed it to Sage.

"Come on, Lucky, just a few more hours to go," he replied. "Besides, this is all Jack's fault. He shouldn't be leading these ladies on the way he does."

Lucky laughed in spite of herself.

Chapter 30

WHAT'S WRONG WITH this woman? Nate thought as he glared at Sylvia Stone. She lounged lazily in the chair of the sitting room and couldn't seem to string a coherent sentence together. She held a coffee cup in her hand. Nate wondered what was really in the cup.

"I just want to go over your movements again on the night Ms. Stone . . . Hilary . . . died. Can you just tell me that?"

Sylvia yawned. "As I said before, I can't really remember. All I do remember is being bored out of my skull at that stupid book signing and having to watch Derek act like he ran the show. I think I fell asleep. I came back here with Audra. She gave me a lift. Derek, of course, had to watch over Mummy and hold her hand all evening."

"You didn't like your mother-in-law very much, did you?"

Sylvia shot a look. "She was a royal witch and you can spell that with a B."

"Oh?" Nate remarked pleasantly. "Why exactly do you say that?"

"Well, she didn't like me. That's for sure. She was *furious* when she found out we were married. For once, Derek did something on his own before asking Mummy"—she spoke the word in an affected tone—"for permission." Sylvia stretched and took another sip of the brown liquid in the mug. "But it was too late. Hilary couldn't do anything about it. And I told her so." Sylvia barked a mirthless laugh. "It was *so* classic. She even offered me money to go away."

"What did you say to that?" Nate asked in a neutral tone.

Sylvia wiggled her shoulders. "I told her no way was I going anywhere. And I told her when she popped off, Derek and I would get everything. Why should I settle for any less?"

Nate's eyebrows rose.

Sylvia, as if realizing she had gone too far, shut her mouth. Angrily, she said, "Don't get any ideas. I didn't kill her. Plenty of times I wanted to, but it wasn't me."

"And your husband? How did he feel about his mother?"

Sylvia rolled her eyes. "Derek loves Mummy. Although why I can't imagine. She treated him like a lapdog or a servant. He'd spent his whole life trying to please his mother while she put him down in front of other people. It was so pathetic. And he just refused to see it."

"After you came back to the Drake House, what did you do then?"

"Nothing. I got undressed and fell into bed. It was an absolutely grueling day, believe me. It wasn't fun being a camp follower for Hilary."

"Did you hear anything while you were in your room?"

Sylvia shook her platinum blonde head. "Not a thing. I slept like a baby."

"Hmm," Nate replied. *More likely passed out*, he thought. He'd be willing to bet her coffee mug was filled with alcohol.

"And your husband?"

"What about him?"

"What did he do?"

"Oh, he worried about Mummy all night. Popped down to her room a couple of times to make sure she was all tucked up."

"Did he by any chance argue with his mother?"

"I doubt it."

"Why?"

"Because," Sylvia drawled, "if he had, he would have been in tears and I would have had to listen to him whine half the night."

"I see. Okay. Could you ask your husband to step in?"

"Sure," Sylvia replied lazily, rising from the chair. "He's hiding in his room right now, crying over Mummy." She floated out of the room.

Nate sighed. All the money in the world wouldn't tempt him to trade places with Derek Stone.

"AH'VE DECIDED TO come back," Nanette announced in a haughty voice.

"Okay," Lucky replied cautiously, relieved that the work load would be lighter now that the dinner hour was approaching, but frankly wishing Nanette had stormed out, never to return.

"Ah've decided to rise above it all. To take the high road. I don't know what that dreadful woman's problem is, but I certainly didn't deserve that kind of treatment."

"Well, I agree, Nanette. And I am sorry about what she said to you, but you were wrong to assault her."

Nanette's eyes widened. "And what exactly was I supposed to do? Put up with that creature's nasty mouth? Not on your life!" she exclaimed.

Lucky glanced over at the cash register. Jack had a smile from ear to ear.

"I'm sure she's just upset your grandfather isn't interested in her. But that's not my problem." She smiled seductively in Jack's direction. "He's smart enough to recognize a desirable woman at least."

Lucky cringed, unwilling to think about her grandfather's desires. "Well, the dust has settled and hopefully everything will go smoothly now. Did you remember to bring in your social security card and your driver's license, by any chance?"

"Whaaat?" Nanette shrieked.

Sophie was in the kitchen helping Sage chop vegetables. Lucky in her peripheral vision saw Sophie peer through the kitchen hatch at the sound of Nanette's voice.

"Y'all told me I had twenty-four hours!"

Lucky took a deep breath. "Yes, you're right. I did. Please make sure you have them tomorrow then."

Nanette sniffed and headed for the cash register and Jack.

The bell over the door jingled as Barry entered. He waved to Jack, but Jack only had eyes for Nanette and didn't notice his arrival. Barry grabbed a stool at the counter, where Lucky was organizing placemats and silverware.

"Lucky," he whispered.

She smiled and moved closer to his stool. "Why are you whispering?"

"Oh." He sat up straighter. "Sorry. Wasn't aware I was." Then as if remembering why he had wanted to speak, he said, "I have some news."

Lucky spoke quietly in response. "About Hank?"

"Shhh." Barry glanced over his shoulder. Jack and Nanette were busy talking at the cash register. Lucky was sure Nanette was bending Jack's ear in complaint. At the moment, only two people occupied a table by the front window.

Barry nodded. "He called me. I guess with all my calling around, I must have hit the right person. No one admitted to knowing where he was, but somebody must have contacted him."

"Well, that's great," Lucky replied.

Barry shook his head negatively. "Not really." He leaned closer over the counter. "He refused to come back to town."

"What? Why?"

"I don't know." He shrugged. "But he asked me to meet him this afternoon in Bournmouth. I guess he's staying there."

"Well, maybe he'll tell you more in person. You'll at least be able to talk to him and maybe talk him into coming back to town and not running away."

"Is there any way you could come with me?"

"You want *me* there?"

"Yes," Barry said in a very serious tone. "You'll be able to get more out of him. I know him. He'll get defensive if I ask him questions point blank. Women are always better at that kind of thing."

Lucky smiled in spite of herself. "That's true. Men never seem to want to explain the details of anything. But assuming I can get away for a couple of hours, won't Hank be mad if you show up with me in tow?"

"Maybe. I don't know. But I just have the feeling you're the right person to ask."

"Okay. Let me see what I can do." In truth, she'd be relieved to get away from the Spoonful for a while. Between Nanette's fight with Flo, Meg's sulking and Jack's behavior, she felt ready to throw in the towel. "Let me ask Sophie. See what her schedule is."

"Thank you, Lucky. I really appreciate the moral support. Something's just not right with him."

Chapter 31

DEREK STONE SAT stiffly, his back straight, in the chair across from Nate, his posture the very opposite of his wife's.

"Once again, Mr. Stone, I'm very sorry for your loss."

Derek nodded. "Call me Derek, please." His face was pale and covered with a sheen of perspiration. Dark circles under his eyes testified to a sleepless night.

"How are you feeling today?'

"Oh . . ." Derek waved a hand limply in the air. "I just . . . I just can't accept that she's gone." His voice broke as if he were about to burst into tears.

Nate spoke quickly, regretful he had offered sympathy. He hoped to keep the man on track with an explanation of his movements. "I'll be brief," he said in a businesslike voice. "I just want to go over your movements again during the day and the night of your mother's book event."

"Uh . . . well . . . I . . . we were already here that day, at the Drake House."

"What day did you arrive?"

"Uh, two days before . . . before the day scheduled for the book signing."

"Why was that?"

"What?" Derek looked confused.

"Why did you arrive two days before the event was scheduled?"

"Oh, I see. Mother wanted to see the area. Didn't I tell you all this before? She was planning on purchasing a home here and just wanted to get the lay of the land. I drove her around each day. She wanted to have a look at the town and the scenery and see if she still felt the same."

"Your mother's arrival must have generated some interest."

"Yes, she's very well known. But we were very private about her coming here before the book signing. She hadn't had a moment's peace since her book was released and she felt it important to get some quiet time."

"I understand someone . . . a woman . . . tried to see your mother."

Derek eyebrows rose. "What?"

"You don't remember?"

"I'm sorry. I don't understand."

Nate sighed. Was the man suffering memory loss? "A woman came to the Drake House asking to speak to your mother. Mrs. Drake called upstairs to let you know."

"Oh, yes. That's right," Derek agreed.

"What was that about?"

"She was . . . just a fan. She was hoping to get a picture taken with mother and have her book signed."

"What did you tell her?"

"I wasn't about to disturb Mother. The woman must have seen the ads in the newspapers and took a chance that we were staying here. I told her she'd have to come to the book signing and Mother would be happy to autograph her book."

"And did she?"

"Did she what?"

"Did she come to the book signing?" Nate repeated his question patiently.

"Oh. I can't recall." Derek stared into space. "At least if she did, I didn't notice her. There were so many people there that night."

"What was her name?"

"Her name?"

Nate sighed again. Why was the man repeating every question instead of answering? His patience was wearing thin.

"Yes, did she give you her name?"

"Oh. No. I don't think I asked her for her name anyway."

"And then what? What else did you do the day of the book signing?"

Derek rubbed his forehead. "Uh . . . well, we didn't go for a drive that day. Sylvia slept late, I believe. We had a late lunch downstairs. Then I think Audra went over her notes about Mother's upcoming schedule and then a little before six o'clock we went over to that restaurant for the event."

"I see." Nate scribbled in his notebook. "What else did you do that day?"

Derek shook his head. "Nothing, really. I chatted with Mother a bit. Did some reading. That's about it."

"Did anything out of the ordinary happen that day? Anything you recall that could be helpful."

Derek mopped his forehead. "I can't think of anything."

Nate felt as if he were slogging through mud. "And that night, after the event. Several people heard your mother arguing with a man. Was that you?"

"Me?" Derek almost jumped out of the chair. "Oh, no. Mother and I never argued."

"They heard voices around nine forty-five to ten o'clock and the maid swears she heard an argument closer to ten thirty. That wasn't you?"

"No. I've already told you. I said good night to Mother and went straight to bed."

"And what time was that?"

"Ten o'clock, I believe."

"And you never heard any raised voices?"

"Certainly not. If I had, I would have investigated right away if I thought someone else was in Mother's room."

Nate sat silent, studying Derek Stone. If Derek had argued with Hilary Stone, he wasn't going to admit it. Not right now at any rate.

Chapter 32

"THIS ALL FEELS very cloak-and-dagger, Barry. I don't understand."

"Neither do I," Barry replied. They sat together on the park bench by the duck pond. Barry pulled a paper bag out of his pocket. Reaching in, he threw small hunks of bread onto the surface of the pond. Several ducks swam toward them as soon as the crumbs hit the water. At the far end, model boat enthusiasts stood at the edge cheering as they raced their sailboats in the breeze.

Hank had described to Barry the exact place they should sit and wait for him. Their bench was secluded from the road. Lucky checked her watch. "What time did Hank say he'd be here?"

"Three o'clock. He's very prompt, I'm sure he'll show up." No sooner had the words been spoken than Lucky spotted a tall figure walking slowly around the edge of the pond, a baseball cap pulled low over his head. Hank sauntered over and sat as though completely unaware that two friends sat waiting for him.

"Lucky! What are you doing here?" He spoke without turning his head.

"I asked her to come," Barry replied. "I wanted some help figuring out what's going on. What the hell, Hank? You couldn't tell me you were going out of town? You can't tell me why or where you're staying? I thought we were friends."

"Of course we're friends." Hank touched the pocket of his shirt, then shook his head in confusion. He sighed. "My glasses. Can't seem to find them." Hank turned to them. "I didn't think anything through. I was so upset, I had to get out of town. I wasn't thinking. Then . . . when I heard the news about Hilary . . . after what happened, I didn't want to come back. I was afraid Nate would think I had something to do with it."

"Well, this is silly, Hank," Lucky interjected. "I don't think Nate really suspects you of anything, but your staying away looks very questionable. Tell us what's going on."

Hank took a shaky breath and rested his elbows on his knees. Hilary . . . Hilary Stone, or whatever she's been calling herself, she's my ex-wife."

"We figured that out," Barry replied.

Hank looked up in surprise. "How did you find out?"

"We went to your house," Lucky answered. "We knew you weren't there, but we were hoping to find a clue to tell us where you had gone, what happened. We found the wedding photo." Lucky waited for a response from Hank, but he remained silent. "You were seen at the Drake House the night of the murder. People there heard an argument between her and some man. Hank, you've got to come back and tell Nate what happened."

"You don't think I'd do anything like that, do you? Murder my ex-wife?" Hank laughed mirthlessly. "Although to be honest, I've thought a lot about doing just that over the years. But believe me, I'm completely innocent."

"Does this have anything to do with why she chose Snowflake as a place to buy a house?"

Hank nodded. "'Fraid so." He took a deep breath. "I might

as well tell you the whole story. At least the part I know about. Hilary was Hilary Means in those days. Hilary-Means-to-an-End. That's what I used to call her after we split up." Hank fell silent for several moments. "I was very much in love with her. She was a smart woman. We worked at the same newspaper in those days. We were married for a few years before I realized things were falling apart. Hilary didn't think I was ambitious enough. She had her sights set on something higher up the food chain, at least as she perceived it. I was covering a story out of town, and when I came home, there was a note and all her things were gone. She had lined up her next guy . . . this publisher she'd been with all these years. I guess that's who broke up our marriage."

"Was she a journalist in those days too?" Lucky asked.

"Hilary? No. She was an assistant to the editor. She wasn't a writer."

"Well, she is now. She's written a bestseller. She's famous."

Hank was silent for a moment, then turned to look at his friends. "Hilary never wrote a damn thing."

"What do you mean?" Barry asked.

"*Murder Comes Calling* is my book. I wrote it." Hank laughed bitterly. "Hilary had the foresight to take my only copy of the manuscript with her when she took off. I spent two years of my life writing that book and then I spent the next two years trying to get it published. I didn't have any résumé as a fiction writer. I didn't know anybody in that business. Couldn't get anybody to publish it and the whole self-publishing thing hadn't really started back in those days. At the time, I figured she had just taken everything out of pure meanness. I never figured . . ."

"That one day she'd claim it as her own?" Lucky asked. "But why now? That was years ago. Why did she wait so long?"

"I have no idea. Maybe she thought I'd be dead by now. Or maybe so much time had elapsed, she hoped I'd forgive her or at least not make a fuss. To be honest, I had kind of given up on my book. I lost heart after she left and I shredded all the drafts. I was so broken up then I just couldn't get the wherewithal to tackle a project like that again. Plus, I was still working at the paper full-time and I just . . . well, I just kind of gave up on ever getting published. Then . . . well, you know the rest."

"Oh, Hank, how terrible. How could she do that to you?"

Hank shook his head. "The woman is . . . was . . . completely amoral. I didn't figure all that out at the time. I thought she was the most beautiful woman I had ever met. I figured I was a lucky dog to find someone like her. I just couldn't see what she was made of. You see, the way Hilary thinks is . . . anything's fair for the taking. There were never any consequences for her. If she could better her situation in some way, no matter what was involved, no matter who got hurt, well, she'd just brush it off and figure it was her due. Was her due, at any rate. Looks like she stepped on the wrong person's toes. Maybe she just got what was coming to her."

"Well, if that's the case, she must have figured you'd put it together, especially once the book came out."

Hank laughed. "Hilary never thought too far ahead. I heard all about her husband, the big publishing mogul in New York. I'll bet he had no idea the woman couldn't string a sentence together. She figured she'd rest on her laurels, but her husband wants to make money and no doubt she's been under pressure to produce another book."

"Oh, I didn't think of that," Lucky said. "You knew she was married to her publisher?"

"Oh, yeah. Word filtered through the grapevine at my newspaper. A couple of people couldn't wait to tell me." Hank shook his head. "That's the real reason she came to Snowflake. I'm sure nobody around here could figure out why she'd pick our little village to settle in. She came to offer me a deal. That's what I was doing at the Drake House. I almost didn't go. If I could turn the clock back, I never would have gone there that night."

"What time were you there?'

Hank sighed. "I don't know. I was only there about five or ten minutes. I left a little after ten, I guess."

"What kind of deal was she talking about?" Barry asked.

"If I would agree to write a sequel to the first book, she'd pay me off if I kept quiet. She'd pay me a lot of money."

"What did you say to her?"

"I told her to go to hell," Hank shouted, suddenly angry. "She ripped my heart out years ago, she stole the product of all my hard work. I was a mess for a long time after that. And then to add insult to injury, she pretends it's her book and her big-shot husband publishes it. She famous and rich and I'm just the jerk who got taken."

"You could've blown the whistle on her," Barry offered.

"Yeah, right. And who would believe me? I didn't even have a copy of the damn thing. It wasn't copyrighted. All the hard copies were gone. I'd just look like a sour grapes ex-husband who got dumped. I'd have no way to prove it was mine. Besides, I don't care anymore. I don't need the money. I'm fine, my life is comfortable. I gave up writing a long time ago."

"I still think it's terrible," Lucky replied. "Talk about taking someone to the cleaners."

"Believe me, if she had just stolen money or things, it wouldn't have hurt anywhere near as much."

"So that was one of the arguments people at the Drake House heard that night."

"I guess so. I guess I was pretty loud. I lost it. I was so upset. And Hilary just sat there, smiling, like a regal queen as if I'd be so hungry for her attention and her money that I'd just let her steal from me again. Unbelievable!"

"Look, Hank, you should come back with us. There's no need for all this hiding out in Bournmouth. If you told Nate your story, I know he'd understand. He's under a lot of pressure and he's got to talk to you. Somebody in that group killed her. Somebody went into that room between ten o'clock, the time you were there, and five minutes to eleven when the maid went in to pick up the tray."

"That's who found her? The maid at the Drake House?"

"Yes. Whoever killed her had to be one of those people in her entourage. Her publicist, her daughter-in-law, her son . . . one of them. But Nate has absolutely no clue which one."

Hank looked up. "Her son? Hilary had a son?"

"Yes. Why?"

"Oh, nothing. Just surprised, I guess. I tend to forget how many years have gone by. I knew she had a daughter, but I don't know whatever happened to the kid."

"A daughter?" Barry asked.

Hank nodded. "Yes, before I met her. Hilary came from Bournmouth originally. She was young then. She gave the baby up for adoption. Refused to have anything to do with the girl. Didn't want to hear about her. Just forgot all about it. That was Hilary all over. I was surprised when she told me. No feeling though. No regrets. Just like it was a fact of her life."

"I wonder if the girl ever tried to find her parents, or her mother?"

"That I don't know. There are ways now that that can be done, but I think both parties have to be willing to be found," Hank replied.

"That's so sad," Lucky mused. "Maybe somebody should try to find her. She has a right to know her mother's dead." Lucky thought about her own parents and couldn't imagine what it would be like to not know where one came from. "It's horrible to think she might be trying to find her mother and then to learn she was dead before she could make contact . . ."

"Knowing Hilary, the kid might be better off. I know the state tried to contact her about the little girl. The baby was adopted, but something happened. Hilary would never say, but something had happened to the adoptive parents and the little girl was going to be put into the foster care system if another family couldn't be found."

"What happened to them? To the parents?"

"I don't know the details. All I know is there was a fire. Their house burned down and I think they both died."

"How old would the baby have been then?"

"Well, let's see. Hilary and I were together five years and she had the girl about five years before that, if I remember. So maybe the little girl was nine or ten at the time."

"Ten years old? The poor little thing. She's given up for adoption and then loses her family like that?"

"Yeah, I agree. Didn't bother Hilary a bit though. She still wanted no part of the kid. And come to think of it, that kid would be about forty years old by now."

"But those are the things that mark people for life, Hank. For all we know, that daughter has spent her whole life hoping her mother would come for her. It just breaks my heart to think about it. Do you know where they placed her afterward?"

"No idea. Maybe somebody adopted her again or she became a ward of the state—institutionalized."

"Institutionalized?" Lucky said. "What a horrible word. Why couldn't another family be found?"

"Well, there were . . . some questions, I think. There was some doubt that the girl was all right in the head if you know what I mean. Hilary started calling her the 'bad seed.' That was her idea of humor. The details, I just don't know. The people from the state did make an effort to reach her, but Hilary wouldn't talk to them. I remember that much. I tried to get her to open up about it, but I didn't have any luck."

"Look, Hank. Come back with us. There really isn't any need to be hiding out here."

Hank shook his head. "I can't. I don't want to go home just yet. I just want my privacy. I'm telling you both this stuff in confidence. I don't want the whole town to know I was once married to her and I was taken for a fool."

"That's better than being arrested for murder," Barry said. "Where are you staying, by the way?"

"I'm not going to tell you. If you don't know, you won't have to lie if Nate questions you."

Barry sighed. "I wish you'd reconsider. You haven't done a damn thing wrong."

"Hank . . ." Lucky hesitated. "I don't know if I should tell you this or not."

"What's that?"

"This wasn't in the papers. They think Hilary Stone was strangled with a telephone cord."

Hank groaned and put his head in his hands. "Just like my book."

Chapter 33

"I GUESS WE got no choice. We'll head back to town." Barry looked over at Lucky behind the wheel. "Lucky? You okay?"

"I'm fine. I'm just thinking about the daughter. If this child was placed in state care and if she's around forty years old now, where would she be?"

"She could be anywhere. Grown up, maybe married with children of her own. How old was Hilary Stone anyway?"

"The papers said she was sixty-four."

"You're thinking that somebody should notify the girl that her mother's dead?"

Lucky nodded. "I do. I think if it were me in that situation, I would certainly want to know. Don't forget, some people live their whole life and never wonder, and then one day they just turn a corner and have to find their adopted child or the parent who gave birth to them. And sometimes there are siblings that they want to meet, or sometimes twins are separated. It's all so sad."

"I don't know how you'd go about finding anything out. I'm sure adoption records aren't public information anywhere."

"I have heard somewhere about a website where people

can post their information, and if the other party is also searching, they can connect. But we don't even know her daughter's name or the name her adoptive parents gave her. If we could find that, we might be able to locate her."

"Didn't Hank say that Hilary came from Bournmouth originally? Maybe the baby was born here."

"It's a good bet. And we know her maiden name—Means. That's a start. Maybe we should talk to Nate. He has the authority to find this stuff out."

"How are we gonna do that and not tell him we've been talking to Hank?" Barry demanded.

"Good question. Maybe that's not such a good idea." Lucky leaned her head back against the headrest.

"You realize we'll really be in the doghouse if Nate finds out we met with Hank and didn't tell him."

Lucky cringed. "You're right. There's got to be another way. I remember my mother talking about a . . . what did they call it in her generation? A home for unwed mothers? It was here in Bournmouth, I think. It was called the . . ." Lucky shook her head. "It's on the tip of my tongue. It's named after a woman and it was a refuge for pregnant girls or women that had no place else to go." Lucky sat forward. "I remember now!" she exclaimed. "It was the Dorothy Banks Home. That was it. I wonder if it's still here." Lucky turned the key in the ignition. "Let's go find a phone book."

"There's a post office and a municipal building we passed on the way in. They'd have some kind of a local directory. If not, one of those little shops further on."

Lucky pulled out onto the street. She made a U-turn in front of the park and drove back the same way they had come into town.

"I see it, just up there on the right," Barry said. "If you pull over, I'll run in and ask."

Lucky pulled into a short-term parking space in front of the building and Barry climbed out and hurried up the stairs. She drummed her fingers on the steering wheel. Hilary Stone, a young woman, if she had no other option, would probably have stayed at a place like the Dorothy Banks

Home to have her child. And the Banks Home must have acted as a go-between for adoption services. If only she had the name of the daughter, she could search for a birth certificate. That would have to be a matter of public record. She looked up and saw Barry returning down the stairs. He climbed into the car.

"It's called the Banks Family Center now. They're in the phone book under Banks, but one of the clerks told me it's the same place. It's just a few blocks away."

Lucky glanced over at Barry. "Should we give it a try? I doubt they'll give out any information but it wouldn't hurt to ask."

"Sure," he replied. "I'm up for it. I don't see how this helps Hank, but if it worries you, let's go."

Chapter 34

"HOW MUCH LONGER are you planning to keep us here?" Audra stood in the center of the room, her arms crossed, an edge of anger in her voice.

"Please, take a seat," Nate answered flatly.

Audra huffed. "Very well. But I have to remind you I do have a very busy schedule. Hilary Stone was not my only client and I am under pressure from many directions. I have to get back to New York as soon as possible."

"I understand that, believe me, Miss Klemack. The sooner I'm able to interview everyone, the sooner I can complete this investigation and the sooner you'll be able to go home."

Audra sighed heavily and collapsed into a wing-back chair across from Nate. "What is it you think I could possibly tell you?"

"I'd like to go over the statement you made the morning after Ms. Stone's death, if you don't mind."

"All right."

"Now, you said that you arrived at the Spoonful around five thirty that evening."

"That's correct."

"And who were you with?"

"Well, we all came together. I mean, we all arrived at the same time, but I drove over in my car from the Drake House with Phoebe. She's Ms. Stone's personal assistant. And Derek brought Sylvia."

"Derek drove his own car?"

"Yes. Well, no. He has a rental car while he's here."

"And how did Ms. Stone arrive?"

"Derek installed Sylvia, I'm sure just to annoy us, and then returned to bring Hilary over when the event was about to start."

"I see." Nate scribbled in his notebook. He had heard all this before but was continuing to question everyone involved until he found a chink, a flaw in one of their stories. "Did anything unusual happen at the book signing?"

Audra shrugged her shoulders. A blank look on her face. "No. Nothing out of the ordinary. There were mobs of people but everything was as usual. Hilary spoke for a while and answered questions and then began to sign the books that people had purchased." Her brow furrowed.

Nate looked at her questioningly. "You remembered something?"

"Oh, yes. It was nothing though. A package was delivered to the office and I gave it to Derek before the book signing. It was a personal delivery for Hilary and I had forgotten about it. Left it in my car. I told Derek to give it to his mother when he brought her back to the inn."

This was the first Nate had heard of a package. "What kind of a package?"

"Oh, just a large envelope."

"And do you remember who it was from?"

Audra thought for a moment. "No. Sorry. I don't remember. Wherever it was from, I didn't recognize the name, so it didn't stick in my mind."

"And where is that envelope now?'

"Oh, I imagine it's in Hilary's room."

"I see." No large envelope had been on the list of items from the victim's room.

Nate cleared his throat. "Several guests here have remarked that they heard an argument, or raised voices, sometime close to ten o'clock that evening. Another witness has reported hearing an argument in Ms. Stone's room later, around ten thirty. Possibly a man and a woman arguing. Did you hear anything?"

"I heard voices. I just assumed it was Derek and Sylvia going at it again. Mostly it's Sylvia. I didn't pay any attention."

"And what time was that?"

"I have no idea," Audra replied blandly. "I didn't check my watch. I was really too tired to think about it."

Nate nodded. "Okay. That's all for now. I may need to talk to you again."

Audra's face took on a long-suffering look. "Just please let me know when I can get back to my office."

"I definitely will," Nate replied.

Chapter 35

THE BANKS FAMILY Center was a remodeled rambling Gothic structure. Originally a grand family home, now jutting wings had been added on either side, and a new entryway diminished some of the Victorian feel that it once had. A signpost in the lawn halfway up the circular drive pointed to a visitor parking area on the side of the building.

Lucky turned to Barry. "This is a crazy thought, but do you think if you had the name of the mother, you could search for a birth certificate that would show the date of the birth?"

Barry shook his head. "I kinda doubt it. Especially years ago. Now, with computers, maybe everything is scanned and you can search for a particular name. But I still don't think it can be done. You'd have to be government of some sort or police to access a record like that. Even so, maybe it still can't be done. You'd have to have an approximate date of birth or location or social security number or something to go by."

"I'll bet you're right." Lucky tossed her keys into her purse. "Let's go inside and see what we can find out."

They approached the freshly painted white double doors and entered a pleasantly comfortable lobby filled with roomy armchairs and sofas. Several women with small children waited in the lobby for appointments. A woman in a pink smock manned a wide reception desk. The walls were hung with photos from days gone by. Lucky stopped to look. A black-and-white photograph of two nurses in a room lined with cradles smiled at the camera. "Look at this, Barry."

Barry whistled under his breath. "It looks like a regular baby factory."

"What a terrible time these women must have had. The stigma of an unplanned pregnancy, families that might have turned their backs on them, even teenagers, no place to turn to, no chance of child support from the father, so little hope. Thank heavens times have changed, and women, if they decide to, can find a way to keep their babies, without fear of job discrimination or social shunning. It's so sad to see these newborns all lined up like that. Like an orphanage. Like a baby storage warehouse." Lucky steeled herself and headed for the front desk. The woman in the pink smock smiled as she approached.

"Hello." Lucky smiled, wondering if the woman perceived her as a possible unwed mother. "I'm trying to locate a child, a child that might have been born here perhaps forty years ago. Is it possible that any information like that would be accessible?"

The woman's eyes widened. "How long ago did you say?"

"I believe about forty years ago. I'm trying to contact an adoptee with information about her mother."

"Oh, I see." The woman glanced at Barry, who had followed in Lucky's wake. He stood up straighter and looked down to make sure the buttons on his shirt were all in place. "Do you know the name of the person . . . child? Are you sure that child was born here at the Banks Center?"

"I don't know for sure, but I believe so."

"Well, forty years ago was a long time. Things have changed a lot. Now we offer all sorts of family services and counseling. And providing shelter to unwed mothers isn't the main thing we do now. I really doubt we'd even have those records in our archives. Information about births was always reported to the state. But it's confidential. Even if a child was born here, we couldn't possibly give out any information. If you're the adoptee or the birth mother, there are avenues to request information from the Vermont Adoption Registry. I can give you their number and website and you could try talking to them."

"I see. It's as I feared. I only have the name of the birth mother, but not the child's name or birth date."

"Ah." The woman shook her head. "You'd have to at least have the birth date. Then you could go through public records for births on that day. But that could be a real chore. Unless, of course, the mother filed a request for nondisclosure."

"What does that mean?" Lucky asked.

"Well, you see, the law changed about, oh, twenty years ago to make it possible for adoptees, adoptive parents and birth family members to access adoption information in Vermont. But you'd have to prove you were in one of those categories because the records are still confidential. The parties involved would both have to consent. If the mother requested nondisclosure, her information would be kept confidential. But even that might not hold up in court anymore. If there were a good reason, say health issues, for example, a judge could order that the mother's information be made available."

"I understand. Then I guess there'd be no way for me to locate this person."

"There is another avenue," she offered.

"Oh? What's that?"

"There's a database. It's called ConnectAdopt. I don't know much about it. I'm not sure which organization maintains it, but people who want to find biological family members post information, birth names if they were given one, birthdates, city and state, whatever they actually know or were told. Often someone is looking for them too and people connect on their own. It's a marvelous service. It always brings tears to my eyes when I read some of the stories."

"Well, that's something. I could do that. You never know. You see, the birth mother has just died. I certainly didn't know her well at all, but I have just learned she had a child that had been put up for adoption and it occurred to me that this girl, this woman, I mean, might want to know."

"Yes, you're right. Some people spend their whole life wondering and hoping. Some of them never care and some actually aren't even told they were adopted. There are thousands of stories. It's really fascinating, if it weren't so heartbreaking most of the time."

"Well, thanks for your help. I do appreciate it."

"You might also want to contact the Vermont Adoption Registry. I know they can't give you any information but perhaps they could suggest an alternative. It's a long shot but . . . here," she said, taking a pen off the desk. "They're right here on Main Street in Bournmouth." She jotted something on a piece of notepaper and passed it across the desk. "Here's their phone number."

"Thank you. I appreciate this."

"Good luck, dear. I wish you the best."

"THAT'S AMAZING," SOPHIE remarked. "She stole his book and published it as her own." The Spoonful had closed for the evening. Sage was in the kitchen, cleaning up for the night. Meg was lending a hand while Sophie waited for Sage to be finished with his work. "Isn't that illegal?"

"I don't know about that. I don't think it's a criminal matter. But Hank would have to sue her and be able to prove it. And there's no way he'd want that kind of publicity. I'm sure of that." Lucky took a sip of her tea. "But, Sophie, please keep this under your hat. It will probably all come out eventually. Hank will have to return to town sooner or later."

"He's crazy to take off like that. It just draws attention to him. I'm sure Nate's getting very hot under the collar about it."

"I'd really like to try to locate this woman—Hilary's daughter. It's been preying on my mind. I can't put it into words, but I can't escape the thought that she wants to find her birth mother. Maybe she's wanted that her whole life. She needs to know."

"How in heaven's name are you going to be able to do that?"

"Well, I'll check with the Vermont Adoption Registry, but I don't really expect to get anywhere with that. Today, I ran into a wall. But I realized I do know one thing. According to Hank, as least as far as he remembers, her adoptive parents died in a fire in Bournmouth about thirty years ago. There must be a record of that fire. It would have been in several newspapers. Then at least I might be able to find out her adopted name."

"But if she ended up back in the system, her name could have changed again, she could be married, with a different name now. Unless you have access to really confidential databases, it would be impossible to find her."

"I know." Lucky nodded. "But I feel I should at least try. If I have no luck, then I can break down and tell Nate about it. He would be able to find her, I'm sure."

"Maybe. It might even be tough for him to sort through."

"I think I'll do what the woman I spoke with today suggested. Contact the Registry. And then I might try to find out more about that fire. It must have been in all the papers."

"You're thinking the library in Bournmouth might have local papers on microfilm? What about the *Snowflake Gazette*?"

"Was it even in existence thirty years ago? I don't think so. I seem to remember what a big deal everyone thought it was when it started. We were just starting high school then, maybe almost twenty years ago. And I'm not even sure about the time frame but it's worth a try, don't you think?"

"Sure. I'll drive over with you. Can you get away tomorrow afternoon?"

"I think so. Now that Nanette's running things here."

Sophie made a rude face.

Chapter 36

LUCKY GLANCED UP at the murals on the ceiling, admiring the dark ornately carved moldings that surrounded the images. "It's beautiful, isn't it, Sophie?"

Sophie agreed. "I haven't been here for such a long time." She chuckled. "Probably since we were kids in high school."

"I used to come a lot in high school, but I haven't been back for a visit since I've been living in Snowflake. It's a shame. It's such a great building. Wish we had something like this in our town."

"I know, but at least we have our little library. It's something." Sophie glanced around. "Let's find someone who can help us." She spotted a woman at the information desk, dressed in dark clothing with a spiky blonde haircut. Sophie nudged Lucky with an elbow. "She looks like she knows what she's doing."

They approached the librarian and explained what they were looking for.

"Oh, that's interesting." The woman leaned over the counter. "I remember my mother and grandmother talking about that fire. It must have been pretty shocking for the town in its time."

Lucky relished the smell of polished wood and old books and a faint odor of something else. What was it, she thought, then recognized the pungent odor of the glue used to repair bindings. "Do you remember anything about it? Or the people involved?"

The blonde woman shook her head slowly. "No, not a thing. I was pretty young when it happened so I didn't really pay much attention." She laid her pen across the notepad she had been writing on. "But come on, I'll take you to the little room we use for viewing and I'll order the film from the archives." She came out from behind the oak counter and indicated they should follow her. "Do you know the actual date you're looking for?"

Sophie shook her head. "Sorry, no. We have an idea it was about thirty years ago, give or take a few."

"That's quite a ways back. I'll have to search, but I do think we have it . . . hopefully you'll find what you're looking for. Follow me." She led them to the rear of the main space, through a door that opened into a small modern cubicle with three microfilm viewers set across a counter. Three plastic chairs with aluminum legs faced the counter. "We have plans to digitize this stuff, but it hasn't happened yet. Money's always the issue, isn't it? But that far back, nobody's bothered." Indicating the chairs, she said, "Have a seat. I'll be back in a little while and I'll make sure you can thread it in with no trouble."

"Thanks," Lucky replied. She sighed and sat heavily in one of the molded chairs. Sophie did the same. She looked at Sophie. "This may be a wild-goose chase."

"Could be. But now I'm curious too. Besides, we do know that it really happened. Hank remembered the state trying to contact her mother and he remembered about a fire. If the little girl was ten at the time, it would have been approximately thirty years ago. But Hank might have blown the story out of proportion too."

"What do you mean?"

"Well, maybe nobody died. Maybe the fire story was repeated so many times, it just grew and took on a life of its own."

"Then why would the state be trying to contact the birth mother if the adoptive parents were still alive? Why else would they do that? If the child had been adopted and that home was no longer there and the state couldn't figure out what to do with the little girl."

"There could be any number of reasons. Maybe one of the parents died and the other parent was no longer up to the task of raising a child that wasn't theirs."

"I never thought of that. How horrible though. To give a child a home and then send her back. Can people do that?"

Sophie shrugged. "I have no idea how the whole thing works."

They heard the door to the main room open and the woman with the spiky blonde haircut entered. She held a sturdy cardboard box of microfilm reels in her hands. "Here you go," she said. "I'll thread the first one in so you can see how it's done." Her fingers moved deftly. "Think you can do the next one?"

"Sure," Lucky offered. "I've done these before."

"Great, when you're finished, please bring them all back to me at the front desk. This first one starts at the beginning of the year, thirty-one years ago. Might be a good idea to start there." She turned away. "Good luck," she said as she closed the door behind her.

Sophie pulled her chair closer to the viewing screen. "I'll bet this was front page news, don't you think?"

"I would think so, even though it was just a local story." Lucky patiently scrolled through each page. "Hey, look at this. The *Gazette* was just a weekly back then. That might make our search easier."

They stared intently at the screen as each page flipped by. Lucky rubbed her eyes to stay focused. When they had scrolled through the first year, Sophie removed the reel and threaded a second one in.

"Here we go. This is the beginning of the year—January."

Sophie returned to her chair. Lucky continued their search. Neither spoke as they watched the pages flip by.

Sophie groaned. "Stop for a second. My eyes are crossing. I don't know how you can look at this stuff and not have your brain swim inside your skull."

"I know," Lucky replied, not taking her eyes off the viewing screen. "But I think we're almost through this year. I'm not seeing anything about a deadly house fire."

"Well, since we don't know the date, best thing would be to finish this year and then move to the next one. If there's nothing there, we can go back two years and forward two years. That would be the logical way to approach it."

"Oh!" Lucky exclaimed. "I think this is it." She peered at the screen. "Look at this—December twentieth. Just before Christmas."

"What do you know?" Sophie breathed. She moved closer to the screen and read out loud. "'The fire at 49 Poplar Street was first reported at eleven p.m. on the night of December twentieth. Mr. and Mrs. George Ellers and their daughter Georgina were asleep in the upstairs bedroom when a neighbor walking his dog heard glass breaking and spotted fire in a downstairs room.'" Sophie looked at Lucky. "Georgina? They must have named her after the dad."

"Look. There's a picture of the firemen removing a body. How gruesome!" Sophie remarked. "Story continued on page ten, it says."

Lucky scrolled forward and they read together in silence. Finally Lucky spoke. "They did die. It says the parents were pronounced dead at the scene."

"Anything about the little girl?" Sophie asked.

Lucky shook her head. "This doesn't mention her. I would assume she survived if they didn't mention her death." She sat back in the chair and stared at the screen. "So assuming we're right, the little girl, Georgina, lived through the fire but the parents died." Lucky heaved a sigh. "This still doesn't tell us what eventually happened to her."

"Assuming this *is* Hilary's daughter. We're making some jumps here."

"Maybe, but Hank did say there was a fire, and it was in Bournmouth. And this is the right time frame. It's a decent bet. And it gives us an address. Right here in town. Let's go check it out."

"What good will that do?"

"How much do you want to bet there's a neighbor who'd remember more?"

Chapter 37

LUCKY PULLED TO a stop under a large elm tree. New spring shoots cast a pale green wash over the street. She checked the house number to her right. "That's 80 Poplar." She turned in the opposite direction and scanned a manicured lot. "If that piece of property doesn't belong to the house next door, that could have been where the house once stood."

Sophie leaned across and stared. "If that's the case, then the neighbors must be taking care of it. It looks more like a small planned play area for the kids. There's a lovely lawn and a garden I can see from here. And it's the only gap in the street."

"The city must have torn down what was left of the house. Maybe nobody wanted to buy the land and rebuild on the same spot."

"Superstitious, probably. If a couple died there, it might linger in people's memories." They were silent a moment staring at the green space. On the lawn, two children, a boy and a girl, played with a bright pink ball while a young woman seated at a bench looked on. "What do we do now?"

"Let's go talk to her," Lucky said, indicating the woman who was watching over the two children.

"In for a penny, in for a pound," Sophie remarked.

They climbed out of the car and walked across the street. The young woman they had noticed was wearing a loose-fitting top. She was pregnant. She watched them with curiosity as they approached.

Lucky spoke first. "Hi. I'm wondering if you can help us."

The woman smiled. "Sure, if I can."

"It's kind of a long story, but we're hoping to locate someone who knew the family that once lived here. This is the lot where the house burned down, isn't it?"

The woman opened her eyes in surprise. "Whoa. That was a long time ago. I have heard all about it"—she hesitated—"my mother and my aunt talked about it for years." She squinted her eyes against the sun. "You know that the people who lived here died in the fire, don't you?"

"Yes, we read about it. Their name was Ellers, right? But they had a little girl, didn't they?"

"I guess." She shrugged. "I really can't tell you very much." She glanced behind Sophie. "Ally, stop that. You're not supposed to hit your brother." The young woman turned back to them, "The person you should talk to is my aunt. She'd remember that fire. She's right across the street. She's always lived in that house." The young woman nodded in the direction of a blue two-story colonial-style house, the same one Lucky had parked in front of. Lucky heard a wailing cry and a small boy careened past and flung himself into his mother's lap. The woman put her arms around him and absently stroked his head. "Shh, baby." She looked over at the young girl, who was bouncing the ball on her foot like a soccer ball. "Ally, get over here, right now!" She turned back to Lucky and Sophie. "Go ahead and knock on her door. Her name's June. Tell her you just met me. I'm April." She smiled suddenly. "All the women in the family are named after months. I broke the mold with Ally here." She nodded in the direction of the little girl, who had ignored her mother's command. Lucky would have offered to shake her hand but the young woman had her hands full.

"Thanks. That's very kind of you. We appreciate it," Lucky replied.

"No problem." The woman had pulled out a tissue and was wiping tears and various other juices pouring out of the little boy's nose.

They turned away and left the garden. "I should never have kids," Sophie muttered. "I think I'd be tempted to kill them."

Lucky laughed. "I'll remind you of that someday soon."

"I can hear the 'I told you so' now," Sophie whispered as they climbed the stairs to the blue house.

Lucky rang the bell and a solidly built woman in a house-dress and apron opened the door. Her hair was gray and curly and pulled off her face with a headband.

"Hi. Are you June?"

The woman nodded.

"We were just talking to April, your niece." Lucky indicated the opposite yard where the young woman was packing up to leave.

"Oh, yes?"

"We're hoping to find someone who knew the family who lived across the street years ago."

"Ah." The woman's face fell. "Yes, the Ellers family. What about them?"

"Well, we know they died in the fire. But we're wondering if you might know what happened to their little girl?"

The woman stared at Lucky silently, then sighed. "You better come in." She opened the door all the way and ushered them into a room filled with sunlight and bright colors, a neat but pleasantly lived-in room. "Have a seat," she said, indicating the sofa. The woman took a chair opposite. "Liz Ellers was a good friend of mine. She was a really lovely woman. So the whole thing hit me really hard. To have that happen right outside your door and to lose a friend." She took a deep breath. "It doesn't matter how many years go by, I still think of her sometimes."

"It's nice that the lot isn't overgrown. It looks well tended."

"Yes. We all chip in. Everyone on the street. It's a nice place for kids to play. We don't want to see it go all to seed. And nobody's wanted to rebuild on that spot anyway after what happened."

"I can understand that."

"But you wanted to know about their little girl?"

Lucky nodded.

"To answer your question, I don't know what ultimately happened. She was given over to the state authorities after Liz and George died. She was probably sent to Salisbury."

"Salisbury?" Lucky asked, shooting a glance at Sophie.

"Salisbury Retreat. Now it's a hospital and an outpatient clinic for all kinds of mental health issues."

"I've heard of it," Sophie offered. "But wasn't it used for other things?"

"Oh, yes. It was a dumping ground for all kinds of people. They dealt with everything. Alcoholism, drug addiction, depression. Lots of people got put there just because their families didn't want them around for whatever reason. They took in unwanted children, so maybe that's what finally happened to the child if they couldn't get her adopted a second time." June looked up quickly. "You knew she had been adopted, didn't you?"

"Yes." Lucky nodded. "We had heard."

"Liz wanted children so badly and tried for a number of years, but finally gave up hope. That's when they adopted Georgina. That's the name they gave her." She smiled at the memory. "They used to argue, Liz and George." She looked up at them. "In a good way, I mean. Liz wanted to name the baby after her own mother, but George, her husband, was insistent. So Georgina it was. Liz was so happy when she brought that baby home. For a while at least."

"Did something go wrong?" Sophie asked.

June stared at Sophie for a long minute. "I don't know how to put this into words, and it sounds like a terrible thing to say, but I always felt there was something wrong with that child. She didn't seem to . . . connect with other kids."

"Was she just shy?" Lucky asked.

"Possibly. Whatever was going on with that girl, believe me, it wasn't the fault of Liz and her husband. You couldn't have found nicer people. They loved that little girl just as if she were their own," June continued, "but after a while even Liz had to admit there was something off. She was withdrawn and strange. Daydreaming and doing odd things . . ."

"Odd, how?" Lucky asked.

"Well, one time she locked one of the neighborhood kids in their cellar and didn't tell anyone. The little boy's parents were frantic that entire day. They were finally ready to call the police. Georgina had told her mother . . . Liz, that she had a new friend in the cellar. At first, Elizabeth thought it was a . . . what's the name they use for that? An imaginary friend. That's what they call it. Now, that's accepted at a certain age, but the girl was way past the age when that would be normal. She thought her daughter was just making things up, but as the day wore on, it started to nag at Liz so she decided to go down into the cellar. That's where she found the little boy. He was terrified, poor little thing. Liz was horrified to think what could have happened to him. He was too frightened to cry out, and if she hadn't gone down to the cellar, who knows?" June shook her head. "Liz had to tell the boy's parents where she found him. It was just awful for her. After that, people really viewed the girl as strange and no one would let their kids play with her." June continued, "And then she liked to play with matches. That was worrisome to her parents. They finally had to get rid of all the matches in the house and lock up the rest. They even threatened to punish her if she played with matches again. That's why . . ." She trailed off.

Lucky waited, allowing the silence to lengthen, hoping the neighbor would continue. Finally she asked, "Are you saying that the little girl might have started that fire?"

June's jaw clenched. "I can't say that. I really can't, but . . . how is it she was the only one to survive the fire? They found her out in the backyard, not up in her room. How did she get out there? Was she wandering around the house at night? The Fire Department felt the Christmas tree was the cause of the blaze. Those things, if they get dried out, they can go up like a bomb, all that pine sap. I shouldn't say this, but I've often wondered if that little girl was fooling around with matches in the middle of the night and ended up setting fire to the house and killing her parents." She held a hand over her mouth. "I know it's an awful thing to say, but all these years, I've wondered."

LUCKY TURNED THE key in the ignition and drove down Poplar to Main Street. Then she pulled the car over and turned off the engine. "What are you thinking?" she asked Sophie.

"Whew! We just got an earful. You know that woman's probably talked about that fire and the little girl for years. I have to say, I have *never* heard anyone talk about a kid like that."

"I don't know," Lucky said, "I'll play devil's advocate here. People always want to blame someone when something bad happens. Something like that, something horrible and inexplicable happening to people you love and care about. That little girl, she's a woman now. She isn't here to defend herself, so I'd keep an open mind. We really don't know. And like June said, the firemen thought it was caused by the Christmas tree. That can happen. They went to bed, maybe they forgot to turn off the Christmas lights, even a spark can ignite them. I'd take it all with a grain of salt."

"I don't know." Sophie shook her head. "She also said that the little girl was too quiet, strange even."

"Maybe you'd be strange if your own mother didn't want you and you knew you were adopted. We have no idea how old she was when she was adopted. But did anything else she said strike you?"

"Like what?"

"The Salisbury Retreat." Lucky waited.

"What about it?"

"The woman they found strangled in the woods. She was a psychiatrist . . ."

Sophie gasped. "At the Salisbury Retreat! That's right.

That went right over my head." Sophie was quiet a moment. "What are you thinking?"

"It seems like too many threads are coming together. This child, Georgina, whoever she is now, could very well have spent many years at Salisbury. Maybe she even grew up there. And now her biological mother is strangled. Both women—Dr. Cranleigh and Hilary Stone—were killed in the very same manner."

"Maybe. But that's a huge place. And you don't even know that's where the girl got placed. She could have been adopted by another couple. She could have been placed anywhere in the state. This doctor and the daughter might not have had any contact with each other. And how would you find out anyway? Those records are extremely confidential."

Lucky shrugged. "It doesn't hurt to ask. You never know what you'll find." She turned the key in the ignition and made a U-turn heading toward the other side of town.

Chapter 38

NATE PULLED HIS cruiser into an empty parking space at the side of the Drake House sheltered by the bordering hedges. There were plenty of spaces to choose from, now that Barbara Drake's first-floor tenants had all been released from questioning. Nate was certain none of them had had any involvement in either of the two murders. He climbed out of his vehicle slowly and walked toward the front entrance of the bed-and-breakfast. He pushed open the door and almost collided with Derek Stone.

"Ugh." Derek let out a grunt as if the air had been knocked out of him. He took two steps backward.

"Mr. Stone," Nate said, "you seem to be in a hurry. Going somewhere?"

"Oh!" Derek stared at Nate, his eyes wide. "Uh, no. Just stepping out for a walk, that's all." His eyes were still red-rimmed, his complexion pale and pasty.

"I'm glad I caught you though." Nate smiled.

"You are?" Derek stuttered. "Why?"

"Oh, just a couple more questions. Why don't we step into the sitting room here." Nate gestured toward the large front room with a fireplace at the far end. The space offered several seating arrangements of overstuffed couches and chairs. "Please." Nate gestured, indicating Derek should enter first.

Derek plopped onto the nearest chair. "What was it you wanted to ask me?"

Nate took a chair opposite and leaned forward. "When I asked you about the details of the night of the book signing, you neglected to mention that Audra had handed you a large manila envelope that had been delivered to the New York office. It was addressed to your mother."

"Oh, yes?" Derek wiped his forehead. "Yes. That's right. I guess it just slipped my mind."

"What did you do with that envelope?"

Derek's eyes grew wide. "Well, I . . . uh . . . I gave it to my mother. It was addressed to her."

"When did you give her that envelope?"

Derek shook his head. "I don't really . . . no, I do remember. I brought it to her room and left it on the desk."

"When was that?"

"It was . . . when I came back here to take my mother to the book signing."

"I see. Did she open the envelope at that time?"

"No. We didn't have time. There was just enough time to get to the event."

"Well, do you have any idea where that envelope might be now? It wasn't among your mother's possessions in her room."

"It wasn't?"

"No."

"Well, I can't imagine . . . I guess someone must have taken it. We were out that evening at the book signing. I brought Mother back and checked on her a little later. But I don't remember seeing it. Perhaps she packed it away in her suitcase?"

"No. I'm afraid she didn't." Nate waited to see if Derek would offer any further information. Derek sat up straighter. "You don't think—"

"I don't think anything, Mr. Stone. I'm merely curious what happened to that envelope. Do you remember who it was from?"

"Uh, no. No. I don't. I don't think I even glanced at it. It was addressed to Mother at our New York office, that's all I remember."

"So you wouldn't mind if I have a look in your room, would you?"

"No. Of course not. I have nothing to hide." Derek heaved a sigh. "I want you to get to the bottom of whoever did this to Mother."

"Thank you." Nate rose from his chair.

"Is there anything else?"

"Oh, yes, one little thing."

"What's that?"

"I asked you about the woman who was waiting in the lobby, who you say was a fan. Did she by any chance give you her name?"

Derek shook his head from side to side. "I already told you, she didn't."

"It's just that Barbara Drake seemed to recall you talked to her for several minutes outside on the entryway."

"Oh. That. Yes. She was just going on and on about how much she loved *Murder Comes Calling*. I thought I'd never get rid of her. Mother was always pestered by people like that."

Nate pulled a photo out of his pocket and held it up for Derek. "Is this the woman you spoke with by any chance?"

Derek stared at the photo.

"Mr. Stone? Do you recognize this woman?"

"No."

"This isn't the woman you spoke to that day?"

"I . . . I don't know. I suppose it could be. It's hard to say from this photo."

"All right," Nate relented. "You're free to go." He turned away and started up the stairs.

Derek's eyes followed Nate's progress to the second floor.

* * *

SOPHIE PEERED UP through the windshield at the hulking red brick monstrosity of a building. "Downright Gothic," she shuddered. "Can you imagine the horror of being confined here a hundred years ago?"

"Definitely dreary," Lucky remarked.

"I hope times have changed."

"I hope *treatments* have changed. Maybe they've even stopped using chains and electroshock therapy." She smiled. "Come on, let's see what we can find out. Let's start with locating Dr. Cynthia Cranleigh's office."

They entered a remodeled lobby, paved in tile with pastel walls and music emanating from hidden speakers. Lucky noticed a stack of newsletters on a long table just inside the door. She picked one up and tucked it in her purse. A smiling woman, this time in a blue smock, greeted them from across the lobby. "May I help you?" she called.

Lucky raised a hand in greeting. "No thanks, we're fine." Nudging Sophie's arm, she led the way to a bank of elevators at the rear of the lobby.

"Do you know where you're going?" Sophie hissed.

"Not a clue, but I didn't want to be told Dr. Cynthia is no longer with us. And then we'd be asked what our business is. I'm hoping she has an office somewhere in this building and maybe we can get a little information if she has a receptionist or an assistant or something."

"Sounds like a plan," Sophie agreed.

At the edge of the lobby, near the elevators, Lucky spotted a glass-enclosed directory. She quickly scanned it and noted the name "Cranleigh" under the Department of Psychiatry. Suite 304. She pressed the UP button on the elevator pad and waited. Thirty seconds later, the doors opened, and several people spilled out, including a man on crutches with his leg in a cast. Lucky stepped back quickly to give him room. Once the way was clear, she and Sophie stepped inside. They were alone in the elevator. Lucky hit the button for the third floor and glanced at her friend as the elevator lumbered upward.

Sophie whispered, "I think this elevator only looks modern. Maybe there's a little guy in the basement powering it with a foot pedal."

Lucky giggled in spite of herself. "Behave yourself and don't make me laugh."

Sophie winked and made a zipping motion with a finger across her lips.

The doors opened to a long empty corridor. They followed the images of footprints laid on the tile to the end. Several closed doors stood on either side of the corridor, numberless, but next to the last door was a nameplate, CYNTHIA CRANLEIGH, M.D. Lucky knocked once on the door and entered.

A desk dominated the center of this room. The walls were lined with plastic armchairs and seats in vibrant colors. "Hello," she called.

"I'm here," a disembodied voice called back. "Just give me a minute." They heard scuffling noises and a head appeared at the desktop. "Hang on." A woman of sixty-plus years with a head of very short silver hair rose from the floor behind the desk. She leaned on top of it. "My back gets stiffer every day. Sorry about that, just dropped a bunch of files. What can I do for you?" She peered over her glasses at them.

"We . . . uh . . ." Lucky wasn't sure how to begin. "Did you work for Dr. Cranleigh?"

"Yes, dear." A shadow passed over the woman's face. "I did. For fifteen years. You know she died, don't you?"

"Yes, we know. We live in Snowflake, where she was found."

"Oh! I see." The woman sat heavily in the chair behind the desk. "So you're not patients of hers then, are you?'

"No." Lucky shook her head. "We . . . well, this is rather a long story. You may not know this but another woman was murdered in Snowflake a few days ago in the same manner. A friend of ours is implicated and we think there might be a connection."

"Another woman?" The gray-haired woman peered intently at them. "My name's Fern, by the way."

"I'm Lucky, Lucky Jamieson and . . ." She turned to Sophie.

Sophie smiled. "I'm Sophie DuBois."

"Well, you've piqued my interest. How 'bout a cup of tea? I was just about to take a break."

"Sure, we'd love that."

"Come on in the back. We have a teeny kitchenette back here." She opened the door behind her and led them down a short corridor. A door to the left stood open. Lucky peeked inside as they passed. Bookshelves lined the walls; the lighting was dim and comfortable. A large desk stood on one side and, on the other, a sofa filled with brightly patterned pillows and a wing-back chair. A box of tissues was placed on a small table in front of the sofa.

Fern noticed Lucky's interest. She turned back. "That's the doctor's office where she saw her patients." She opened a door at the end of the corridor. It led into a small room with a sink, a small counter, a round table and three chairs. "Have a seat." An electric kettle was steaming on the countertop. Fern reached up and retrieved three mugs, filled each one with a teabag and then poured boiling water into the mugs. She unplugged the kettle and relayed the mugs to the table with a sugar bowl. "Milk or cream?" she asked.

"No, thanks," Lucky and Sophie answered in unison. The room had an aroma that reminded Lucky of a teachers' lounge in elementary school. An ever-mysterious inner sanctum where grown-ups gathered.

"Sorry, I don't have any lemon to offer you." She dipped a teaspoon of sugar into her mug. "So tell me all about this woman in Snowflake. Are you talking about Hilary Stone?" Fern asked.

"That's right. You see, they died within a few days of each other and they were both strangled. I can't help but think there's a connection between Ms. Stone and Dr. Cranleigh. That's what brought us here. A possible connection." Lucky took a sip of her tea. It was delicious, some sort of mint and orange flavor. "We've also learned that the author, Hilary Stone, had a daughter years before, maybe forty years ago, who was given up for adoption. I've been trying to trace her."

"Why?" Fern asked.

"Because . . . well, this is hard to put into words. I lost both of my parents a couple of years ago in a car accident. That's part of it, and I can't help but think this girl, this woman now, might have wanted to find her mother and someone needs to let her know that her mother is dead."

"Hmmm. Maybe. Happens a lot. You'd be the bearer of sad news."

"I know, but I still think she'd want to know, don't you?"

"Could be. Not everybody feels that way. I've seen a lot, working in this system." She waved an arm that seemed to indicate not just the building itself, but the institution, the mind-set, the bureaucracy. "You know, adoption records are strictly confidential. The laws have changed in recent years and there are extenuating circumstances that could be involved, but I certainly wouldn't know anything about adoption. Dr. Cynthia wouldn't have either."

"This little girl was adopted, but when she was nine or maybe ten, her parents died in a house fire." Lucky noticed a shift in Fern's expression. "She was named Georgina Ellers after the adoption." Lucky remained silent, watching the woman. "You know who I'm talking about, don't you?"

Fern groaned and put her face in her hands. "I knew it. I knew it had something to do with her."

"She was a patient of Dr. Cranleigh's?"

Fern's jaw tightened. "I can't tell you that. I can't give you the names of Dr. Cynthia's patients."

"You don't have to. We'd just like to know how to contact her."

"I can't help you. I have no idea where she is now."

"Now?" Sophie asked.

"She took off." Fern stared at them a moment, then seemed to make up her mind. "Hell, what difference does it make. This is it for me. I'm retiring. This is my last job. I'm packing up Cynthia's office. I only have a few more days here. By all rights, I shouldn't even be here today, but I want to get this finished. After that, I'm sure they'd let me go anyway, but it's all right, I'm ready." Fern cradled the mug of tea in her hands. "I thought the world of Cynthia. She was so caring about all her patients. She wasn't one of those shrinks that just throw pills at people. She really went the extra mile whether they had insurance or were stone broke. She didn't care what their situation was, but she really cared about Georgina. She had treated her off and on for years."

"Was she institutionalized?"

"No, no, nothing like that. The girl had spent her life in a series of foster homes, none of them were ideal situations. She . . . how can I put this? She had problems. A certain imbalance, I guess. She never seemed to have a solid footing. No wonder, considering what happened to her and how she had to grow up. She came here through a state-funded community mental health program. She lived in the area, managed to hold down a job, but I always felt she was one who could easily go off the rails. Cynthia took extra pains with her." Fern looked up quickly. "You know the police have been here, don't you? Asking about her patients?"

Lucky immediately pictured Nate in her mind's eye. "From Snowflake?"

"Yes. His name was . . ." Fern glanced around as if Nate's card would be available. "It's on my desk . . ."

"Nate Edgerton."

"Yes, that's it. He's been here a couple of times. The first time after they found Cynthia." Fern shivered. "I still can't get over that. That Cynthia's gone. I've been crying my eyes out ever since. She's the only reason I've stayed here as long as I have. I could have retired several years ago, but I stayed because of her."

"You said 'a couple of times'?" Sophie interrupted.

"Yes. He was asking about your famous writer too. If there had been a connection between Cynthia and her. I told him there wasn't. I had the names of all her patients over the years and I had never heard that name. He insisted I check and I did, but my answer was still the same. Of course, I'd no way of knowing that the writer woman had a daughter she had given up for adoption."

"It was only through a fluke that we found out about the child and the adoption." Lucky looked over at Sophie. "I think we'll have to find a way to tell Nate."

Sophie nodded once.

"And then there was that other man who came by. I told the policeman about him."

"Another man? Who was it?" Lucky asked.

"Said he was an investigator, hired by some attorney in New York. He came by a couple of times. The first time, Dr. Cynthia wasn't here and he tried to get me talking about Ms. Ellers, he called her. I told him where to get off. He came again after they discovered Cynthia in the woods . . ." Fern's voice caught and tears sprang to her eyes. She waved her hand in front of her face, "Sorry. It just comes up and grabs me sometimes. I wouldn't talk to him. Told him to get lost."

"Who was he working for? Did he say?"

"Oh, I guess he did, but I don't remember now. He told me the name of the attorney, but he wouldn't say who had hired this attorney." Fern laughed. "Ha! Confidential, he said. I didn't like his attitude. I told him our records were confidential too and he could contact the police if it was so important." Fern gathered up the empty mugs and placed them in the sink. "Maybe he did. I'd have no way of knowing." She turned back to them. "You have to understand. Cynthia never talked about her patients, she was very ethical that way. I don't want you to get the wrong impression of her. But . . . sometimes she'd ask me what I thought. Maybe because I'm an old lady and I've lived a long time. She'd lay out a hypothetical situation and get my reaction." Fern smiled. "But I could read between the lines. This woman . . ."

"Georgina Ellers?"

Fern looked up quickly, "Yes, that's right. She had always wanted to know why her mother had given her up. She wanted to know who her father was and"—Fern shrugged—"how she came to be on the planet, I guess. But . . . something had happened recently. I don't know what it was. You see, Cynthia herself? She wasn't adopted, but she had no family at all. That much I knew. Maybe she was an only child, or maybe her parents were dead, but I think she had a special . . . concern for her patient because of that. She connected with her in a certain way that might not have been really healthy for Cynthia." Fern continued, "But I did notice that one day Cynthia was disturbed. It was the next day after Georgina had come in. What I think Cynthia was trying to tell me was that Georgina had found her mother. Either she had gotten access to the adoption records, maybe years before, but still couldn't find her mother, or somehow she had recently found her mother. Something had changed and I knew Cynthia was worried about her."

"How could she do that? How could she find out who her mother really was?" Lucky interjected.

"Well, an adopted child does have the right to inquire, especially if the mother didn't require nondisclosure of information. And even then, there are ways around that." Fern took a deep breath. "Apparently, I got the impression Georgina was much worse in recent months. I don't know what she told Dr. Cynthia in her sessions. Cynthia would never give me details about her patients, but I had access to the notes. I . . . I was worried about Cynthia and I took it upon myself to make sure I read her notes about these sessions. I was afraid Cynthia was getting too involved. She didn't tell me as much, but I think that's why she took a leave. When Georgina stopped showing up for her weekly session, I think Cynthia went looking for her."

"Where would she begin to look?"

"I don't know for sure, but to hazard a guess, I'd say New York. And maybe that's where Cynthia went too, but I don't know it for a fact. Cynthia was going way beyond the bounds in checking up on her patient, but like I said, she was getting too involved in trying to help this woman. I think she was afraid of what trauma this could cause to her patient, or maybe she was afraid of what Georgina might do once she found her mother."

Fern's voice choked and tears flooded her eyes. "I tried to talk to her before she left . . . Cynthia, that is. She was such a wonderful woman and a good doctor. She certainly didn't deserve to die like that, alone and murdered in the woods and left like a poor dead animal. Sometimes I can't stop crying."

"Did you think Georgina could be violent?" Lucky asked.

"I really have no idea."

"What did she look like, Georgina? Could you describe her?"

"Oh." Fern's eyes opened wide. "I never met her."

"What?" Sophie exclaimed.

"I never set eyes on her. She always came in for her sessions in the evenings after I left for home. She did manage to keep a job and she always paid her portion in cash, so I never even had to send a bill." Fern smiled. "They're too cheap to pay overtime here, so I certainly wasn't going to stay. I'm not running any charities. If Cynthia had asked me to stay late, I would have done it in a flash, but she was too considerate. She always made sure I went home on time." Fern continued, "I know what I know because I could see Cynthia's concern and I read her notes."

"Do you think we could have a peek at those?" Sophie asked hesitantly.

Fern sat back in her chair. "Oh, no. Sorry, dear. I couldn't. I draw the line at that. Besides, even if I were so inclined, I don't have those files anymore. They've all been shipped to the Records Department."

"I understand," Lucky said. She thought a moment. "You said she had a job. Did you ever know where she worked? Was it here in Bournmouth?"

"Oh, I'm sure she lived locally and probably worked here too. I don't know where, but I think . . . I think Cynthia once mentioned something about her being a waitress, if I'm not mistaken."

Lucky and Sophie exchanged a look. There was no need

of words. They both immediately thought of Nanette. Lucky spoke first. "We really appreciate your time. We really do. I think maybe locating this daughter will be up to the police. I don't know if there's anything else we can possibly do."

"Well, frankly . . . my advice? I'd stop looking if I were you. Lord knows, it didn't do Cynthia any good."

Chapter 39

LUCKY FILLED THE dishwasher with the last load of dishes from the evening. Sophie had returned to the Spoonful with her and had stayed on to help. Nanette had gone for the day and Jack was in the office counting receipts. She could overhear Sophie filling Sage in on the details of their excursion to Bournmouth that afternoon.

Meg finished straightening the chairs at all the tables. "Need anything else, Lucky?"

"No, we're fine, Meg. You can take off if you like."

"Okay," Meg replied.

Lucky looked up. There was an odd tone to her voice. "Everything okay, Meg?"

"Fine," the girl answered abruptly and pushed through the swinging door into the corridor.

What now? Lucky thought. It felt as if all sorts of negative energy had been swirling around the restaurant all evening. Even Jack had been uncharacteristically silent since she had returned.

Jack poked his head through the doorway. "Good night, my girl. I'm takin' off."

"So soon, Jack?"

"Well, it's three bells already."

"Oh, I thought I'd fill you in on what happened today, if you were going to stick around and have a beer."

"Uh, can't do that tonight. I've got plans."

"Plans?" Lucky's eyebrows raised.

He grinned. "Yup. I have a date."

"A date?" Lucky almost dropped the mug in her hand.

"What's wrong with that? You think no lady would want to step out with me?"

"Uh . . . Jack, that's not what I meant. You just took me by surprise." She hesitated. "Can I ask with whom?"

"Why, Nan, of course. That's what I call her. Nan. Pretty name." Jack waved as he returned down the corridor. Lucky heard the back door slam.

Sophie peeked out through the kitchen hatch. "Did I just hear right?"

"Unfortunately, you did."

Sage, standing at the worktable, shook his head.

"Sophie, I have to figure a way to get rid of that woman before Jack gets hurt. I don't like any of this one bit. I just can't figure out what she's up to." It hadn't been that long ago that Jack's health was in jeopardy. He still suffered from a wartime post-traumatic stress disorder, but he had been on an even keel for some time and Lucky didn't want to see him lose ground because of emotional upheaval.

A rap came at the front door. Barry stood outside. Lucky walked to the door and unlocked it. Normally only Horace stopped by at closing time, usually because he was taking Cicero for a walk. Lucky was surprised to see Barry at this hour.

"Come on in, Barry. Are you okay?"

Barry nodded. "Oh, I'm all right. Just wanted a chance to talk to you alone. Have you been able to find anything out?"

"A few things. Grab a seat."

"Where's Jack?"

"He's gone already. Believe it or not, he has a date with the infamous Nanette."

"Oh?" Barry's eyes widened. "Old codger. Who'd a thunk it?"

"Don't let him hear you call him old."

Barry laughed. "Well, there certainly seems to be a lot more spring in his step these days."

"Hey, Barry," Sophie called from the kitchen. "We've got some stuff to tell you." Sophie pushed through the door with a tray, three chilled glasses and three bottles of beer. "Sage'll be right out." She placed the tray on the table. "Lucky, I know you don't like beer. Sage has some nice white wine. I'll get you a glass."

"Thanks," Lucky replied gratefully.

When Barry had been brought up to speed with the events of the afternoon, he sat quietly for a few minutes. "This doesn't sound too good, Lucky. Maybe you should give it up. Might be better if you didn't locate this woman."

"That's what I'm thinking," Sophie said, taking a sip of her beer.

"I don't know." Lucky sighed. "I haven't really decided what to do. What is interesting is that Nate was looking for a connection between Dr. Cranleigh, the psychiatrist, and Hilary Stone. They were both killed in Snowflake and in the same manner. We have an advantage because we know the connection is Hilary's daughter. I think we're going to have to tell Nate."

"Please, Lucky," Barry begged. "Please don't tell Nate where Hank is, not yet at least. I promised him I wouldn't breathe a word and you promised him too."

"Well then, you've got to talk to Hank. He's got to come back to town and tell Nate what he knows. I could be totally wrong. The daughter, Georgina, might not be the connection between these two women, but she *must* be. It's way too much of a coincidence."

Sage had joined them and now the four were huddled conspiratorially around the front table. All the lights except for one lamp had been turned off. They all jumped when a sharp rap came at the door. Nate stood outside.

"Uh-oh," Barry said. "Why do I have a bad feeling?"

Lucky froze for a moment. They she rose and opened the door. "Hi, Nate. Come on in."

Nate shot a dark look at the group. "Where's Jack?"

"He left already."

"I see. Well, in that case, I won't stay. But I just want to warn you"—he looked at Lucky, and then glanced at Barry—"I won't be happy if I find out there's a parallel investigation going on here. Especially if anyone in this group"—his look took in the whole table—"is withholding information."

Sage suddenly found the contents of his glass worth studying. Sophie glanced at Barry.

"We wouldn't do that." Barry's voice betrayed his nervousness.

"I would certainly hope not. You know . . . I could have sworn I saw the two of you driving through Bournmouth yesterday afternoon."

"Uh . . ." Barry faltered.

Lucky immediately felt a hot wave of guilt wash over her, but she thought quickly. "I had an errand to do. Barry offered to help me with it."

"Hmm. Awfully nice of you, Barry." Nate didn't look convinced. "Anyone heard from Hank?" Nate was greeted with silence.

"Okay. Here's how it's gonna go. If I don't hear from Hank Northcross in the next twenty-four hours . . . if he doesn't show up in Snowflake, I'm issuing a warrant for his arrest. Hank was present at the scene. His eyeglasses were found shattered in Hilary Stone's room. He had the means and the opportunity, and with a little more investigation, I'm sure I'll figure out what his motive could have been. You can pass that on . . . just in case anyone happens, just *happens*, to be talking to him." Nate turned and walked out without another word, shutting the door firmly behind him.

Sophie was the first to speak. "Whew. Nate's a wee bit upset, I think. And you," she said, turning to Lucky, "you out and out *lied* to him."

"What was I going to say?" Lucky squeaked. "I was

sworn to secrecy. I couldn't tell him Barry and I met with Hank yesterday."

"Did you hear what Nate just said? Hank's eyeglasses were found in that woman's room! This is awful," Barry groaned. "I've gotta call him. He has to come back. We have to tell Nate everything. About the daughter, about Hank's book. Everything. This is getting crazy."

"Look, we know Hank was at the Drake House that night," Lucky replied. "Horace saw him. Other people could have seen him and I think we can assume he was there to see Hilary Stone."

"Yes," Sophie interjected, "but Nate said the glasses were broken. That doesn't sound good. That sounds like maybe there was a struggle."

"Or maybe Hank just dropped them and accidentally stepped on them," Barry argued. "Or maybe they're not Hank's, but Nate thinks they are."

"I just remembered." Lucky caught Barry's eye. "Hank mentioned he couldn't find his glasses the other day. Remember?"

"Did he?" Barry asked. "I don't remember that."

"He did."

"So. That doesn't mean a thing," Sophie said. "It sounds more like he thinks he lost them. Wouldn't he remember if they dropped in the middle of a heated argument with his ex-wife?"

"Let's not speculate," Lucky said. "The bottom line is that Nate is getting upset about Hank's disappearance. It's so foolish that he won't come home." Lucky jumped involuntarily when she spotted a face at the front window. Meg's face was pressed against the glass. She was staring at the group. Lucky rose and unlocked the door. "Forget something, Meg?"

Meg stood with her arms crossed. "No," she answered angrily. "I did not forget anything. I can see what's going on here and I want in."

"What do you mean?" Lucky asked as Meg stormed past her.

"I'm always kept out of all the excitement that goes on around town. Everybody just overlooks me, like I'm invisible, and I'm sick of it. I want to be part of the murder investigation, 'cause I can see that's what you're all doing."

Looks were exchanged around the table.

"See? I know what you're thinking. What could Meg possibly have to offer? You all think I'm just a dumb waitress."

"Nobody's calling you dumb, Meg," Sage answered. "You're young, that's all. We don't want you to get in any trouble with the cops or anything."

"Really? Well, I happen to be the only one here who's actually read *Murder Comes Calling*. Hellloooo!" She stood with her hands on her hips. "In fact, I probably know more about detecting than all of you put together. And even I can see there's a connection between these two murders."

Barry stood and pulled over another chair. "Welcome to the newly formed Murder Investigation Club, Meg."

Chapter 40

"MEG'S RIGHT," LUCKY said. "She's every bit as smart as anyone at this table. More importantly, we need to focus and put our heads together and do what we can to help Hank."

Another knock came at the front door. Lucky groaned. "What now?" She looked up to see Horace with Cicero on a leash. She unlocked the door and let them in.

He stared at the group at the table. "I hope I'm not interrupting anything. Just thought I'd stop by and chat."

"The more the merrier," Sage said. "Welcome to the Murder Investigation Club, Horace, as Barry has so aptly dubbed it. We've decided to investigate on our own to try to prevent Nate from arresting Hank." He stood. "Would you like a beer?"

"Oh, yes, that would be nice. Thank you," Horace replied. "Where is Hank, by the way? I've been hearing lots of rumors." He unsnapped Cicero's leash and pulled over another chair to join the group at the table.

"Hank's out of town and refuses to come back," Barry explained, "but Nate's threatening to issue a warrant for his arrest if he's not back here in twenty-four hours."

"That sounds serious."

"Nate's pretty ticked off, would be my guess," Sage said. He turned to Lucky, "You should bring everyone up to speed."

Lucky glanced at Barry. "What do you think, Barry? Would we be breaking our promises to Hank?"

Barry heaved a sigh. "I know he's sensitive on the subject of his past, and I know he'd prefer not to have people know, but we didn't actually promise that. We only promised not to tell Nate where he was. I vote that we share all information. It's all gonna come out anyway, so it might as well be between people who really care about Hank."

When Horace and Meg heard the story of Hank's past and his marriage to Hilary Stone and the daughter she had given up for adoption, Lucky relayed the information she and Sophie had gleaned that afternoon.

"I can't believe that!" Meg said. "*Hank* wrote that book? Our Hank?"

Barry nodded in response. "Took me by surprise too."

Horace shook his head. "Plagiarism is a serious issue." Cicero growled in his throat as though agreeing with his master.

"I hope I'm not spoiling anything," Meg said, "but in *Murder Comes Calling*, the guilty party is the estranged child."

"Is this a case of life imitating art?" Sophie asked.

"Well, if that's the case here, it's as if Hank's work predicted the future, isn't it?" Horace said. "If he knew Hilary had a daughter that she had given up for adoption, perhaps that gave him the kernel of an idea for the story."

"Unless Hank were the murderer," Barry offered, "which I don't for a second believe. I won't believe it."

"Meg"—Lucky turned to the girl—"I think it's important that we know everything you know about *Murder Comes Calling*, but let's all keep an open mind. It can't be just a coincidence that Dr. Cranleigh and Hilary Stone were strangled with what may have been a similar weapon, but it could be someone copying the book."

"But that's not all," Meg said excitedly. "All the victims were women who worked in fields related to adoptions. A doctor, a social worker and a counselor. There was another victim who knew the crime was going to be committed but didn't tell the police in time and that person had to die too."

"Do we know what these women were strangled with?" Horace asked. Cicero made yearning noises deep in his throat.

"Oh, Cicero," Lucky said. "I'm sorry, boy. I forgot your chicken." She reached down to pat the dog's head. "Hang on." She jumped up and went to the kitchen, returning with a good-sized hunk of cooked chicken for him. He gobbled it instantly and licked Lucky's hand.

"We do know," Lucky offered. "I hate to betray a confidence, but I happen to know both women were strangled with something thin and plastic, probably a telephone cord or something like it."

"Oh!" Meg gasped. "Just like the book."

"Can you tell us about it?" Sophie asked.

"Yes," Meg breathed, straightening her glasses. Her face was flushed. "See, the protagonist is a television reporter and journalist, a writer, like Hilary Stone. The reporter gets an anonymous phone call from a stranger who promises her a tip about the three murders where the victims were all strangled with a telephone cord. She goes to meet this unknown person in the subway, but instead of meeting her informant, she discovers another murder victim, dead and strangled on the subway rails. The last victim knew one of the crimes was about to be committed but didn't tell the police in time and because she, the last victim, knew too much, she had to die too." Meg paused for breath. "It's very confusing because at first you're sure it's the ex-husband of the first murder victim, but the final twist comes at the end and it's a shocker. The killer is the first victim's estranged child, who's targeting everyone who had a hand in putting her into foster homes. It's so weird that Hilary Stone had an estranged child too!"

"How many victims?" Sophie asked. "Please, let's hope there are no more."

"That's fascinating," Lucky said, "but unless the real murderer is trying to copy the book, I don't know if the novel is really relevant." She shook her head. "When I heard about the daughter, I really wanted to locate her because . . . I don't know, she had been given up so coldly, my heart just went out to her, but now I think we've got to consider the possibility that . . ." Lucky trailed off.

"She's the killer," Sophie finished.

"That could be," Lucky agreed. "We just don't know. But I think we should assume she's here in Snowflake, and she's one of the women who made sure she was close to Hilary Stone in some way. And if she did kill her own mother, the next question is, did she kill her psychiatrist because her doctor knew too much?" Lucky looked around the table. "I don't know about anyone else, but I'm convinced that one of these women who are here, on the scene right now, one of them is the daughter of Hilary. I wanted to find her because . . . well, as I said, I felt it was important someone tell her. But if she's already here, and I'm starting to believe she is, we still have to identify her for the obvious reasons. We have to band together. If we combine forces, we should be able to figure out which one of them is Hilary Stone's mysterious daughter."

"Who's in?" Barry asked. "Raise your hand if you want to help Hank." He looked around the table at their faces.

One by one each person raised a hand. "We'll do whatever we can to clear Hank's name," Sophie said. "I'm sure he had nothing to do with this."

"Well, we only have twenty four hours. You heard Nate," Sage said. "Once he issues a warrant, Hank is sure to be picked up. Wherever he's staying, he must have to go out for food or fresh air. He could be easily spotted. Bournmouth's not that big."

"Do you suppose the doctor thought the daughter was capable of murder?" Horace interjected.

"That's what I think," Sophie said. "Dr. Cranleigh wanted to stop her before she lost control."

Lucky looked around the table at their little group. Barry's spirits seemed to have lifted. "Are we jumping to a horrible conclusion? I'm not totally convinced that Hilary's daughter is guilty of these murders."

Horace reached across the table and held Lucky's hand.

"I think you must seriously consider that possibility. You could be putting yourself in grave danger."

Lucky nodded. "I know, it's occurred to me too, Horace." Lucky sipped her wine. She had almost forgotten that Sophie had poured her a glass. "But this is what I think we should do. Each of us can take one person to target. Someone has to find out how long Derek Stone has known his wife. They married fairly recently. Audra, the publicist, told me she was hired for this job recently too, but she had her own company before that. Phoebe, well, I just don't know how best to approach her."

"That's too weird," Sophie remarked. "That would mean that if Sylvia is really Georgina Ellers, then she knowingly married her half brother."

"That's true," Horace replied. "Could she be that diabolical . . . that's if Sylvia really is the person we're looking for."

"And Audra . . . it seems if she works for the publishing house, they might have just assigned her to Hilary for this trip," Sage offered.

"Yes, but how long has she worked for the publisher? What if we find out she's only had her job for a couple of months?" Lucky took a deep breath. "What we do know is that Georgina Ellers, if that's still her legal name, is approximately forty years old. That's based on the fact that she was reported as being ten years old when the fire killed her adoptive parents. She's entered her middle years, but she could still appear to be very young. Anybody have any thoughts on how old those three women are?"

"That's a tough one," Sophie replied. "They all seem to be right around that age. Audra's very sophisticated and Sylvia looks like nine miles of bad road, but they and Phoebe could all be around that age. That doesn't help us a bit."

"Why don't I call Barbara Drake," Lucky said, "and let her know we're available to deliver food if any of her second-floor guests would like that? It'll give us a chance to spend more time over there without arousing suspicion. Besides, I think Barbara would appreciate the offer."

"Won't she think it's weird you're willing to do that?" Sophie asked.

"I don't want to say anything about this to Barbara, not yet anyway. I'll think of something to tell her. Exactly what, I don't know right now, but I'll come up with something. She wants to get to the bottom of this very badly too. And for one thing, we can trust her. We know who she is. Barbara grew up in Snowflake."

Horace cleared his throat. "I've spotted Derek walking around town early in the morning. I can strike up a conversation with him and try to find out about his wife."

"Meg and I can deliver food if Barbara's open to that and talk to Audra and maybe Phoebe. Find out whatever we can," Sophie offered.

"I feel terrible not being honest with Nate," Lucky said. "I'm just not sure he knows about Hilary's daughter. And I'm sure he doesn't know that Hilary stole Hank's book."

"That's all he'd need right now," Barry said. "Hank's motive for murder."

"True," Sophie said, "but Nate has resources we don't have. He may be on the same track we are because we know he talked to Dr. Cranleigh's assistant in Bournmouth."

"And speaking of which . . ." Lucky looked around the table. "I almost forgot to mention this. Another thing that Fern, Dr. Cranleigh's assistant, told us was there was someone else asking for information about Hilary's daughter."

"Who?" Sage asked.

"He identified himself as a private investigator working for an attorney, but wouldn't say who hired the attorney. Fern claimed she didn't tell him anything. She was very suspicious of him."

Horace shook his head. "Who would have hired an investigator? Certainly not Hilary Stone. She had no interest in the child, as far as we know. And it certainly wouldn't be the doctor who was killed. That wouldn't make any sense. She must have already known her patient's story. Who else is left?"

"Stone's husband, the publisher?" Sophie asked.

"That's assuming he even knew Hilary had had a daughter," Sage said, "and even if he knew, why would he have any interest?"

"It might have nothing to do with Hilary Stone," Meg offered. "What if it was a relative of the two people who died in the fire?"

"Thirty years later?" Barry asked. "That doesn't make any sense."

Meg looked crestfallen. Lucky reached across and patted her shoulder. "Don't lose heart. You have some good ideas."

"What should we do next, Lucky?" Barry asked.

"Are you good with cars, Barry?" Sage asked.

"Uh, sure."

"Well." Sage smiled. "They have two rental cars. Maybe you can make sure they're temporarily disabled. Nate's restricted them to town, but they'll be getting stir crazy. They'll be easier to approach if they're on foot."

"Good idea." Barry slapped the table in glee. "I'll take care of that tonight when they're all asleep."

"I'll see what I can learn from Audra tomorrow," Lucky said. "I think we all have our assignments." She looked around the table. "There's someone else we should think about." The others looked at her expectantly.

"What's that?" Sage asked.

"Nanette." She waited for their reaction.

"Oh!" Sophie exclaimed. "Right. Just who is she? She arrived out of nowhere. Nobody knows anything about her. And didn't you give her an ultimatum to produce some real identification?"

Lucky groaned. "Yes. Yesterday. I've got to get on her case again."

"She's the right age," Horace added.

"And her hair is definitely dyed," Sophie added. "She's recently arrived in town."

"True," Horace offered, "but if so, why is she here instead of trying to get close to Hilary Stone? Did she have any interest in coming to the book signing?" he asked Lucky.

"Never said anything about it," Lucky replied. "And she

didn't come. Although it was very crowded, I'm sure I would have noticed her. But she definitely warrants more investigation." She turned to Sophie. "I have an idea about that. I think it's something we can take care of but we can talk about it later."

Sophie nodded in acknowledgment.

Lucky turned to Meg. "What do you say we adjourn the first meeting of the . . ." she smiled, "the Murder Investigation Club. We'll meet here tomorrow . . ." Lucky remembered her plans with Elias for dinner. "Sorry, I can't be here tomorrow night, but the night after. We'll meet after closing and compare notes. Anybody second that?" Lucky said.

"I'll second," Horace announced. Cicero barked to make it unanimous.

Chapter 41

MEG WALKED VERY quietly down the corridor. When she had first arrived at the Drake House, she peeked through the front window and saw Phoebe watching the news on the television in the front sitting room. Audra sat at the other end of the room, near a reading lamp, her feet propped up on an ottoman with a book in her hands. She wasn't sure where Derek or Sylvia were, but she assumed they were in their bedroom. She grasped the doorknob to Phoebe's room and, summoning her courage, turned it. She peeked inside, fearful someone else might be there, even though she was sure Phoebe was still downstairs. A suitcase rested on a folding hammock. The lid was propped against the wall. Meg quickly stepped inside the room and left the door ajar. In case anyone saw her, she could always claim she was checking for dishes to be picked up. She glanced around the room. Everything in it was neat and orderly, except the desk. Papers were strewn across the top. Meg hurried across the room and quickly leafed through the papers. Several large envelopes, all addressed to Phoebe Hollister or Lexington Avenue Publishing at the New York office, were stacked to the side. Meg riffled through the papers on the desktop. Everything seemed related to travel arrangements, car rentals, invoices and the group's travel schedule. Nothing looked out of the ordinary. She opened each drawer and checked its contents. Nothing of note. She had just picked up the large envelope on top of the stack to check its contents when she heard a floorboard squeak. She dropped the envelope on the desk. It slid to the floor. Someone was coming. She picked the envelope up quickly, returning it to the stack on the desk and did her best to rearrange the loose papers. A small white business card caught her eye. She picked it up. CYNTHIA CRANLEIGH, M.D., SALISBURY RETREAT, with an address and telephone number. Her heart was beating fast and her hands were shaking. Why would Phoebe have the doctor's card? She slipped the card into her pocket. She listened again, not daring to breathe, but heard nothing. She hurried out to the corridor and picked up her tray. She looked both ways. The corridor was empty. She was sure she had heard footsteps and the creak of a floorboard. She took a deep breath to calm her nerves. Maybe it was just her imagination.

She approached the doorway to Room 4, Sylvia and Derek Stone's room. She knocked and entered when Sylvia called out, "Come in."

Sylvia sat at the dressing table, still in her silk gown even though the day was almost over.

"Excuse me," she said quietly.

Sylvia turned in a flash, an angry look on her face. "Oh, it's you. Well, come in. Don't just stand there gawking. What have you brought us tonight?"

Meg smiled with difficulty. "I have a serving of cream of asparagus and a carrot and ginger soup for you and your husband."

"Well, put them over there." Sylvia gestured airily to the small table in the corner of the room." She smiled suddenly. "I have to admit, your restaurant's food is the best there is around this town."

Meg smiled in return and placed the tray where Sylvia had indicated. She could feel Sylvia's eyes on her back.

There was something quite intimidating about the woman. She was beautiful, but there was a hardness to her. The platinum blonde hair didn't quite go with her complexion, as if she were masquerading as a Hollywood icon of years before. Meg could definitely smell hard alcohol in the room.

"Sit down, sweetie, and talk to me," Sylvia said. "Tell me what's going on out there."

Meg was taken aback. "Excuse me?"

"Have a seat. No need to run away."

"Uh, all right." Meg nervously wiped her hands on her skirt. She had no idea what possible common ground she and Sylvia Stone could have.

"So," Sylvia announced, turning from her mirror. "Have the police found any leads?"

"Uh, well, I don't really know." Meg hesitated. What was Sylvia thinking? That she, Meg, had some inside track to the police investigation?

"I know that big guy . . . what's his name?"

"Nate? Nate Edgerton?"

"Yes, that's it. He's the chief of police, right?"

"Yes."

"Well . . ." Sylvia smiled slyly. "We heard you people at the restaurant are pretty friendly with him. Don't tell me you don't overhear everything that goes on there."

"I don't hear very much. Mostly everyone just ignores me. But Nate hasn't come in too often lately."

"Oh. That's too bad." Sylvia smiled widely. "I was hoping we'd be allowed to go home soon. Holding us here is just ridiculous!"

"Yes, ma'am," Meg replied.

"After all, there's only one person in our little group who really has a motive."

Meg's ears perked up, but she wisely kept her mouth shut.

Sylvia waited expectantly for Meg to respond, but when no words were forthcoming, she continued. "It's Audra."

"Audra?" Meg asked.

Sylvia leaned forward, and her silk dressing gown fell open, leaving a gap that showed lacy black underwear. "Everyone knows she's having an affair with Derek Stone." She waited for Meg's reaction. "Derek Stone, *Senior*. You get my drift?"

"Oh!" Meg was taken aback at this confidence. "You mean . . . your . . . father-in-law?"

"Yes, the old goat. Can you believe that?" She leaned forward again and in a confidential whisper said, "I swear, I think Hilary wrote that book to reclaim some territory because Audra would like nothing better than to take Hilary's place. Disgusting! That's where the police should be looking."

"Is that true?" Meg breathed, unable to remain quiet.

"Oh, yes. It's true all right."

"Have you told this to Nate Edgerton?"

Sylvia batted her eyes a few times. "I hate to be the bearer of gossip. They might think I was trying to draw attention away from myself."

Meg couldn't resist. "Did you have a motive too?"

"Me?" Sylvia shrieked. "Certainly not. What possible motive could I have to want Hilary dead?" She sighed heavily. "She was a royal pain but I could deal with her easily enough." Sylvia turned back to her mirror. "Thank you, dear. I'll see you tomorrow."

Meg had been dismissed. "Good night." She rose from the settee and, carrying her tray with bowls and saucers, stepped into the hallway and shut the door behind her.

What was that all about? she wondered. *If she expects me to tell Nate about Audra's affair, she can just do her own dirty work.* Occupied with her thoughts, Meg walked toward the stairway. Her back stiffened. She heard it again. The creak of a floorboard. She turned quickly. No one was there. The sconce lights were dim and barely illuminated the other end of the corridor. Was that a shadow? She shook her head. Her eyes were playing tricks on her. She stepped carefully down the stairs, balancing her tray. In the front entry she heard voices in the kitchen. She pushed through the swinging door. Barbara and Mrs. Partridge were in the kitchen washing up. Barbara turned when she heard Meg enter.

"Oh, Meg. I forgot you were still here." Barbara moved

forward and took the tray from her. "I'll take care of these. It's late, you go on home now."

"Thank you, Mrs. Drake." Meg smiled.

"Call me Barbara, please."

"Oh, okay," Meg said, "Barbara." She picked up her purse and lifted it to her shoulder. "Good night." Meg left by the kitchen door and stepped out into the garden. The moon had risen high and cast an eerie glow over the bushes. If she hurried, she could be home and in bed by ten o'clock. She stepped along the flat stones laid out in the earth and reached the road. It wasn't far to her home and normally she wouldn't have minded the walk but she couldn't shake the feeling that someone had been listening to her conversation with Sylvia in the corridor. And then there was that creaky floorboard. She shivered, realizing she had forgotten her jacket. She considered turning back but she was too tired. She'd retrieve her jacket in the morning. She passed under the shadow of a spreading tree. That's when she heard it. Rustling in the bushes by the side of the road. A shiver of fear ran up her spine. She began to walk quickly, doing her best not to panic and break into a run. The sound was probably just a possum or a squirrel. Some little creature that would be more frightened of her than she of it. She stopped and took a deep breath, willing herself to be calm. It was just her imagination. She took a step forward, but before she could move, strong hands pulled her backward into the bushes. Something tightened around her neck. She gasped for air, struggling helplessly against her attacker. Her feet slid on wet leaves. She reached out to grasp at branches but they slipped out of her hands. Then everything went black.

Chapter 42

ELIAS HELD THE door open as Lucky stepped into the Mont Blanc Restaurant at the Resort. "Have you dined here before?" he asked.

"No. Never. It's gorgeous. Look at those chandeliers, how they catch the light." She had agonized over what to wear this evening. All her clothes were everyday things that she wore to work or around town. She had a serviceable black skirt and a few sweaters, and a black suit, but somehow nothing was quite right to wear to a restaurant like this. In desperation she had called Sophie, who had rushed over with the perfect dress. It was a silk sheath in a deep rose color with a low-cut neckline. The color set off her fair complexion. She wore a garnet necklace that had belonged to her mother.

"I'd much rather look at you this evening, not the chandeliers." Elias smiled. He patted the small jewel box in his pocket to reassure himself it was still there. Tonight would be the night, he had promised himself. The more he thought about it, the more nervous he became. If his schedule, or Lucky's, had allowed, he would have taken her out of town for a romantic getaway, but barring that, this setting was the best one available.

A waiter hurried forward to seat them. He held the chair for Lucky and produced two leather-bound menus. The waiter recited a list of their special dishes of the evening and Elias ordered a bottle of white wine for their table.

"What would you like?" he asked.

"Oh, it's so hard to choose. Everything sounds fantastic. I think I'll have the duck breast with cherry marinade."

"Good choice. I'll order the pasta in a cabernet sauce." He smiled at her. "I'm so glad I could drag you away for an evening out. You must be getting sick of my cooking."

"Not at all. I love the things you cook. I'm just surprised you wanted to come here. It's so expensive."

"Once in a while it's fun to splurge."

Lucky couldn't help but wonder what had spurred Elias's decision, but she decided to relax and enjoy the evening and not ask any questions. It wasn't every night she was taken out to a restaurant she couldn't afford.

"What's wrong?" Elias asked.

Startled, Lucky said, "Nothing. Nothing at all. Why do you ask?"

"It's just that you looked like you were drifting away, lost in thought."

"Oh, I'm sorry. It's hard for me not to think about these murders and everything that Sophie and I have found out. Plus, I feel absolutely terrible about not being honest with Nate." On the drive up the mountain to the Resort, Lucky had filled Elias in on their meeting with Hank and everyone's willingness to become involved.

"You should feel terrible," Elias remarked, half in jest. "When are you going to come clean?"

"I think very soon. I'm sure Nate's way ahead of us, but the one thing he might not know about is Hilary's daughter and the fact that she was given up for adoption. And then there's Hank's book that Hilary Stone stole."

"You realize that you've all made some pretty big jumps in logic, don't you?"

"What do you mean?"

"Well, you're assuming that Hilary's daughter is this Georgina Ellers, right?"

"Yes, she has to be."

"Why, because two people died in a house fire?"

"Yes. How many house fires were there in Bournmouth where people actually died? It's bigger than Snowflake, but it's hardly a metropolis."

"Well, to play devil's advocate, Hank's memory could be very faulty. It has been a lot of years. Maybe it wasn't a house fire. Maybe if, *if* something happened to these adoptive parents, even if they did actually die, Hank might have mixed that up with the story of a real fire where two people actually died. It has been known to happen. Memory is a funny thing, especially since he didn't have any personal involvement."

Lucky arranged and rearranged the linen napkin on her lap. "Well, that's a good point. But taken along with the fact that someone named Georgina Ellers was a patient of Dr. Cranleigh's who was killed in the same fashion, that's a huge connection. It has to be real."

"Like I said, I'm playing devil's advocate. It could all be fact but there could be holes in your logic."

"I'll give you the possibility of that, but I really don't think so."

"Besides, I don't like the idea of your trying to find someone who could be dangerous."

"That's what everybody else thinks, but I'm not so sure. I'm kind of trusting my first instinct."

"That her daughter should be informed?"

"Yes. Absolutely. What if this poor woman has been in turmoil her whole life about not knowing her mother, not knowing why she was given up, just wanted to find her mother and make that connection?"

"Yes, and if she's one of the women who was close to Hilary Stone, then she already knows her mother is dead."

Lucky sighed heavily. "True. I wouldn't be telling her anything she didn't know. That's if she is on the scene in Snowflake."

Elias reached across the table and grasped Lucky's hand. "Let's forget all this just for tonight. I see our waiter approaching with a large tray."

Lucky smiled. "Okay, I'm starving. You won't get an argument from me."

"Just promise me you'll talk to Nate right away and tell him everything?"

Lucky nodded. "I will. I think it's time. I promise I'll talk to him first thing in the morning."

Their waiter materialized at the side of the table and served them with a flourish.

Lucky smiled across the table. "Thank you. This is a wonderful treat. Not just to be waited on, but in such luxurious surroundings."

She sliced a small piece of breast and dipped it in the cherry sauce. "Mmm. Delicious. Try yours." She waved her fork at his plate.

Elias smiled. "You need some more wine." He filled each of their wineglasses a second time. Then he reached across the table and clasped her hand. He held it tightly. "Lucky . . ."

"Yes?" She looked across the table at him.

"I wanted to come here tonight because . . ."

A shadow fell across the linen tablecloth. Their waiter stood over them with a phone in his hand. "Ms. Jamieson?" he said.

"Yes?" she answered in surprise.

"A call for you."

Lucky looked quizzically at Elias, then took the phone. "Hello?"

It was Sophie. "Oh, Lucky, I'm so sorry to interrupt your dinner."

"What's wrong?"

"It's Meg. She's been attacked outside the Drake House."

"What? Where is she?"

"We have her in the car. We're outside the Clinic. I was hoping Elias could see her here."

"Of course. Is Meg all right?" She glanced across the table at Elias. He looked at her quizzically.

"I think so. Just pretty shook up."

"We'll be right there." She ended the call. "It's Meg. She's been hurt at the Drake House. They're waiting for us at the Clinic."

"Oh!" Elias said, quickly sliding the box back into his pocket. "We'll have to go."

"What were you going to say before we were interrupted?"

Elias shook his head. "Uh, nothing. We can talk later." He gritted his teeth in frustration. He had finally worked up his courage only to be interrupted, but this call was far more important.

Chapter 43

"I DON'T KNOW what happened," Meg moaned, holding her head. "I was talking to Sylvia in her room. Derek wasn't there." Meg looked up at the concerned faces, "Boy, I got an earful too."

"Hold still," Elias ordered, checking Meg's pupils. "You need to rest. I think you're fine but you've had a terrible scare and your throat is bruised." He turned to the others. "I don't like this one bit. I hope someone's already called Nate."

"Barbara Drake did," Sophie answered.

"Please let me finish," Meg begged. "Anyway . . . Sylvia was telling me all about Audra and why Audra of all people was hired for the job instead of someone in-house. She said she's sure Audra is having an affair with Hilary's husband, Mr. Stone, Senior." Meg continued, "And while she was talking, I had the feeling that someone was in the hallway. I was sure I heard a floorboard creak. Somebody was listening to Sylvia. So I left the tray in the kitchen and went out the back door and started walking down the road. Then . . ." Meg stifled a sob. "I felt this thing around my neck and everything went black."

"This is horrifying," Sophie said. "Someone tried to strangle you, Meg." She turned to the others, "Meg left her jacket in the kitchen. Barbara spotted it and ran outside to catch up with Meg. When she heard the scuffling in the bushes, she started yelling. She had a flashlight and I'm sure she scared off whoever had attacked Meg."

Lucky felt the room spin around. "She saved your life, Meg. You can't go back there. Somebody obviously felt you were a threat. Maybe they overheard you talking to Sylvia and were afraid you found something out."

"I can't imagine what. It was all just gossip." Meg took a deep breath. "The next thing I remember, I was lying on my back and someone was screaming. And then Barbara was helping me walk back to the house."

"I never should have let you get involved."

"You couldn't have stopped me, Lucky." Meg started to slide off the examining table. "Oh, my neck hurts. Anyway, everybody heard Barbara yelling to Mrs. Partridge and they all came running down the stairs."

"Were they all there?"

"Yes, I think so. I was a little woozy. Derek was in his pajamas and even Sylvia came to see what was going on. Then Audra came down and . . . I don't think I saw Phoebe though. She might have been there and I just didn't notice."

"I want you to stay home tomorrow and maybe the next day," Lucky said. "I don't want you coming back for a while."

"Oh, no. I'm not staying away. I don't want to miss anything."

"Well, we're taking you home. I just want to make sure you get there safely. And I should probably have a word with your mother. You're not going back to the Drake House. Not after this."

"No!" Meg insisted. Then she saw the look on Lucky's face. "Let me tell my mother, okay? I promise I will." Meg slipped her sweater back on. "But we can't disband the Murder Investigation Club."

Elias raised his eyebrows. "The what?"

"Oh," Lucky said. "Well, everyone's become involved

somehow. Barry and Horace and Sage too. And I told you that Hilary didn't write *Murder Comes Calling.* It was Hank's book and she stole it."

"Giving Hank a very good motive to murder her."

"Except he didn't," Meg said. "I'm sure our Hank would never do anything like that."

Elias nodded patiently. "Of course not," he said, "but I don't know what Nate would think."

Meg continued, "Hank wrote it. Hilary stole it and then married this publisher, Stone, and claimed it as her own. Hank told us—"

Elias interrupted her, "When are you lot going to talk to Nate?" Lucky could hear a note of anger in his voice.

Lucky looked at Sophie and Sage. "I guess tonight we will. If he's on his way here."

"Nate's ready to issue a warrant for Hank's arrest," Meg said. "That's why we've been trying to help."

"You're withholding information from the police in a murder investigation." Elias looked at all of them. "Are you all crazy?"

"Elias, listen," Lucky said. "Hank swore Barry and me to secrecy. He just wasn't up to coming back to Snowflake to cope with this. I forgot to tell you the most important thing. The reason Hank was at the Drake House that night was because Hilary asked him to meet with her. She wanted him to agree to write a second book for her. She promised to pay him but she would take the credit. Needless to say, he became very angry and refused," Lucky said.

"Well, it's unfortunate that Hank was on the scene and had an argument with this woman, but none of you have any business sticking your nose in this." His statement was greeted with dead silence.

Meg rubbed her forehead. "I almost forgot." She reached into her pocket and retrieved the doctor's card she had found. "Look what I found in Phoebe's room."

"What is that?" Lucky asked. She took the card from Meg's hand and gasped. "Dr. Cranleigh's card!' She looked at Meg. "And you found this in *Phoebe's* room?"

"Yes." Meg nodded.

Lucky turned to the others. "How could Phoebe possibly have this card?"

Elias sighed. "I think it's high time you shared these little tidbits of information with Nate." He waited for a response, and when none came, he shook his head. "I give up."

"Hey," Sage said. He peeked out into the hallway. "Someone's at the front door." He looked around the room. "It's Nate. I better let him in."

"Go ahead," Elias said. "I think every one of you needs to tell Nate everything you know. It's high time the Murder Investigation Club was disbanded." He glared at Lucky. "Before somebody really gets hurt."

Sage reentered the room with Nate in his wake. Nate's face was grim. "Okay, let's all sit down someplace and have a nice talk."

Chapter 44

AFTER LUCKY AND Barry had confessed their part in the cover-up to Nate, with Meg filling in the rest of the details, Nate sat in gloomy silence. "And Hank claims he wrote this book, the one that Ms. Stone claims for her own?" Meg nodded. "Does he have any proof?"

"No," Lucky answered. "Hilary Stone stole his only manuscript. And then Hank destroyed all the drafts."

"Interesting." Nate looked around the room at all their expectant faces. "Thank you for that. That I did not know. Not sure if it changes anything, but in case you're interested, none of you have fooled me one bit. I'll say this once. I know where Hank is staying. I really don't have time to drive over to Bournmouth again this week. I can do so if he still refuses to come in voluntarily to answer some questions, but if I have to, I'll go over there with sirens and handcuffs if that will bring him to his senses. Do I make myself clear?" This last was said with great volume.

Barry cringed. "I'll call him tomorrow."

"Make sure you do." Nate looked around the room. Meg, Nate and Lucky occupied the few available chairs in Elias's office. Sage leaned against the windowsill while Sophie sat on the arm of Meg's chair, her arm around the young girl's shoulder.

"Now, Meg. I want a promise from you that you won't go back to the Drake House. This was no joke. I'm going to have to go over there now and question those people. You have no idea how lucky you are that Barbara followed you out. And for your information, I know about Hilary Stone's estranged daughter."

"How do you know?" Sophie asked.

Nate opened his mouth to reply and then firmly shut it. "None of your damn business."

"Have you been able to trace her?" Lucky asked.

"No," Nate grumbled. "But it's in the works. I am checking out all those people staying at the Drake House. I don't think some random stranger killed the psychiatrist or Ms. Stone. It was one of the people who are there right now. That's why they're not leaving town until I figure out which one of them killed those women."

"We think Phoebe is Hilary Stone's daughter," Sophie said.

"On what basis?"

Lucky passed the doctor's card to Nate. Nate stared at it for a long moment but didn't reply. He tucked it into his pocket.

"And what about the private investigator who went to the Salisbury Retreat?" Sophie asked.

"I know who he is and who he's working for," Nate replied.

"You do?" Meg asked. "Who?"

"That's none of your business either, little lady. You have your orders. You are not to go near that place. Is that clear?"

"Yes," Meg said. Her face was bright red with humiliation.

"I'll have the information I need very soon to make an arrest and I would really like all of you"—he paused and sighed—"to stay the hell out of my investigation!" Nate rose and turned back. "Can I make that any clearer?" Everyone shook their heads negatively but remained silent. Nate slammed Elias's office door behind him.

Sophie sighed heavily, "I'm glad that's over with."

Elias stared at Lucky. "Uh-oh. I know that look."

"What?" she replied. "I was just thinking."

"Better you don't. Better you listen to Nate."

"Who do you think hired a private investigator? And why?" she asked the room in general.

"Could Hilary have hired an investigator herself? But why?" Sophie asked.

"Maybe she had a change of heart?" Lucky offered.

"About her daughter?"

"Maybe. Yes. Maybe she finally became curious as to what happened to her."

Sophie said, "Do you think Derek could have hired him?"

"Why would he do that?" Lucky answered. "Besides we don't even know that Derek knows he has a sister . . . half sister."

"That's true," Sophie mumbled. "Maybe Hilary confided in Hank years ago because it wasn't that far back in her past. But after all these years . . . why would she bother to tell her current husband and she might not want to tell her son in any case. Especially if Derek was curious and would like to contact his half sister and Hilary didn't want to raise that specter, to have all that come back to haunt her. Or maybe Hilary's husband got wind of the child and wanted to find out more because Hilary wouldn't tell him the truth."

"We could speculate forever," Lucky said. "We just don't have any facts."

"I'm glad you've all finally come to that brilliant conclusion," Elias commented. "However, it's now after eleven o'clock. I have an early morning and I'd really like to get some sleep." He stood and opened the door. Sage, Sophie and Meg filed out of his office.

"We'll give Meg a ride home," Sage said. "I want to make sure she gets there safely."

"Thanks, Sage," Lucky replied.

Elias grasped Lucky by the arm and pulled her back into the office. He held her close. "I worry about you, you know."

"I know you do, but you shouldn't. I'm a big girl. I can take care of myself."

"Yeah, right." He heaved a sigh. "I'm really sorry our romantic evening flopped."

"Me too. It was absolutely lovely. Thank you, Elias."

"Well, we'll try again another night," he said, remembering the ring in his pocket. This certainly wasn't the right time, he thought. Once again, the romantic moment he had been hoping for would just have to wait.

Chapter 45

LUCKY HAD CONSIDERED trying to gather information over the phone, but finally decided her best course of action was to speak to someone directly at the Adoption Registry. If she showed up in person, they'd have to talk to her. It was a last-ditch effort to see if there was some route through which she could firmly identify Hilary Stone's daughter. She agreed with the others that Phoebe could be the person they were trying to identify. Otherwise, why would Phoebe have Dr. Cranleigh's card? But she still wanted to do everything she could to be sure.

Her face burned, remembering Nate's reaction to their attempts at investigation the previous evening. She rationalized her actions to herself. Her visit here had nothing to do with investigating the murders. She had her own personal reasons for wanting to locate this woman. Was it possible Hilary's daughter was criminally insane? Was it possible she had murdered her psychiatrist and her mother? Lucky shivered, envisioning the possibility. If that were the case, then all the more reason to discover her identity. On the other hand, perhaps too many people over the years had stood in judgment. Perhaps she played no part in the fire that killed her adoptive parents. Dr. Cranleigh may have been worried about what Georgina might be capable of, but perhaps she was merely concerned about emotional trauma to her patient. Georgina Ellers, or whatever her current name was now, might possibly only be guilty of wanting to connect with her mother.

She found a parking space half a block away from the Vermont Adoption Registry and climbed out of the car. The Registry maintained a branch office in Bournmouth equipped with databases containing all the state's information available in their main office at the state capital. She hurried down the street and entered through a heavy oak door. She found herself in a small waiting room. A young woman sat behind a long wooden counter, tapping at a keyboard and staring at her monitor. She looked up as Lucky approached.

"Hi. Can I help you?" She smiled.

"I hope so. I'm trying to locate an adoptee who would be approximately forty years old now. I know adoption records are confidential but this is a rather unusual situation."

"I see. Are you an adoptee or a relative?"

"No. Just a friend."

"Well, maybe you should talk to Steve. Steve Lambert is my supervisor. I'll buzz him and let him know you're waiting." She rolled her chair back and reached for the phone, pressing a button. "We do maintain a voluntary registry where adoptees and birth parents can post whatever information they might have . . ."

"What sort of information?"

"Oh, it could be anything. Sometimes an adoptee may actually have a birth certificate, but it could be any information they've been given about the birth family. The thing is you must be what we call a birth family member, an adoptee yourself, or a guardian of an adoptee . . . or even a descendant of a deceased adoptee, and eighteen years old to request identifying information." A buzzer sounded and she picked up her phone.

"There's someone who's asking for information. Can you

see her?" The young woman waited, then said, "Okay." She hung the phone up and turned to Lucky. "Steve will be with you in a sec."

"Thanks. I appreciate your time." Lucky turned away to take a seat, but before she could sit, a door opened at the rear of the room and a bespectacled young man came into the waiting area.

He approached and offered his hand. "Hi, I'm Steve. What can we do for you?"

"I was hoping for some information or at the very least I have some information that perhaps you could post on your registry for adoptees." Lucky decided to give her original reason for wanting to locate Hilary's daughter. "I've recently learned that a woman who died in Snowflake this past week had a daughter whom she put up for adoption. I . . . was trying to find this woman because I thought she might want to know that her mother is deceased."

"Ah, I see." Steve grimaced. "I'd be happy to take whatever information you have, but if you're not a family member, we can't give you any information. The law was changed years ago to make it easier, but those records are still confidential."

"I was afraid that was the case."

"Hang on, let me grab a notepad." The young man leaned over the counter and pulled up a yellow legal-sized pad of paper. Lucky spelled Hilary Stone's name, and gave him the name "Hilary Means." She also told him the approximate year of the birth, and the names of the deceased adoptive parents. "The name she was given at the time of the adoption was Georgina Ellers, but of course, that might have changed."

"Sorry I can't be of more help. But I'll check our site and see if either of those two names appear, and if they do, I'll request that they contact me. You know . . ." He trailed off. "In many cases, neither the parent nor the child ever gets curious enough to inquire. They never look back. Maybe fifty percent of the time."

"That's rather sad, don't you think?"

"Who knows. It's not for me to judge. If you like, you can check our site yourself. It's adoptconnect.com and you can read some of the entries. You might find it helpful." He pulled a second sheet of paper from the pad and jotted down the link.

Lucky slipped the paper into her purse. "I have heard of that before. I will have a look at it. Thanks for your time."

"No problem." The man smiled and held the door open as Lucky exited.

Lucky reached the sidewalk. The sky had grown dark. Spring rainstorms were usually pleasant sprinkles but these clouds looked threatening. She buttoned her jacket and hugged her purse tighter as a brisk wind assailed her and hurried back to her car. So far, this trip had been an exercise in futility. The best thing she could do would be to return to the Spoonful before the dinner rush and forget all about her search.

She pulled the car door shut and started the engine. She reached over and grabbed her purse. The newsletter she had taken from the table in the lobby of the Salisbury Retreat was still there. She hadn't been able to shake the feeling that Fern may have known more than she was willing to share the day that she and Sophie had gone there. Perhaps if she spoke to the woman again, alone, she might learn more. It was only a short distance, a few blocks. Easy enough to stop there before returning home.

Chapter 46

LUCKY HURRIED THROUGH the lobby and took the elevator once more to the third floor. She stepped out onto the tiled corridor. The hallway was completely silent and empty. Would Fern still be here? Still working? The door to Suite 304 was closed. Lucky knocked. No answer. She wiggled the knob, but the door was locked. Leaning closer, she held her ear to the wooden panel, but heard no sound at all. Too late. Fern had undoubtedly completed her tasks and was well on her way to retirement.

Lucky retraced her steps and hit the DOWN button on the elevator console. The elevator dinged as it arrived. As the doors opened, she came face to face with the doctor's assistant.

"Well, hello. You again! Were you looking for me?" Fern smiled.

"Yes! I was hoping you were still here."

"Not for long. I'll be finished packing everything by tomorrow, and then that's it for me. You've just caught me. Come on back."

Lucky dutifully followed Fern down the hallway. The woman walked with a pronounced limp that Lucky hadn't noticed on her last visit. Fern turned around. As if she could read Lucky's thoughts, she said, "Polio. When I was a kid. My mother didn't believe in the vaccinations when they were first offered." She shrugged. "I survived though."

Lucky nodded in response. She waited patiently while Fern fished a ring of keys from her pocket and unlocked the office door. "I was just grabbing some lunch down in the cafeteria." Fern dropped her purse on the desk and turned back. "Now what can I do for you?"

Lucky looked around the outer office. Stacked boxes, head high, were lined along the walls, all taped and labeled. "You've done a lot. What's going to happen with all this?"

"Well, the files have already been sent to the Records Department. This is all Cynthia's books and personal stuff. It's going into storage until her lawyer can figure out what to do with it. She might have had a will, that I don't know. The rest of it belongs to the Salisbury." Fern shot a sharp look in Lucky's direction, waiting for her to get to the point.

"I came back to see you because . . . well . . ." Lucky pulled the newsletter from her purse. "I noticed this in the lobby the other day. It looks like the Salisbury Retreat hosts community events on occasion. You know, where some of the residents or patients work or volunteer."

"That's right. Sometimes they hold bake sales or rummage sales. Annual picnics in the summertime." Fern smiled. "We still have those." She indicated the newsletter, "It's PR, you know. On the one hand, it's good for the patients who are being treated here and it's community outreach." Fern chuckled. "Would you believe this place used to be called the Institute for the Criminally Insane?"

"Yes." Lucky smiled. "I think I knew that. It's a rather forbidding name."

"You can say that again!" Fern exclaimed. "Who the hell would want to eat a cupcake from a place like that?" She laughed. "But what are you getting at?"

"Where could I find some of the older newsletters?"

"You're thinking that this girl . . . this woman . . . Georgina might have been involved with the events?"

"Yes, and there may have been photos or group photos of the volunteers."

"Oh, I'm sure there were." Fern pulled her keys out of her pocket. "Come on, I'll take you down to the administrative offices and introduce you to Helen. She's the woman in charge of that. She's got a file cabinet full of those newsletters."

"That's fantastic. Thank you!" Lucky replied.

Fern locked the door behind them and together they headed back toward the elevator bank. As they rode down, Fern explained, "Helen's a friend of mine. She's actually in the basement. They didn't want to give her a fancy office on the first floor. Don't ask me why. This place is run by a bunch of old fuddy-duddies. They don't think what she does is that important."

"And you do," Lucky stated.

"Sure. It is important. I may have my gripes about this place, but the Salisbury does a lot of good. It's important that people in Bournmouth see it as a positive contribution. Otherwise, you'd have the townspeople on the front lawn with torches in the middle of the night."

Lucky laughed out loud. "Terrific image."

"Here we go," Fern said as the elevator doors opened. She limped down yet another tiled corridor toward a door at the end. "Helen! It's me. Put that liquor bottle away, I'm bringin' a visitor."

Helen wore a big grin as they turned into her office. She swiveled in her chair, away from a long worktable where photos were laid out. She smiled at Lucky. "Don't believe a word she says. I'm a complete teetotaler."

"This is Lucky. She's the one who came to see me the other day with her friend."

"Oh, yes." Helen's face became serious. "Fern told me about the murder of that famous writer in Snowflake. Just like Dr. Cranleigh. You're trying to find one of our patients?"

"I'm hoping to. Everyone I've talked to is suspicious of her. But I'd still like to find her." Lucky deliberately neglected to mention that Hilary's daughter was possibly already in Snowflake and well aware of her mother's death.

Helen nodded. She appeared to be the same generation as Fern and wore a bright pink blouse over a pair of black slacks. Her fair hair was cropped very short and her nails were painted in a color that matched her pink top.

"Lucky's hoping that maybe one of the newsletters has some photos with names. You know the kind of thing I mean, don't you?"

"Oh, sure," Helen replied. "I take a lot of the pictures myself for these events. We want to make the hospital seem a friendly place, full of active people. Not just a dumping ground for neurotics or psychotics, you know. I always try to get the names of everyone for the newsletter, especially the volunteers. They work pretty hard for these things and it means a lot to them to see their pictures and their names in the newsletter. Good for self-esteem in my opinion."

"I can understand that."

"Here, I'll show you some of our older photos. You can see what this place looked like back in the dark ages." Helen pulled a heavy binder down from a shelf above the worktable. "I like to keep these around to remind myself why I'm doing this job." She opened the binder to display page after page of photographic reproductions in black and white of depressed-looking people. Even allowing for a modern perspective of clothing or good grooming, it was obvious these patients were suffering from mental or emotional issues. "They used to line up these folks and take pictures of them. Why, I have no idea. They'd hardly be good advertising for mental health," Helen remarked. "Even in the early 1900s, you were legally insane if your behavior was anything other than what was considered normal. People were diagnosed as being maniacal, or suicidal or melancholic. Some diagnosis, huh?"

"Now the catch-all phrase is paranoid schizophrenia," Fern remarked bitterly. "All the vets in this country are diagnosed that way, no matter what kind of problems they're having. Lazy damn shrinks. Not like Dr. Cynthia."

Helen reached over and squeezed Fern's shoulder in sympathy. She turned to Lucky. "This has hit my friend hard."

"I can't say I blame her."

"There were some hardworking, ethical doctors who really tried to keep these people with chronic problems from being dumped in a place like this, but none of their efforts were really significant. Even in the later years of the twentieth century, only four patients were actually released to return home. Can you believe that? The majority were senile and at the end of their lives. Rotten way to spend your life and your last years, wouldn't you say?" Helen remarked rhetorically. "Now, thank heavens, it's all different. We have programs for just about everything. We serve the gay and lesbian community, we have an addiction program. We have both inpatient and outpatient programs. We do have adults with severe and persistent mental health issues, but we like to think of ourselves as a safety net rather than a last resort." Helen replaced the heavy binder on the shelf, "But I'm sure you're not interested in all that history. You'd like to find a picture of this girl."

"Yes." Lucky nodded. "If she was a regular visitor here, whether as an outpatient or not, she could have had her photo in a newsletter. I may have to come back another time though because I do have to get back to work soon."

"Where do you work?" Helen asked.

"At the By the Spoonful Soup Shop in Snowflake. It's my business."

"Oh, I've been there!" Helen exclaimed delightedly. She turned to Fern. "Remember the time my niece came to visit and we drove all over?" She turned back to Lucky. "That's a great little restaurant."

Lucky smiled. "I think so. I hope you come again."

"I'll do that. I will." Helen smiled. "But if you're in a hurry, I can loan you my CDs. I like to be organized. I keep hard copies of all the newsletters and I have them on my hard drive, but I also keep CDs, just in case my computer up and dies or something."

"Oh, would you?" Lucky asked. "That would be fantastic."

"Just return them to me in good shape, will you? I'd hate to have to rerecord all that stuff again. What time period are you interested in?"

"I'm thinking just the last few years. We know she lived

and worked locally and saw Dr. Cranleigh during that time. If she was involved in any events, I think it would be then."

"Good thought. Okay." Helen moved to a file cabinet on the other side of the room. Lucky watched as her fingers clicked though stacks of plastic CD cases, moving several to the side. She lifted out a pile of six and wrapped a rubber band around them. "Here you go. No rush, just bring them back when you're done."

"Thank you. I will. I really appreciate this." Lucky smiled. "I'll take good care of them."

"Nice to meet you, dear. I'll make sure I say hello the next time I'm in Snowflake."

Chapter 47

"I'M TERRIFIED, LUCKY," Barbara Drake said. "I don't know what's going on in this house. If anything had ever happened to Meg . . . I can't even think about it."

"You're not to blame," Lucky replied.

"What's so frightening is that we could have found the poor girl dead in the woods last night. It was just sheer luck that I spotted her jacket and ran after her." She shivered, rubbing her arms. "My other guests have all checked out and I'm stuck with that lot upstairs. It must have been one of them. Anyone could have easily slipped out the front door and waited by the side of the road." Barbara shivered again. "I can't bear to think about it."

"Me neither. But I'll be the one coming over from now on. I can't have Meg put in any danger." Lucky looked over Barbara's shoulder and spotted Audra in the lounge, reading a magazine. "You know, while I'm here, I might as well let them know what our specials are for the next few days."

"Please," Barbara said, "be my guest. It's wonderful you're willing to do this."

"Well, it's not that big a deal and these are special

circumstances." Lucky didn't mention she had an ulterior motive in being so generous with her time. "I see Audra. I'll check with her."

Lucky approached the armchair where Audra sat. She still wore her black pants suit and high heels. Maybe it was the only outfit she had packed. "Hi, Audra. I'm just checking if you or the others would like some soup specials for lunch. I'm making another trip over in a few hours. I thought I'd ask now while I'm here."

"Oh." Audra looked up from flipping through a fashion magazine. "Anything is fine with me. Just no carbs, please. You'll have to ask the others though. I have no idea what they'd like. Do you have a martini soup? That might be a good one for Sylvia," she answered sarcastically.

Lucky struggled to keep her tone neutral. "I assume you've heard what happened to Meg, our waitress, last night."

"I did. Are you sure it wasn't some weirdo passing by? Or maybe an ex-boyfriend?"

"I can't imagine anyone wanting to hurt Meg. Did you happen to hear anyone moving around last night?"

"Only Phoebe. I heard her door open and shut. A couple of times. Then our landlady started yelling for help. Scared me half to death. I thought someone else had been murdered."

"Audra." Lucky sat in the armchair next to the blonde woman. "I hope you don't mind my saying this, but you don't seem very concerned about Hilary's death."

"What the hell is that supposed to mean?" Audra flipped the magazine closed.

"Just that it must be tough. You'll be out of a job now and—"

"Oh, I'm not worried." Audra waved her hand airily. "I've had an offer from the publishing house to do more work for them." She smiled slyly. "So if you're implying I had a motive to kill Hilary, you're wrong. I won't be affected at all. And if you're really curious about motives, have a look at Sylvia. Hilary hated her. She was furious when Derek married Sylvia."

"Was that a sudden thing?"

"I'll say!" Audra leaned closer. "Sylvia gave up an

important career . . ." Audra said, her voice dripping with sarcasm. "As an exotic dancer. Derek picked her up in one of those clubs. They had a weekend fling and ran off to a justice of the peace. Hilary was apoplectic. She was never crazy about Junior and now this. She even tried to buy Sylvia off, but it was no go."

"When did that happen?"

Audra looked at her curiously. "Why are you asking?"

"Oh, no reason. I thought I heard someone say they were newlyweds."

"Hah! That's a good one. It was three weeks ago. But trust me, romance played no part. Sylvia saw dollar signs and Derek saw . . . well, you can imagine."

"Was Ms. Stone difficult to work with?"

Audra shrugged. "Not particularly. I do have to say, I've been amazed at the success of this book. I don't think even her husband thought she had it in her."

"Really?"

Audra smirked. "Well it certainly made him sit up and take notice, didn't it? Maybe that's why she wrote it."

Lucky wondered if Audra had a point. If Derek Stone, Senior had been losing interest in his wife, what better way to get his attention. Especially if Sylvia's gossip was correct and he was having an affair with his publicist. "You've been in this business a long time, haven't you?"

"Well, I've done this type of work for a while, but Derek"—she hesitated—"that's Mr. Stone, Senior, helped me set up my company officially about a month ago and then hired me for this project. He's been absolutely wonderful."

Lucky was sure he had. The gossip Meg extracted from Sylvia must be true.

HORACE SAT ON a park bench near the edge of the Village Green, very close to the pathway he had noticed Derek Stone using the morning before. He reached down and patted Cicero's head. "Get ready, boy." Cicero wagged his tail in anticipation. Horace finally saw Derek's round figure approach in jogging clothes. Derek was walking though, not jogging. Horace waited until Derek was ten yards away and then leaned down to the dog's ear. "Go get him, Cicero."

Cicero barked once and raced toward Derek. When Cicero reached his goal, he continued to bark, running in circles around the man. Horace knew Cicero wouldn't hurt a fly. For the dog, it was all in good fun. Derek stopped in his tracks and made shooing motions with his hands. He looked frightened. Finally, Derek started to yell. "Somebody! Help! Get this damn dog away from me!"

Horace jumped up and ran after Cicero, grabbing his collar. "I'm so sorry. Don't let him scare you. He just wanted to play."

"Well, he has a strange way of showing it." Derek's face had blanched and he was sweating profusely. "Why isn't he on a leash? Don't you people have leash laws here?"

"I sincerely apologize. Why don't you take a seat for a minute. Let Cicero sniff your hand, so you won't be a stranger."

Derek was visibly annoyed. "Fine. I'll sit for a minute. But keep that mutt away from me."

Horace's immediate reaction was to put Derek in his place. How dare he call Cicero a mutt. Cicero was a noble canine. But to say what he really felt would ruin the moment he had worked for. Horace slipped a treat from his pocket and passed it to Cicero as soon as Derek looked away. "You look like you've been running a little too hard."

"Just trying to keep the weight off," Derek replied as he patted his paunch. "Doing the best I can while I'm stuck here. Is there no workout club or gym in town?"

"No, I'm afraid not." Horace thought it best not to mention the facilities at the Snowflake Resort. "Excuse me, but you're Derek Stone, aren't you?"

"Yes, I am." Derek looked surprised that someone would know his name.

"Yes, I thought so. I heard you speak at your mother's book signing. You did a wonderful job of keeping everything under control."

"Thank you." He sniffed. "Not everyone has appreciated my efforts."

"I am very sorry for your loss. It's such a terrible thing to lose someone."

"Yes." Derek nodded sadly and looked down. His shoulders began to shake.

Was he crying? Horace wondered. He hadn't meant to elicit this much emotion from the man. "I'm very sorry," he repeated.

"Thank you." Derek wiped his nose on his sleeve. "My mother was an amazing woman, so talented, so strong. I admired her and loved her so much. I'm just heartbroken. I don't know how I'm going to cope now that she's gone."

"You've worked with your mother for a long time?"

"Oh, yes. While she was writing, she'd ask my advice and we'd bat around ideas for this book and the next one."

"I see." Knowing what he knew about Hank's claim, that Hilary hadn't written a word of the book, Horace wondered if Derek was out and out lying, or completely delusional. "Then it's really doubly hard."

Derek started to sob again. This time loudly. Horace felt in his pockets and pulled out a handkerchief, offering it to Derek.

"Thank you. I'm sorry. I didn't mean to get this worked up. I was out running to get my mind off of all this. I can't stand being here another day. I don't know how long the police will insist we stay in Snowflake. And I can't possibly leave until they release my mother's body. It's just ridiculous."

"I guess they're no further along in their investigation?" Horace asked.

"Country bumpkins, that's what they are. I mean, really! I should insist they call in real crime scene investigators. They have got to get to the bottom of this. This should never have happened to my mother."

"Did someone mention you're a newlywed? Congratulations. That should be some comfort in such a difficult time."

Derek snorted. "Yes. Sylvia and I were married three weeks ago. Mother was very angry. She had . . . well, she had chosen someone she wanted me to meet. She was very insistent but . . . well, Sylvia just swept me off my feet."

"Ah," Horace replied noncomittally.

"But now . . ."

"Yes?"

"Well, I wonder now if I was too hasty." He looked at Horace; his eyes were red-rimmed. "Do you think I was?" he asked earnestly.

"Well, not if you're in love. Not if someone that special comes into your life. If that's the case, then you didn't make a mistake."

Derek's brow furrowed. "I don't know. I just don't know anything anymore."

Horace felt terribly sorry for Derek.

SOPHIE PICKED UP a basket at the entrance to the market and sauntered casually down an aisle, pretending to peruse the products on the shelves. She had been following Phoebe Hollister through town, as Phoebe stopped at the pharmacy, the bakery to purchase some cookies and now at the market, where Phoebe stood at the end of the aisle choosing a bottle of vitamins.

Sophie turned her head to make sure Phoebe was still within range. Her timing was unfortunate because at that moment, Phoebe looked up and stared directly in Sophie's eyes. Sophie looked away quickly and moved to the other side of the aisle, where a selection of hand lotions were on display. There was movement in her peripheral vision. She looked up quickly. Phoebe was gone.

Sophie replaced the item on the shelf. Her basket was now empty. She walked slowly to the front of the store, where she could see the two checkout stands. She knew Phoebe had placed a few items in her basket so she would have to go through the checkout line to pay. Phoebe wasn't there. Sophie walked around to the next aisle. No Phoebe. "Damn," she muttered. *How did I lose her?* she thought. She had been trying to orchestrate a moment when she could casually strike up a conversation with the woman, but so far, she had been forced to hurry to keep up with Phoebe's travels through town.

Sophie walked the width of the front of the store, peering down each aisle in search of Phoebe. She had disappeared. Sophie sighed and spun around to leave. Phoebe was standing directly behind her, inches away. Sophie almost knocked foreheads with her.

"I hope you don't think you've fooled me."

"Wha . . ." Sophie was speechless.

"You've been following me all over town."

"No I haven't . . ."

Phoebe bared her teeth in a poor imitation of a smile. "I'm only going to say this once . . . stay away from me."

Sophie could feel her temper flare. "Look you . . . don't you think you're being a little paranoid? I'm doing my shopping and—"

"Oh, really?" Phoebe snatched the empty basket out of her hand and flung it to the ground. Sophie held her breath. How far would this woman go?

Phoebe pressed a hand on Sophie's chest, pinning her against a shelf with a swift movement. A few cans of soup rattled to the floor. "Stay away from me," she muttered darkly, "or I'll make you very sorry."

Phoebe spun on her heel, dropping her shopping basket, and fled from the store.

Sophie took a shaky breath, trying to regain her composure. *What was that all about?* she thought.

Chapter 48

LUCKY STRAIGHTENED UP the last of the chairs. The dishwasher had been loaded and everything was in place for the next day. Sophie sat at the worktable in the kitchen, chatting with Sage. Meg had busied herself replacing the water in all the vases of forsythias while Jack stayed in the office organizing the receipts of the day.

Lucky breathed a sigh of relief that the day had gone smoothly. No further upsets with Nanette, who had managed to behave herself all day and had left at the first opportunity. She had flirted with the customers as usual and spent too much time at the cash register with Jack, but otherwise the day had been relatively peaceful.

Jack pushed through the door from the corridor. "All's well, my girl. I'll go to the bank tomorrow and take care of the cash."

"Thanks, Jack." She squeezed his hand. "Are you heading home now?"

"Well, I . . . uh . . ." His face brightened as he heard a rap on the front door. Nanette stood outside.

Lucky, confused, turned back to her grandfather. "Why is she here now?"

"Uh . . . we have a date." He smiled. He hurried over to the door to let Nanette in.

"Hellooo, everyone." She waved to Sage and Sophie in the kitchen. Sophie raised a lackadaisical hand in response.

Meg had just pushed open the swinging door from the kitchen. She carried a heavy vase of flowers in her hands.

"Ah'm so glad y'all here right now, 'cause Jack and me, we have a very important announcement to make."

Jack was beaming. Lucky felt a knot forming in her stomach.

"Jack and I are engaged."

Meg dropped the vase she was carrying. Glass shattered and water spilled across the floor. Complete silence enveloped the room for half a minute.

"Well, y'all can say something nice, can't you?" Nanette snarled.

"Engaged?" Lucky could barely choke out the word. She looked at her grandfather, "Jack, tell me this isn't true!"

"What do you mean?" he said. "Nanette and I have been very happy together. I feel like I have a new lease on life."

"You've only known her for a week!"

"Now, Lucky dear, y'all can't be all possessive about your dear grandfather. He's a real man and he's got a right to have a real life, if you know what I mean."

Lucky felt her blood boiling. She wanted to rip the woman's throat out.

"And once Jack and I have tied the knot, then we can see about changing some things around here, can't we, Jack?" She simpered up at him.

Lucky's heart fell somewhere down around her feet. She turned to her grandfather, "Jack, you can't be serious about this."

"Ah'm standin' right here. There's no need to talk about me like I'm not in the room," Nanette shouted.

"I'm not talking to you, you . . ." Lucky trailed off, unwilling to completely alienate Jack.

Jack stepped forward, "Lucky, my girl. It's gonna be all right. I know this is kind of a shock to you, but you don't have to worry about a thing. We'll all be a big family and we can work out our differences." He looked down at Nanette. "Ready for our big night out, sweetheart?"

"Ah sure am, Jack darlin'."

"Well, let's go then. It's almost three bells." Jack put an arm around Nanette's waist and ushered her out the door. Nanette turned back and smiled slyly at Lucky as she exited.

Lucky felt like her heart would break. Sophie and Sage were staring at her through the hatch. Meg hadn't moved since the vase shattered.

"Is it too late to fire her?" Meg asked.

LUCKY SAT AT the round table with her head in her hands. Sophie had brought her a cup of tea and sat next to her. Meg was busy sweeping up the broken glass and mopping the water spill. Sage kept his distance in the kitchen.

"This is a nightmare. Where did this woman come from?"

"Hell?" Sophie asked.

Lucky nodded. "That about sums it up. This can't be real. Jack has taken leave of his senses."

"He's just flattered, that's all. But you're right. What is her game?"

"Sophie, if Jack goes through with this, she could be running the restaurant."

"But it's your business, isn't it?"

"Yes." Lucky's shoulders slumped. "Technically, yes. But what am I going to do, kick my grandfather out? It was in my parents' name, but he started it with them years ago. Gave them seed money and he's worked here since he retired. I can't deny it's his business too."

"Can't you put your foot down and keep her in her place?"

"I can, but can you imagine the tension that will cause? I love Jack. He's my only family. I don't want to make his life miserable. I don't know what she's up to, but I know in my gut she's up to no good. Is she trying to take my poor grandfather for all he's worth? He doesn't have that much. What does she want?"

"Maybe she's just a control freak. Maybe she hates other women, I don't know." Sophie shrugged. "Did she ever bring in her identification?"

"Oh," Lucky groaned. "She didn't. My brain is fried. She should have brought it in days ago. That's it. My mind's made up. I'm giving her the boot tomorrow morning and I'll pay her for her time and be rid of her. Even if I have to physically throw her out. I don't care what Jack says. I can't have her working here no matter what. If Jack wants to marry her, that's his business, but she's not working here until I see some proper identification."

"Speaking of which, how does she plan to get a marriage license without identification anyway?"

"Good point." Lucky smiled in spite of herself. "There's hope yet."

Lucky spotted movement at the front door. It was Horace with Cicero on a leash and Barry bringing up the rear. She stood and unlocked the door for them. "I hope we're not late for our meeting," Horace said.

"Sorry, Horace," Lucky said. "We haven't had a chance to tell you about Meg's being attacked. We're all under orders now from Nate to stay out of his investigation."

"Oh, no!" Horace's face paled. "What happened?"

"I heard about it today, Lucky," Barry said. He turned to Meg, "Are you all right?"

"I'll tell you both all about it," Meg answered. "But I don't see why we have to disband the Murder Investigation Club. No harm in sitting around and chatting about it." She glanced at all their faces. "Is there?"

ONCE EVERYONE HAD gathered around the table, Meg very formally called the meeting to order. She filled Barry and Horace in on her conversation with Sylvia and Sylvia's gossip about Audra. She finished with the story of finding

Dr. Cranleigh's card in Phoebe's room and her attack and their meeting with Nate.

Barry's face turned white. "Meg, you can't go back there. Why would someone want to hurt you?"

"Maybe they heard me talking to Sylvia. In fact, I felt like someone was listening in the corridor but I can't be sure. But just before I went to Sylvia's room, I had a peek in Phoebe's. I knew she wasn't there because I saw her downstairs when I arrived. I started to search her desk. But I got out of there quick when I thought someone was coming. That's when I saw the business card. Maybe whoever did this thought I had learned something I wasn't supposed to know."

"I agree with Barry," Horace said. "Lucky, you've got to make sure Meg stays safe."

"I will," Lucky agreed. "I'll be delivering everything from now on."

Meg's face fell. "Lucky, that's not fair. I didn't do anything wrong. You can't cut me out of everything."

"I'm not, Meg, believe me. I'm not cutting you out, but this is getting too dangerous." Lucky's tone brooked no interference. She turned to the others. "Okay, my turn now." She explained going back to the Salisbury Retreat and borrowing discs of old newsletters in hopes of finding a photo of Georgina Ellers. "I'll start going through those soon. It's a long shot but you never know."

"It sounds to me like Phoebe's the person we've been searching for," Sage said. "You're not sure?"

"I'm sure," Sophie said. "That woman scared the hell out of me today."

"I guess I am too," Lucky said, "but I'd like to find some definite proof. I also had a chat with Audra this morning. Mr. Stone, Senior, helped her set up her business just a month ago, even though she claims she's done this work for years. And Derek found Sylvia working as an exotic dancer. He whisked Sylvia off to a justice of the peace just three weeks ago and Hilary tried to buy her off."

Horace spoke up. "I waylaid Derek on his morning run.

What I heard confirms that. I actually felt terribly sorry for him. He's really broken up over the death of his mother."

"Well, I took care of Derek's car a couple of nights ago in the wee hours," Barry said. "He won't be driving anywhere for a while."

"What about Audra's car?" Sophie asked.

"I didn't get a chance. Sorry. Maybe I should go back and make sure that one's out of commission too." He looked around the table. "Look, are we being ghouls? Sticking our noses into everyone's life like this?"

"I don't think so," Sophie piped up. "We're doing this to help Hank. The finger of suspicion shouldn't be pointed just at him."

"So what are we left with?" Sage asked. "Audra might have had a motive to get Hilary out of the way. Sylvia probably hated her mother-in-law, but why would she need to kill her? She's married to Derek. Hilary couldn't do anything about that."

"Oh, I don't know," Lucky said. "She could have made their lives miserable. Eventually it might have torn them apart."

"Well, Derek doesn't strike me as a man in love," Horace said, "more like a man who's waking up from a bad dream."

"All the more reason he wouldn't want his mother dead. Besides, do we know anything about his financial situation?" Sophie asked. "Did Mommy hold the purse strings or is Derek a trust fund baby?"

"I don't know how we'd ever find that out, unless one of the three starts to blab." Lucky stirred her tea.

"Sylvia could have a motive because if Hilary dies, maybe Derek inherits quite a bit," Barry said.

"What do we really know about Phoebe?" Lucky looked around the table.

"She is kind of the dark horse, isn't she?" Sophie remarked. "It's easy to overlook her, she's so . . . what's the word . . . taciturn even though she always seems to be bossed around by the others."

"I'm sure Nate's questioned all of them, he must have

some information about her," Lucky replied. "And Dr. Cranleigh's card in her room looks very suspicious."

"Yeah, good luck getting anything out of Nate. And now that Jack's tied up with . . ." Sophie trailed off.

Lucky groaned. "Go ahead, finish your thought."

"Well, all I meant was that Nate comes in a lot to chat with Jack, but if Jack's not here, I can't see how we can learn anything," Sophie finished.

"If only Fern had actually met Georgina Ellers at some point . . ." Lucky said.

"Ah," Horace replied. "Yes, if she had met the daughter, we wouldn't be sitting here guessing. But are we convinced this mysterious daughter is even around, much less targeting her own mother and her psychologist?"

"Nothing we can show Nate as proof, that's for sure," Lucky answered.

"Maybe . . ." Meg started to speak.

Everyone turned to her.

"Well, I can't get over the fact that these murders have been committed just like in the book. Just like in *Murder Comes Calling.*"

"So for whatever reason, the murderer is a copycat. She . . . or he is using the book like an instruction manual," Lucky said.

"That's really crazy," Sophie volunteered.

"But if Hilary's daughter is crazy . . . didn't you say Hank told you Hilary referred to her as the bad seed? Maybe Hilary knew something," Sage said.

"How could she? She gave that little girl up as an infant," Sophie answered

Meg sighed. "But in the book, the murder weapon is a telephone cord and the estranged child is the culprit. As it stands now, Hank looks like the prime suspect, since he wrote the book."

"I have a question," Horace asked. "Have you found out anything about Nanette?"

"Soon, Horace." Sophie smiled. "Lucky and I have a plan."

Chapter 49

NATE TAPPED HIS pencil against the battered green blotter of his desk. The station was closed. Only a nightlight at the front desk and his metal desk lamp relieved the darkness. His thoughts strayed to Derek Stone, Hilary's husband. Usually the first person any cop would look at, but in this case, several people had confirmed his presence at the New York dinner. His driver took him home that night and his housekeeper heard him come in. Hilary Stone had been killed sometime between nine forty-five and ten fifty-five that night. Perhaps the maid at the Drake House was accurate, that she heard an argument at ten thirty. She was the only one who claimed to have heard that, but he was inclined to believe her.

Did the stolen manuscript play into this, he wondered. Certainly could be enough to send somebody around the bend, knowing someone else took credit for their hard work and reaped the rewards. In spite of Hank's erratic behavior, Nate just couldn't picture him acting in such a violent way. He shook his head and finally picked up the phone. This was something he needed to deal with. He checked his notepad and dialed the number of Derek Stone's Manhattan townhouse. He was curious what Stone's reaction would be to Hank's claim that he was the real author of *Murder Comes Calling*.

Chapter 50

LUCKY DUG INTO the still hard earth at her parents' gravestones. The phlox had come back early and was promising blooms but the bed needed weeding. It was the only positive thing she could think to do this morning. She had been saving small pots of pansies in her kitchen through the winter months that she hoped to use at the cemetery. Today was as good a day as any. The worst of the frosts were over, and these new plants could get an early start.

Her anxiety over Jack's announcement the night before had kept her awake half the night. There was that, and her anger. She slammed the trowel into the earth to loosen it up and pulled up stray bits of wet grass. There was her fear for Jack, that he was making a fool of himself over this woman, and then there was her intense dislike of Nanette. Was it justified? *Yes*, she thought, *it's certainly justified. The woman is manipulative, bullying and just plain evil. But what does she want? Does she really want to marry Jack and take over the Spoonful?* And what options did she, Lucky, have? What could she do? She loved Jack with all her heart and wanted him to be happy, but she was sure he could never be happy with a woman like that. His head was just turned. He was lonely and he was flattered, but that didn't constitute a relationship. And what if this marriage actually took place? Would that give Nanette real leverage in making decisions about the restaurant? She knew in her heart of hearts that Nanette would wield power with no holds barred, and Lucky would have to fight her every step of the way. The infighting would be vicious and Jack would be very unhappy. The way things were shaping up, the only real option she might have would be to bow out gracefully. If she left the business to Jack and Nanette, Sage would never stay. The Resort would give anything to get his talents. He and Sophie could stay in the area, but where could she herself go?

She took a deep breath. The way she was feeling, she'd maul these little plants. She carefully placed each into its prepared spot and gently filled the earth around them. A vision of her mother's face rose up in her mind's eye. She sat back on her heels. "Mom, what should I do? What can I do?" she whispered. She could imagine her mother's response. What would she say? If she were here, she'd probably say, *Let it run its course. It will all work out in the end.* In her mind, she replied, *Sounds good, Mom, but I don't think I can hold my temper much longer.* She imagined her next step. Walk into the Spoonful, take Nanette aside and fire her? There'd be a scene, but so what? Too bad if Jack was unhappy. He could do whatever he wanted in the future, but there was no reason she had to keep the woman around.

Maybe, she thought, *we've spent too much time looking at the wrong people*. Maybe Nanette was the woman they should be investigating.

Chapter 51

LUCKY AND SOPHIE waited impatiently. Lucky had made an excuse and left the restaurant early, with Meg promising to close up. Sage had volunteered to drive Meg home while Sophie had traded her car for another belonging to a work friend at the Resort. Since both Sophie and Sage came and went from the Spoonful at various times, Nanette would recognize their cars. They were now parked a block away from the Spoonful near the Village Green, but close enough to see any car leaving the small lot behind the restaurant.

"There she is," Sophie whispered.

"Why are you whispering?"

Sophie laughed. "I have no idea." She turned the key in the ignition and waited as Nanette pulled out onto Broadway. Then she turned on her lights and eased the car out of its parking spot.

Nanette drove slowly down Broadway. It seemed she was heading out of town, but when she reached the Old Colonial Road, she turned right and took the winding two-lane road for the next mile and a half. Sophie followed. There were no other cars on the road. Lucky was sure they couldn't be seen in the dark, but she was still concerned.

"Slow down," Lucky said. "We don't want her to spot us."

"Okay." Sophie complied and allowed a great deal of space between the car she was driving and the car ahead of them. Another car came speeding up behind them. Sophie checked her rearview mirror. "He's moving fast, he's going to want to pass us."

"Let him. Just slow down some more. He'll get the hint."

The other driver passed them in a roar and went out of sight at the next curve. "Where'd she go?" Sophie asked.

Lucky peered ahead. "She's ahead of us. Don't worry. Just don't get too close. I don't want her to spot us." They could see the taillights of the car that had passed them on the road. Suddenly that car sped up and passed Nanette's. "Stay way back."

"Look, she's got her signal on. She's turning." They had driven about three miles. "Doesn't look like she's heading for Bournmouth."

As they passed the turnoff, they saw Nanette's car moving slowly down a dirt road. "Where's she going?"

"I don't know. But as we went by, I thought I saw a light further in, like a cabin maybe."

"What should we do?"

"Drive on a little and pull over. We have to investigate."

Sophie didn't look thrilled at the prospect. "Are you sure about this? We promised Nate."

"I know we did, but this is about Jack and the restaurant, not the murders. We have to figure out what she's up to."

"Okay," Sophie agreed reluctantly.

"There's a good spot." Lucky pointed. Sophie's headlights had illuminated a small cleared patch near the edge of the road. "We'll be safe here. We can walk back."

"This is making me very nervous, Lucky. She scares me."

"Sophie, we have to find out where she's going and why. I want to know if this is where she's living. She told me she was driving over from Bournmouth and looking for an apartment in town, but if she's living here, then she lied to me and she's hiding something."

Sophie turned off the engine. The road was dark. No cars passed on either side. The moon was only half full and barely shed any light in the dense woods next to them. They climbed out of the car and walked quickly back to the lane that Nanette had taken.

"I wish we had a flashlight," Sophie whispered.

"Me too, but I think if we're careful, we'll be able to see if there's a cabin or an RV or something in the woods. The moonlight shone onto the dirt lane in patches, highlighting a pathway through the blackness of the woods. They walked slowly and quietly. The night had grown quite chill and their breath blew out in front of them in small puffs.

Sophie grasped Lucky's arm. "You're right. I see a light."

"Good. Go in that direction. Hold on to my arm. I knew I saw something. It's a small cottage."

"We're like Hansel and Gretel in the woods, following bread crumbs."

The windows of the tiny cottage were all lit. Two of the curtains were open. Lucky could see movement in the windows. "Be very quiet. I'm going to try to get close and see who's in there. I'll bet there's more than one person. I can't imagine a woman wanting to live alone in the woods like this."

"Don't get too close. I'm getting nervous. She's just the kind that would have a shotgun and ask questions later."

"Shhh," Lucky whispered. "Stay back. I'll get close to the window and see who's inside."

"Are you sure?" Sophie hissed.

"Yup. Stay back. Stay inside the trees."

The cottage sat in a clearing. Three wooden steps led up to a front door, where an outside light beamed. Lucky approached one side of the house. An elongated square of light fell on the ground. She could see the edge of a wall cabinet. This room appeared to be a kitchen. Staying clear of the area where the light fell, she tiptoed as quietly as possible toward the window. She held her breath and peeked quickly up over the sill. Two people sat at a kitchen table,

Nanette and a man. The man was thin with a gaunt, weather-beaten face. He wore a denim jacket over a flannel shirt. Nanette had a pad of paper in front of her and was writing on it. Lucky ducked her head quickly before she was spotted. She moved silently to the other side of the small house. A lamp shone in a bedroom. The furniture was basic, a double bed and only one bureau. Two suitcases sat on the floor. She heard footsteps and the creaking of wood and suddenly the door to the bedroom was flung open. Nanette entered, laughing loudly. The man followed. He was tall compared to her height. He grasped her by the arm and swung her around, pulling her close. He was silent as he nuzzled her neck and shoved her toward the bed. Nanette shrieked. Laughing, she fell backward onto the bedclothes.

Lucky had seen enough. Carefully she stepped away from the window. She turned and headed in the direction where Sophie waited. Her foot struck a branch, snapping it loudly. She hurried toward the trees. Just as she reached the darkness of the woods, she heard the sash of a window flung open behind her.

"Who's there?" Nanette shouted. Lucky kept moving. She was inside the tree line now but had lost her bearings. She couldn't find Sophie.

"Sophie?" she whispered, moving to her right, sure of the spot where Sophie should be waiting but she couldn't see her in the dark. "Sophie?" she hissed again, terrified of being heard.

"Over here," the whispered answer came back.

Lucky moved toward the sound of Sophie's voice. A hand grabbed her arm. "Get down."

They heard the door of the cottage slam open. The thin man with the weather-beaten face stood on the threshold, a shotgun in his hand. They hunkered down behind a bush, fearing to breathe. The man stood, his eyes scanning the woods for several minutes waiting for a sound or the sight of an intruder.

Lucky felt Sophie shift. "Stay still," she whispered.

"My foot's gone numb," Sophie hissed. "Pins and needles."

"Shhh." Lucky squeezed Sophie's arm. She peered through the branches and held her breath. Finally, the man stepped inside and shut the door. They heard the click of a lock.

Sophie started to move. "Wait," Lucky said. "Give him a few more minutes."

"I have to stand," Sophie whispered. "My foot's . . ."

"Okay. But move very quietly and slowly back to the road."

They stepped gently and slowly through the brush, reaching the narrow lane they had followed toward the house. Once on flat ground, they began to run and didn't stop until they reached the car. They climbed in quickly and Sophie turned the key. The engine came to life and the tires made a squealing noise as she drove onto the road.

Lucky didn't take a deep breath until they were a quarter mile away from the cottage.

"What did you see?" Sophie finally asked.

"Nanette and a strange man. And it's anything but a platonic relationship."

"Oh, great," Sophie mumbled.

Chapter 52

LUCKY CLIMBED THE stairs to her apartment and locked the door behind her. She hung her sweater on a hook in the closet and dropped her purse on a kitchen chair. The light on the answering machine was blinking. She hit the button and Elias's voice filled the room. He must have wondered where she had gone after work. Should she tell him that she and Sophie had followed Nanette to a cabin in the woods and spied on her? Doubtful. He'd never approve. Still, she didn't regret their decision. She was relieved she had discovered the extent of Nanette's lies and misdirection. They still had no way to find any further information, but maybe she could confide in Nate and ask him to run the license plate on her car. The next problem was how to tell Jack.

Her muscles were stiff. She felt drained, not from work, but from the emotional turmoil she had been going through all week, worrying about Jack and the tension at the restaurant. There was also the possibility that Phoebe Hollister was Hilary's daughter. Phoebe couldn't be ruled out. Why else would she have had Dr. Cranleigh's card? Whoever Hilary's daughter turned out to be, the thought that she could be the bad seed her mother had dubbed her sent shivers up Lucky's spine.

She hadn't had a chance as yet to look at the CDs that were stacked on the desk in the living room. She sighed and walked down the hall. Helen from the Salisbury Retreat had labeled each disc with the months and years of the newsletters she had recorded. The first began in January, three years prior. She slipped the first disc into the drive. Lucky clicked through the pages. Judging by the monthly dates, there were only six newsletters per year. Various articles were written by voluntary contributors. Other entries were interviews of heads of departments and staff doctors. Occasionally a more widely disseminated article was reprinted if the hospital felt it pertinent to their patients or the community. Each publication contained several photos. Many were of the building and grounds. She kept scrolling through and eventually came to some group photos where the names were listed. Some of the events were rummage sales, two blood drives, several open sessions for flu shots and one bake sale hosted by a local ladies' auxiliary.

An hour passed as she carefully checked each newsletter. Finally she slipped the last CD from the stack into the drive. She rubbed her eyes and forced herself to focus. If only Georgina Ellers had been active at the Salisbury Retreat. This was such a long shot, but it was possible she had willingly or perhaps not so willingly been a volunteer to man a table or pass out flyers. So far, each photo had listed all the names of people in the group photos. The name "Georgina Ellers" was so firmly in her mind that she almost missed it. She gasped and scrolled back.

A dark-haired woman stood next to a table of used books for sale. She held a book in her hand, as if she were about to purchase it. Her name wasn't listed under the photo, but there was no doubt in Lucky's mind that the woman who stood by the table was Phoebe Hollister.

It took a moment for the shock to subside. Phoebe, guarded and unapproachable, had to be Hilary Stone's daughter. This was too much of a coincidence. Lucky had been so focused on the Ellers name, the picture had taken her completely by surprise. Phoebe must have changed her name, or married, changing her surname.

Lucky printed out the page and reached over to the telephone. She dialed Sophie's number. Sophie picked up on the second ring.

"You won't believe what I'm looking at."

"What's going on?" Sophie asked.

"Remember the CDs I told you I borrowed from the Salisbury Retreat?"

"Yes."

"It's Phoebe. There's a photo of her standing in front of a table at a used book sale on the hospital grounds."

"She must have changed her name?" Sophie questioned.

"She must have. It's her. She's Hilary's daughter."

"What's the date on that newsletter?"

"It's . . ." Lucky quickly scrolled to the first page. "Two months ago. What are the odds that a personal assistant from a publishing house in New York was at a hospital in Bournmouth at that time? What are the odds that two women, Georgina, or whatever her name is now, and Phoebe, were connected with the same hospital?"

"I guess anything is possible. But how long has Phoebe worked for the publishing house?"

"I don't know. Nate would know though. He's questioned all of them."

"You have to tell Nate."

"I will. I'm calling him next. I just wanted to tell you first. And we'll have to tell Meg and Barry and Horace and everyone too." Lucky hung up and dialed Nate's home number. When he answered, he sounded annoyed. "I am really sorry to bother you, Nate, but I have to tell you what I found. It could be important."

He listened patiently and then whistled. "What do you know!" he exclaimed. "And how did you come across these old newsletters?"

Lucky explained her last visit to the Salisbury Retreat and her meeting with Helen, the keeper of the newsletters.

"And of course there's Dr. Cranleigh's card that Meg found in Phoebe's room."

"Uh-huh. Thought I told you to stay out of this."

Lucky groaned. "I'm sorry, Nate. You did, but I just thought . . ."

"I know what you thought," he grumbled.

"How long has Phoebe worked for the publisher?"

"Not long. Not long at all." Nate sighed, "Okay, this is interesting, very interesting. Thanks for calling. I'll be paying another visit to Phoebe first thing tomorrow morning."

"Will you let me know what she says?"

Nate sounded dubious. "I have no intention of encouraging your investigating," he replied.

"Oh, come on, Nate."

Nate smiled. "Well, I guess maybe you've earned the right to know. I'll stop in at the Spoonful as soon as I can. Thanks again, Lucky."

Lucky took a deep breath. She shook her head. They had been right about one thing. They were right to assume that Hilary's daughter was on the scene. Lucky rubbed her forehead and thought back to the events of the last few days. Was their logic faulty? It *was* an assumption on their part that Dr. Cranleigh's patient was the daughter of Hilary Stone. But the coincidence of a patient who lost both parents in a fire at a young age was too great. Fern had jumped to the same conclusion and knew immediately that the doctor's patient was the adopted girl, Georgina Ellers. It had to be the same person. It had to be Phoebe Hollister. Granted, it was an intuitive leap on her and Sophie's part, but that one fact was a connection between both murder victims. Was it possible it was only a coincidence that Phoebe Hollister had a connection to the Salisbury Retreat? Lucky shook her head. That was a very, very big coincidence.

Chapter 53

LUCKY HAD TOSSED and turned all night in an attempt to sleep. Dreams or nightmares kept waking her up. If Phoebe Hollister was in truth the woman they had been trying to find, was she a killer who strangled her psychiatrist and her own mother? And if so, how did Phoebe learn who her mother was and manage to penetrate her inner circle? Lucky's dreams were populated with rushing trains and screams in the night. This morning, she'd gladly leave the problems to Nate Edgerton. Hopefully he would keep his word and stop in at the Spoonful later in the morning. She had enough other problems to worry about.

There was no doubt in her mind any longer that Nanette was targeting Jack. He was being set up, but for what reason? Nanette was definitely involved with the man at the cabin, but did she actually intend to go through with a plan to marry Jack? She had to tell her grandfather what she had learned, but when could she tell him and how could she find the words?

When Lucky arrived at the Spoonful, she slipped an apron over her head. She touched the design on the front gently. *No way is this design going to change, Mom, I promise you*, she thought. The warmth of the restaurant took the chill of the morning away. Delicious aromas emanated from the kitchen. Lucky peeked in. Sage was at the stove stirring a pot. He looked up and smiled.

"What are you making today?" she asked.

"I thought I'd try something with carrots and apples for a change." He studied her face. "Heard you had an adventure last night," he whispered.

"Sure did. And I guess Sophie told you why I called late last night. We'll have to tell the others."

Sage nodded. "How are you feeling this morning?"

"Determined."

"Oh?" His eyebrows rose. A big grin spread across his face.

"She's going. We've seen the last of our new waitress, at least as long as I'm here."

"This I gotta see." Sage seemed to have perked up. He grabbed a handful of carrots and began to peel them expertly.

"Is Sophie coming by this morning?"

"She said she would a little later. She wasn't feeling too great earlier."

"Oh? She okay?"

"I think so. Maybe just a touch of the flu."

The phone on the kitchen wall began to ring. Lucky grabbed it. It was Nate. "Lucky, some not so good news."

"What's up, Nate?'

"Our Phoebe's done a runner. She's taken off. Disappeared."

"How? When?"

"Sometime last night. She took a set of keys from Audra's purse and drove away in Audra's rental car. I've got an APB out for her. Hopefully, she'll get picked up soon. I want her back here for questioning."

"Oh, Nate. She must be Hilary's daughter. Do you think she . . ." Lucky couldn't bring herself to ask the question.

"It's not looking good for her. I think she's gonna have a lot to answer for."

Lucky sighed. "I appreciate your calling, Nate."

"I just wanted to keep you in the loop. You're involved in this now, and with Meg's attack, you all need to be on guard. Wherever she is, I doubt she'll be back but do be careful. Keep an eye out in case she does decide to turn up. And warn the others too."

Lucky hung up. Sage was looking at her questioningly. "That was Nate. Phoebe disappeared in the night. She stole Audra's car and took off. Nate said to be on the lookout, in case she decides to come back."

"Holy . . ." Sage rubbed his forehead. "I'm gonna call Sophie."

"Good idea. Can you let the others know too?"

Sage nodded. "I will." He set his spoon to the side and wiped his hands on a dishtowel.

"Has Nanette come in yet?"

Sage shook his head. "Haven't seen her. I'll call Sophie and tell her the news."

Lucky peeked through the hatch. Jack sat at a table by the window reading the newspaper. She whispered to Sage, "I've got to talk to Jack while I have the chance." Lucky was dreading the conversation she needed to have with her grandfather. She steeled herself and pushed through the swinging door, heading for his table. "Jack."

He looked up.

"I'm sorry about the other night." She sat across the table from him and took his hand. "It was just a shock. You know I love you and I want you to be happy more than anything in the world. You know that, don't you?"

"I know that, my girl." He smiled and squeezed her hand in return. "This has all happened kinda fast, I admit, but I think if you get to know Nan, you'll change your mind. Sometimes people just rub you the wrong way."

"Uh, well, first of all, I still have the same problem. We have no valid identification for her."

"I understand. You're right. But she won't have to worry about working anymore, not once we get married. Not unless she wants to. I don't have a lot, but I have my little house and my pension."

Lucky bit her tongue. “Is she here yet?”

Jack checked his watch. “No, she’s a little late. It’s two bells already.”

“Well, I’m sure she’ll be here soon. Uh, Jack. Listen, there’s something I have to talk to you about. Before . . .”

“Before what?”

“Before we open. I . . . last night . . .”

“Oh!” Jack slapped his forehead. “I completely forgot. I’ve got to get to the bank this morning.” He looked across the table, “Can this wait till I’m back? I want to get there and get back early, before it gets busy. Maybe Meg can watch the cash register for a little while? I’ve been so busy, I’ve forgotten to get there all week. Won’t take me long.”

Lucky sighed. “Sure. We can talk later.”

Jack rose and headed for the office, where he had secured the cash.

Lucky straightened out their chairs and went behind the counter to get ready for the day. “Meg?”

“Right here.” Meg peeked through the hatch from the kitchen.

“Jack’s heading over to the bank. Can you take care of the register while he’s gone?” Lucky was determined to take Meg into her confidence about Nanette and everything else she had learned as soon as the right moment presented itself.

“Sure, no worries,” she replied.

Lucky rummaged through the drawer of CDs. Music would calm everyone’s nerves today. She found a soothing classical piece and popped it into the CD player. The first notes had just filled the restaurant when Jack came through the swinging door. His face was gray.

“Jack?” Lucky was immediately alarmed. “What’s wrong?”

“It’s . . . it’s gone.”

“What’s gone?” A fearful chill ran up Lucky’s spine.

“The cash. Our week’s take. It’s all gone.” He clutched his chest. His face contorted in pain. His knees buckled and he fell forward on to the floor.

“Sage!” Lucky screamed.

Chapter 54

LUCKY RACED TO Jack's side. He lay gasping for breath on the floor. His eyes were wide. He looked terribly frightened.

Sage rushed from the kitchen and kneeled next to him. "Jack, can you hear me?" he asked. Jack's eyes fluttered. Sage carefully rolled Jack onto his back and stretched out his legs. He felt for a pulse. He looked up at Lucky. "Call for an ambulance. Right away."

Lucky could barely breathe. She raced to the kitchen phone and dialed the Clinic, praying Elias was there and not seeing patients in Lincoln Falls. Rosemary, the receptionist at the Clinic, immediately put her call through to him in his office.

"I'll take care of the ambulance," he answered. "I can get them quicker than you. I'll be right over."

Lucky rushed back to Jack's side. Meg stood helplessly nearby. Tears were streaming down her face. Sage felt Jack's pulse. It was clear Jack was losing consciousness. "He's breathing but I think his heartbeat is very slow. Do you remember that course we took?" Sage asked.

Lucky nodded. She was so frightened, she couldn't speak.

"I think . . . I think we need the AED. I'll get it."

Lucky felt Jack's wrist. Sage was right. His heart was beating but the rhythm felt very slow.

Sage rushed back with the restaurant's automatic external defibrillator in his hands. He quickly unbuttoned Jack's shirt. He placed the pads on Jack's chest. Before he could turn on the power, Lucky heard the back door slam. Elias came though the swinging door. His eyes quickly took in the scene.

Elias looked up at Meg. "Can you get me a stack of towels from the kitchen?"

Meg rushed away and returned a moment later with several fresh dishtowels. Elias placed them under Jack's head, creating a soft cushion.

Lucky quelled the sob rising in her chest. "He just came through the door and said something about the money being gone, then he went down." She grasped her grandfather's hand.

Elias checked Jack's pulse and breathing. "We're in luck," Elias said. "The paramedics were still in town. They'll be here in a few minutes." He opened his bag and drew out a syringe.

Meg stepped around them and hurried through the swinging door to the corridor. Lucky heard her steps on the wooden floor. She peeked out a moment later. "Oh, Lucky, Jack was right." She held an empty cash bag in her hand. "Looks like someone forced the lock on the drawer."

Sage caught Lucky's eye.

"Nanette," she said. He nodded in acknowledgment.

"Want me to call Nate?" Meg asked.

"Later, Meg. I don't care about the money," Lucky answered. "I just want Jack to get help."

"I'm gonna call him anyway," Meg replied. She marched into the kitchen, her face red with anger. Lucky heard her voice on the phone.

Five minutes that felt like an eternity passed while Elias monitored Jack's vital signs. Lucky spotted the ambulance pulling up outside the windows of the restaurant. "They're here."

"Good," Elias said. "Let's get them in here. I'll call ahead to the ER."

Lucky rushed to the front door and unlocked it. She called out to Meg and Sage. "We can't open today. I've got to stay with Jack. It'll be too much for you two to handle."

"Let me call Sophie," Sage said. "If she can come right over, we can keep going."

"Good idea," Meg offered. "We can close the counter, I can handle the tables and Sophie can do Jack's job. That'll work."

The paramedics entered with their equipment. One of the men nodded to Elias. "Hey, Dr. Scott."

Elias quickly related Jack's vitals and medication to the paramedics, then together they expertly moved Jack onto a gurney, placing an oxygen mask over Jack's nose and mouth.

"The anticoagulant should see him through and he's stable for now, but don't delay."

"We'll get him there fast," one of the men replied.

Lucky was almost in tears as the paramedics lifted Jack into the ambulance. She turned back to Sage and Meg. "You two are the best. But listen, if Sophie can't make it, just close up shop. I'll stay in touch by phone."

"Call us as soon as you know anything, Lucky," Sage said.

Elias put his hands on Lucky's shoulders. "I have two patients waiting at the Clinic. Jack's in very good hands. I'll call the ER and let them know what to expect. They'll admit him right away. As soon as I can, I'll meet you there."

"Okay." Lucky was disappointed Elias couldn't travel immediately but she knew he had a heavy schedule. "I'll ride with Jack then."

"You'd only worry more. Besides you'd be stranded there. It might be better if you followed them to the hospital. As long as you're okay to drive. Are you?" he asked.

Lucky nodded. "I'll be careful. Don't worry about that."

Elias leaned down and kissed her lightly on the lips. "Try not to worry. Drive safely. I'll be there very soon." Elias followed the gurney out to the sidewalk and watched as one man climbed in the rear and the other returned to the driver's seat.

Lucky rushed down the hall, grabbed her purse and hurried out the back door to her car. She said a silent prayer for Jack under her breath. Why had she ever let that horrid woman bulldoze her way into the restaurant?

Chapter 55

LUCKY'S HEART WAS racing as she followed the ambulance to the hospital at Lincoln Falls, the sound of its siren adding to her fear. She wished now she had gone in the ambulance. At least she could be with Jack in case he came to inside the vehicle. He wouldn't know where he was or what happened. On the other hand, Elias was right. If she needed to return to Snowflake for any reason, it was best to have her car handy.

After what seemed like an age, the ambulance lumbered into the emergency entrance of the hospital. Lucky parked quickly in a nearby spot and hurried over to the back door of the van, where the paramedics were lifting out the gurney on which Jack rested. His eyes were open now. True to his word, Elias had alerted the emergency room personnel and a nurse was waiting for them as soon as they entered.

"Follow me, fellows," she said to the two men. She approached Lucky. "Family member?"

"Yes," she replied breathlessly.

"Okay. The doctor will be with him right away." Out of the corner of her eye Lucky spotted a tall man in a white medical coat hurry from a door marked STAFF LOUNGE into the room where Jack had been taken. His hair was tousled and he looked as if he had just woken up. The nurse caught Lucky's look. "We've been on alert all night. There was a bad crash on the interstate." She smiled, "Don't worry, he's in good hands. Could you step over to the window and give his insurance information to the clerk?"

Lucky nodded wordlessly, still panicked about Jack's condition.

"That's a good girl," the nurse said.

Lucky thought, *Girl?* How apt. That's exactly how she felt, as if she were five years old and helpless in an emergency. By the time she completed the paperwork and answered questions at the front desk, the doctor had finished his examination and she was allowed in the room. Jack was conscious although not terribly alert. She rushed to his side and grasped his hand, noticing the plastic bracelet around his wrist.

"I'm so sorry, my girl. I must have given you a terrible fright."

"You did, Jack. I'm just glad you're all right."

"The doc here was telling me some things, but it's better if he tells you, you'll understand better than me."

Lucky turned to the tall man with the tousled hair. His name tag said, HERBERT MCCUTCHEON, M.D. "You're the granddaughter?"

Lucky nodded. "Yes."

"Well, your grandfather's stable right now, but I'm going to admit him. He needs to see the cardiologist and have some tests run. And he needs to be under observation and monitored for the next few days, depending on what we find. The lab technician will be here in a minute to draw blood. We'll check his enzymes and we'll get him to Cardiology for an EKG, but I'm pretty sure he's had a myocardial infarction—a heart attack. It was a mild one but it's a good idea to check out any underlying conditions."

Lucky felt as if a hand were squeezing her chest. "I see. Can I stay with him?"

"Of course. You may have to wait outside the Cardiology

Lab, and he'll be in the Coronary Care Unit, but otherwise, you can stay close. Does he have a primary doctor?"

"Yes. We live in Snowflake. Elias Scott is his doctor."

"Oh, that's good." Dr. McCutcheon turned as a woman in a lab coat arrived with a carryall of tubes. He turned to her. "CBC and a cardiac panel."

The woman nodded her head and approached the gurney. Lucky was immediately concerned that Jack, who always had a reaction to the sight of blood, might have a worse one at the sight of his own blood. The technician wrapped a flexible tourniquet around his arm and asked him to clench his fist. Lucky moved to the other side of the gurney and held his hand. "Just look at me, Jack."

The doctor took notice of her comment. She looked up at him. "Jack served in the Pacific and sometimes . . ."

"I understand," he said. "I've given him something to relax him." He turned to Jack. "No need to be anxious at all. Your granddaughter's staying with you." He stepped to the doorway. I'm on duty here but I'll stay in touch with Admissions and Cardiology. They'll take care of you."

Jack closed his eyes as the technician drew several tubes of blood. When she had finished her work, Jack said, "I'm remembering now. The money, Lucky. It was all gone."

Lucky nodded. "Don't worry about that now. It's only money. We'll get it back or we'll make some more. It's not important."

"I've been such a fool." His eyes filled with tears.

"Stop that." She squeezed his hand. "You were worked on by a professional, Jack. I'm sure of that."

"Can't believe I trusted her. I let her see where I kept the cash, and if I hadn't been so caught up, I would have taken it to the bank a few days ago."

"It's my fault too, Jack. I should have checked. I could have gone to the bank too. I just wasn't paying enough attention. But I don't want you worrying about that now. Please. Just concentrate on getting your strength back." Lucky thought his complexion seemed gray under the neon lights. Even his cheeks seemed to have sunken.

Jack shook his head and groaned. "No fool like an old fool."

LUCKY SPENT THE next few hours trailing Jack's gurney through the hospital. One nurse wheeled him to the Cardiology Department. Another took him to the third floor with his paperwork. The cardiac care nurse helped him undress and made sure he was comfortable in his bed. Lucky waited outside until Jack was set and then she stepped inside the room. The space wasn't private but there were no other patients nearby. She was grateful that Jack would have some privacy at least.

A different nurse entered. "Mr. Jamieson, we'll be giving you fluids intravenously for now. But would you like some water?"

"Uh, yes. That would be nice. But please call me Jack."

The nurse smiled back. "Jack it is then." She gave Lucky an encouraging smile as well. "If you're staying around, you might want to grab something yourself downstairs in the cafeteria. They'll be serving lunch now."

"Okay, thanks." Lucky touched Jack's arm. "I'll be back in a bit, Jack. I need to call the Spoonful and let them know you're okay. I know everyone will be very worried."

"Oh," he groaned. "I don't want anybody worrying about me."

"And I need to call Elias and let him know what's happening. He'll be here as soon as he can."

"Okay, my girl." Jack smiled for the first time.

Lucky leaned over and kissed his check. "I'll be back in a short while." She slipped out the door and headed for the elevators. When one opened, she stepped inside and hit the button for the floor below the lobby entrance and then followed the signs pointing toward the hospital cafeteria. A few people on a lunch break were drifting in but the cafeteria was almost empty. It was quiet enough that she could make some phone calls. She picked up a tray and moved through the glass displays of food. Suddenly she was ravenously hungry. She realized she hadn't eaten even a piece of toast that morning. She chose a helping of meatloaf with mashed potatoes and peas. She smiled to herself, a childhood memory flashing before her eyes of her grandmother's weekly meatloaf. Jack had outlived his wife by many years. No wonder he was lonely and Nanette had been able to turn his head. She should have realized his feelings. She should have made more of an effort to spend time with him, do things with him. She sighed and moved her tray to the cash register, paying for her purchase.

When she finished her meal, she dialed the restaurant. Sophie answered.

"What's happening? How's Jack?"

"He's okay. He's awake and on a heart monitor. They've been running tests and waiting for results. The cardiologist said it was a mild heart attack . . . if there is such a thing."

"Poor Jack. He shouldn't be going through this."

"I agree."

"Meg called Nate, but I guess you know that. He stopped by and I told him about the place we followed Nanette to. I just hope he can find it okay."

"She could be gone by now, Sophie. I've been thinking. She must have broken into that drawer and grabbed the cash last night when we were all out front. I didn't go into the office before we closed up. She's taken off. She had to know we'd figure it out right away."

"Now you know why she didn't want to show you any ID."

"I was an idiot to let her hang around at all. And I should have realized Jack was distracted and made sure that cash got to the bank. I'm kicking myself that I didn't listen to my first instincts. If I had, none of this would have happened."

"Well, stop beating yourself up. The important thing is that Jack's okay. Are you coming back to town tonight?"

"I don't think so, Sophie. I'd feel better if I stayed here. Just in case anything worse were to happen. They told me immediate family can stay after an emergency or after surgery."

"Where will you sleep?"

"There are chairs and a sofa in the waiting room and I'm

sure the nurses will give me a blanket. I'll be okay. I can chat with Jack if he feels up to it. I don't want to dump any more work on you though. I think we should close the restaurant tomorrow, just for one day. I can come home after tomorrow when I'm sure Jack's stable."

"I won't argue with you. Today was crazy busy and then everybody was asking about Jack. Guy Bessette and Horace and Barry and Nate and everyone. They'll probably all troop over to visit him tomorrow. Everybody's been worried sick."

"That might cheer him up a bit. I think he's pretty depressed right now."

"In fact, I'll come over tomorrow morning if you don't need me at the Spoonful and give you a break if you like."

"Thanks, Sophie. I can't tell you how much . . ." Lucky felt her throat tighten and tears came to her eyes. "How much you and Sage mean to me . . ."

"Stop that mushy stuff right now, or you'll have me in tears. We all got a bad fright, but it's going to be okay."

Lucky sniffed her tears back and laughed. "Thanks. Love you," and she clicked off. Sophie was right. This was an awful scare. A scare she was sure would never have happened if it hadn't been for Nanette.

Chapter 56

AN ORDERLY HAD arrived early that morning to wheel Jack back to the Cardiology Department for more tests. Lucky returned to the waiting room and snuggled deeper into the chair, pulling the blanket up to her nose. It was the aroma that roused her. She opened one eye to find a smiling Sophie standing over her, waving a steaming cup of very strong coffee back and forth in front of her face.

"Hey, sleepyhead. Wake up. Look what I brought you."

Lucky groaned and stretched, pushing off the blanket that had covered her during the night. "Oh, thank you!" she mumbled, sitting up straighter and reaching out for the paper cup.

"Be careful, it's hot."

"Mmm. It's good," Lucky said, taking a small sip.

"I can't believe you spent the night like this." Sophie glanced around the room. "Where's Jack?"

"He's in Cardiology right now, but they'll bring him back up. He's doing well actually, but I didn't want to . . . I just felt I shouldn't be far away. Just in case . . . you know . . ."

Sophie nodded. "I understand."

"Elias found me in the cafeteria right after we talked. I was so glad to see him. The ER doctor and the cardiologist were great but having Elias here made me feel so much better."

"Did he stay with you?"

"For a little bit. Then he went to talk to Jack's cardiologist and decided to check on his other patients. We had dinner together and he tried to talk me into coming back to town, but I really didn't want to leave Jack alone."

"I'm sure he understood." Sophie waited. "Anything else happen?" Sophie was well aware of Elias's plan to propose at the Mont Blanc Restaurant, but Meg's attack had put that on the back burner. She had been waiting anxiously for the moment to occur, even though she doubted Elias would pop the question in a hospital cafeteria.

Lucky looked at her friend quizzically. "Uh, no. It was a very calm evening, thankfully. Jack was resting quietly and eventually I nodded off."

Sophie hooked a foot around a nearby chair and pulled it closer, then sat. "Have you eaten anything?"

"No. I'm not hungry. Not yet anyway."

"How's the food here?"

Lucky smiled. "Jack wasn't too excited. He ate a little plain oatmeal and herbal tea." Lucky sipped at her coffee. "This is much better than what they sell downstairs. Thanks!" Lucky took another sip. "I'm so sorry. I feel like I'm dumping on you."

"You're not dumping, not at all." Sophie smiled. "Do you know when they'll release Jack?"

"Not today. I talked to the cardiologist earlier when he made his rounds. With luck in a few days. Maybe. I am glad I stayed though. After all that Jack's been through, I didn't want him to get stressed out and maybe . . ."

"Have one of his spells?"

"Yes, that, but also he feels so bad about Nanette stealing the money and being played like he was. I just wanted to be here to lift his spirits."

"I'm sure you did. What are you going to do today?"

"Well, I think when Jack's back to his room, I might drive home, take a shower, get some clean clothes and come back in the afternoon. As long as the nurses don't object, I'll stay another night, just to keep him company. After that, maybe by then we'll know when they plan to release him."

Sophie's purse slid from the chair arm to the floor. Lucky reached down to right it and noticed a folded newspaper sticking out of the purse. "What have you got? The *Snowflake Gazette*?"

"No, it's the *Lincoln Falls Sentinel*. I picked up a copy when I stopped to get the coffee. Big spread on the murder in Snowflake."

"Don't you mean 'murders' plural?"

"The Cranleigh murder's on page six. The front page is all about Hilary Stone. You'll see."

Lucky rested her coffee container on the windowsill and unfolded the newspaper. A photo of Hilary Stone took up a good quarter of the front page. It was a posed publicity photo that the *Sentinel* had obtained. Hilary was smiling, wearing a soft pastel-colored blouse with an open neckline that displayed her sapphire and diamond necklace.

"It's gorgeous, isn't it?" Sophie said, pointing to the necklace. "I guess she must have loved it and worn it all the time. Must have cost a mint."

Lucky stared blankly across the room. The newspaper dropped from her hand.

"What is it?" Sophie asked, alarmed.

"Sophie . . ."

"What?"

"The necklace. She's wearing the necklace."

"I know." Sophie's brow was furrowed.

"She wasn't wearing it that night."

"The night of the murder?"

"Yes! I remember now." Lucky rubbed her forehead.

"What?"

"Her necklace was on the bureau. When I went in to

deliver the tray. She didn't have it on. I noticed it lying across the top of the bureau."

"Okay . . . so?"

"Derek. Derek lied. That morning when I went back to the Drake House, I was standing right there when he told Nate he went into his mother's room later and helped her take off her jewelry. He said she always had trouble with the clasp. But he couldn't have. I was there in the room when she was still alive. Derek came into her room *after* me. Hilary had already taken the necklace off."

"Well, people say strange things sometimes . . . maybe it was his habit to do that, but with the shock of finding out his mother was murdered, he may have been just babbling."

"No, Sophie. He was upset, yes, but he wasn't babbling. He was stating it as if it were an actual fact. He lied. He was there all right, but he made that up to sound like . . . like it was a perfectly normal visit." Lucky stood and shook off the blanket. She slipped on her jacket.

"Where are you going?"

"To the Drake House. And I'm going to call Nate on the way."

"I'll come with you."

"No, please, Sophie. Could you stay here and tell Jack I'll be back later? Don't say anything about Derek though. I don't want Jack to worry."

"Okay," Sophie replied hesitantly. "I'll stay and visit with him, but then I'm heading back to town. I know you. You'll barge in. And I'll make sure I call Nate and tell him what you said."

"Look, Nate will probably not take me seriously. I know it's a minor thing but it's still a lie and why should he lie about it?"

"It's not evidence, Lucky. It doesn't mean he murdered his own mother, much less a doctor he probably never met."

"We'll find out, won't we?" Lucky grabbed her purse, fished out her keys and turned to her friend. "I'll call you as soon as I reach Nate. I think Nate should question him again."

"Be careful."

"I will. I always am."

"Then be more careful." Sophie followed Lucky to the doorway and watched as she pressed the DOWN button on the elevator panel. A sudden chill ran up her spine. Lucky might have promised, but she didn't intend to waste a second calling Nate herself.

Chapter 57

LUCKY REACHED THE Drake House in record time. She had driven as fast as possible down the two-lane road that led back to Snowflake. She was sure she had broken the speed limit, but it was early enough that there was virtually no traffic. Now would be a good time to call Nate before she went in to find Derek, but what could she tell him? He might not pay any attention to her hunch. And on top of that, what could she say to Derek without tipping her hand? She wasn't sure what she could do, but she wanted Nate to question Derek again and she wanted to be there when Nate did. Nate would still be focused on Phoebe's disappearance. She hoped she could reach him. She quickly dialed the station. Bradley, Nate's deputy, answered on the second ring.

"Bradley, is Nate there?"

"Sure, Lucky. He's in his office."

"Let me speak to him for just a moment, please." Lucky prayed Bradley wasn't in one of his obstructive and officious moods.

"Uh . . ." Bradley hesitated.

"It's important, Bradley."

Bradley sighed heavily, "Oh, all right." The line went silent as Bradley relayed her message. Then Nate picked up.

Nate listened patiently as Lucky quickly outlined her thoughts. "Why would he lie, Nate?"

"I don't know. Where are you now?"

"At the Drake House."

"Damn. I thought I told you . . ." Nate sighed. "How's Jack doing?"

"He's been admitted but he's stable. I stayed with him last night. Sophie's with him now."

"All right. I'll go along with this, but only if you wait for me. I'll come over and have another talk with Derek. It'll be a few minutes though. I'm waiting for a report from the lab. Don't confront him, Lucky. Stay the hell out of this."

"But what if he tries to—"

"That's an order. Stay away from him. I'll be over as soon as I can."

"All right," Lucky agreed grudgingly. Frustrated, she turned off the engine and sat back in her seat. Waiting for Nate might take a long while. Her eyes roamed over the guest and staff parking spots on the side of the house. She sat up straighter. Derek's rental car was gone. The same one that Barry had promised to disable. How had Derek managed to get the car fixed so quickly? Barbara Drake must have enlisted Guy Bessette's help to get the car running again. There were only three other cars in the parking area, now that Barbara's guests had all checked out. An older sedan, a pickup truck that she thought belonged to the Partridges and a small compact car. Had Derek gone out or had Sylvia taken the car somewhere?

The reception area was empty when Lucky entered. She dinged the little bell that sat on top of the front desk and waited. Her eye caught a stack of mail that had just been delivered. She glanced at the envelope that sat on top. Her breath caught in her throat. The name clearly marked on the front was "Georgina Ellers." The return address was a Bournmouth post office box.

Barbara Drake hurried out to the reception area. "Yes? Can I help . . . Oh, hi, Lucky!"

Lucky held the envelope up so that Barbara could see the addressee. "Is this Ginny's mail?"

"Yes. Why?"

She had been totally wrong. She wanted to kick herself. She had jumped to the conclusion that Phoebe must be Hilary's daughter. Georgina Ellers did exist and she had been right here under their noses all along. But how could two women in the same small circle have both had a connection to the Salisbury Retreat? "Where is Ginny now?"

"You just missed her. Derek offered her a ride back to Bournmouth. She had some car trouble this morning. Guy couldn't get over till later and Ginny wanted to get home."

"How long ago did they leave?"

"Just a few minutes ago. I'm not sure but Sylvia might have gone with them." Barbara stared at her. "Why? Is anything wrong?"

"Call Nate. Tell him Ginny's in danger. Tell him what you told me." Lucky turned and rushed to the front door.

"Wait. Lucky! What's going on?"

"I can't explain. Just please call Nate. Tell him that." Lucky pushed through the front door. The pieces had finally fallen into place.

Chapter 58

LUCKY BACKED OUT of the drive of the Drake House and pulled onto the road heading in the direction of Bournmouth. Ginny had been there all along, overlooked, as they all speculated on which of the women surrounding Hilary Stone could possibly be her daughter. Why hadn't she considered Ginny as a possibility earlier? How easy it must have been for her to obtain employment at a busy bed-and-breakfast. Had she been stalking her mother? Or had she just been curious? Or was she determined to introduce herself and ask why she had been given up for adoption? Ginny would have no reason to fear Derek. Especially if Sylvia were present in the car. In fact, perhaps Ginny even thought of revealing who she was to her half brother. A half sibling who might have every reason to want Ginny out of the picture.

The skies had become darker and the rain started, first in big splotches and then a steady downpour. If she drove fast enough, she might be able to catch up with them. Derek would never suspect they could be followed. She hit a deep puddle as she navigated a bend in the road. She hit the brakes quickly and felt the car slide, its wheels spinning.

She narrowly avoided losing control of the car. A sudden surge of adrenaline caused her heart to hammer in her chest. She lifted her foot from the accelerator and guided the car back into the lane. It wouldn't do to go off the road or have an accident now. She drove as fast as possible for the next few miles, biding her time and passing every vehicle on the road ahead as soon as she could. She slowed as she reached the sign announcing the town of Bournmouth. Turning on her blinker, she pulled to the side of the road, letting other cars pass by. She hadn't spotted Derek's car, and with only a few minutes' leeway and the speed at which she had driven, it wasn't possible they could have reached Bournmouth before she had.

Was she wrong? Had there been an innocent reason for Derek to lie to Nate? Or did Derek intend to harm Ginny? The rain was heavier now. She could barely see through the windshield. When she was sure there was no oncoming traffic, she made a U-turn and retraced her route. They had never reached Bournmouth. It confirmed her opinion that Ginny was truly in danger. Other than a few houses along the way, there were no paved roads that led anywhere away from the main route. The only road Lucky knew of was a service road to the rear entrance of the recreation area at the pond. It was possible there were other tracks through the woods that she wasn't aware of, but it was far less likely that Derek would be familiar with them if Lucky herself wasn't.

Fifteen minutes later she reached the turnoff and slowed. She entered the dirt track now turned to mud in the rains. Several yards along, two concrete pillars on either side of the road had once supported a heavy chain. The chain was broken now, its sign warning NO ENTRANCE lying in the mud. Fresh tire tracks were being eroded by the rain. They had come this way.

Lucky hit the gas pedal only to feel her wheels spinning. She was stuck. She yanked the gear shift into reverse and gently backed up. The wheels spun again. She tried to go forward and then repeated the maneuver a few more times. The wheels sank deeper into the ground. "Damn!" She hit the steering wheel with her fist. If only she had something in her trunk that she could use. A couple of short boards. She'd be able to rescue her car from the mud. She glanced out at the trees around her. A few sturdy twigs might even do, but there was no time. There was nothing to be done. She'd have to proceed on foot. She pulled her cell phone out once more and dialed the police station. She had no idea if Nate had ever reached the Drake House. If so, he might have tried to trail her route. He would certainly know of this service road but would he think of it?

The temperature had dropped. She was shivering and her fingers felt stiff. She hit the buttons. Bradley answered again. Before waiting for him to speak and before losing her connection, she said, "Tell Nate I'm on the service road to the pond. He'll know." Then she hung up and climbed out. Her first steps left her in mud that covered her shoes. She pulled each foot out of the wet earth with difficulty and reached the side of the road, where pine needles and leaves gave her an easier pathway. She half walked, half ran along the edge of the road.

By the time she reached the end of the dirt track, her clothes were soaked through. She spotted the roof of the boathouse down below. Derek's rental car was parked to the side, the rear passenger door wide open. Lucky approached it cautiously. The car was empty and no one was in sight. Farther along, to her left, steps crafted out of heavy logs led down to the boathouse. A woman's scream cut through the air.

Chapter 59

LUCKY STEPPED CAREFULLY on each log. She couldn't afford to slip or make any noise. Ginny was in danger but she was still alive. Had Sylvia gone with her husband and Ginny? If so, Sylvia was as guilty as Derek. There were two of them and only one of her.

She reached the side of the building and ducked under the window. Hunkering down, she crawled toward the open door to the wooden boathouse. The sounds of angry voices came to her. She was sure it was Ginny who had screamed, but now Sylvia's voice was unmistakable. Sylvia was shouting in a high-pitched tone that could have cut glass.

"You are such a useless . . ."

Then a moan and Derek's voice. "I can't. Sylvia, please I can't . . ."

Sylvia screamed in frustration. "Do I have to do everything myself? What's wrong with you? You are such a pathetic excuse for . . ."

Derek's response was muffled.

"Just do it!" Sylvia shouted. "Get in the boat and take the rope and the cement block."

Lucky heard a loud crash as something hit the inner deck. Then silence and shuffling sounds inside the boathouse. She peeked around the doorjamb and instantly pulled her head back. Ginny was trussed with rope, a gag in her mouth. She sat in a rowboat that had been lowered into the water. The sound of the crash was an oar that had fallen from its slot in the wall. Derek and Sylvia stood on the wooden planking only ten feet away. Derek was kneeling, a thin plastic cord dangling from his limp hand. He began to sob. "Please don't make me do it again, Sylvia. Please. I can't. I can't sleep. I keep seeing—"

"Shut up, Derek," Sylvia spat. "You are such a worm. You are completely useless to me. Get in the boat." Derek was quiet now.

"Get in," she shrieked.

Lucky heard scuffling sounds and then the splashing of water as the boat rocked back and forth in its cradle. She took a deep breath and peeked again. Derek was now sitting in the rowboat. Ginny's frightened moans could be heard through the cloth gag in her mouth. Sylvia stood, her back to the doorway. Lucky's heart was racing. There was no time. Nate would be too late. Crouching, she rose to her feet and sprinted across the platform. Sylvia turned on her heel, a look of complete shock on her face. Lucky rushed toward her and wrapped her arms around Sylvia's body, her momentum carrying them to the edge of the deck and into the water.

The shock of the cold water numbed her body and almost caused her to gasp, but holding her breath, she kicked upward and surfaced. The rain pelted her face and her hair obscured her vision. She pushed her hair away and turned in a circle. Sylvia's head bobbed to the surface a few feet away. She screamed, "I can't swim!" Flailing, she reached for Lucky, her nails digging into the skin of Lucky's arms. Lucky cried out in pain and pulled away. Sylvia sank under the water and a moment later bobbed to the surface, her mouth opening and closing silently, then she sank below the water again. She was drowning.

Lucky took a deep breath and dove into the murky depths. Sylvia was a few feet away, flailing just below the surface.

Lucky swam closer and attempted to grab her from behind. Kicking hard again, she lifted Sylvia to the surface. Sylvia clutched Lucky's arms. Her panic pulled them both under the water. Lucky struggled to rise to the surface but Sylvia's weight was causing them both to sink. She couldn't release Sylvia's grip. Her lungs felt ready to burst. Her ears were ringing and flashes of light appeared before her eyes. Her feet touched the rocky bottom of the pond. Sylvia would drown them both. She couldn't hold her breath a moment longer. With a last reserve of strength, she raised her knees and kicked Sylvia away. Then she reached out and clutched the back of Sylvia's jacket and pushed up to the surface. When she felt air on her face, she gasped great gulps. Her chest ached from the effort of holding her breath. Before Sylvia could turn and drag them under again, she kicked hard and swam back to the shelter of the boathouse, one hand clinging to Sylvia's collar. Once inside, she guided Sylvia's hands to the first rung of the wooden ladder that led to the platform. When she was sure Sylvia wouldn't sink again, she scrambled up to the deck. Sylvia, gasping and coughing, looked up, pure hatred in her eyes.

"Climb!" Lucky ordered.

Still choking, Sylvia clung to the wooden slats and began to climb. She had lost her shoes. Her feet were bare. When she reached the platform, she fell to her knees and coughed up more water. Lucky scanned the walls of the boathouse and spotted a coil of rope on the far side. She hurried around the perimeter of the platform and pulled the coil of rope off its hook. She'd have to restrain Sylvia until help arrived. Derek presented no danger. He still sat in the rowboat and hadn't moved. Of the two, Sylvia was far deadlier.

Lucky turned back with the rope in time to see Sylvia rise to her feet and sprint for the open door. Lucky rushed after her. Sylvia was heading for the car, trying to escape. Slipping and sliding on the muddy earth, Lucky climbed the log stairway. "Sylvia!" she shouted.

Sylvia turned. Her face was distorted in rage, her hands extended, her nails like claws. She rushed at Lucky. Lucky stepped back, protecting her face with her arm. She wasn't sure she had the strength to fight the woman. As Sylvia lunged again, she stepped aside quickly. Sylvia landed on the muddy ground. Lucky kneeled on Sylvia's back, holding her to the ground. Sylvia struggled to squirm away but Lucky grasped her hands, wrenching her arms back, and managed to tie the rope around one of Sylvia's wrists. Sylvia gave one final push and Lucky flew backward. Sylvia leaped to her feet and started to run. The rope was slipping through Lucky's fingers. Lucky clutched the rope tightly and, with all the strength left in her arms, gave a hard pull. Sylvia's feet flew from under her. She landed hard. Lucky scrambled over to her and tied both of Sylvia's wrists behind her back. She dragged Sylvia closer to the car and lashed the rope around the front wheel. Sylvia was going nowhere. The sound of a siren cut through the rain. Nate was coming.

Chapter 60

LUCKY RETURNED TO the boathouse. Derek hadn't moved. He sat in the rowboat, his face slack, his eyes glazed over. Lucky reached down and removed the gag from Ginny's mouth. She climbed down into the boat and, keeping a close eye on Derek, untied Ginny's legs and arms. "Can you stand up?"

Ginny nodded. "I think so."

"Hang on, I'll get out first, then I can help you."

Lucky climbed back onto the platform, then turned and reached out for Ginny's hands. Ginny grasped on and shakily climbed out of the boat and onto the wooden deck. She collapsed in Lucky's arms. "Thank you."

"Come sit down." Lucky led her to the wooden bench built into the side of the boathouse. "Nate's coming. I just heard the siren."

"I . . . I was so stupid. I never thought . . ."

"That they were in league?" Lucky asked.

Ginny nodded. She glanced at Derek, who hadn't moved. "He's my half brother. I knew it, but I didn't think he did. I wanted to tell him. How did he know?"

"Lucky!" Nate bellowed, his voice echoing through the boathouse.

"In here, Nate. It's all clear."

Ginny began to cry. Lucky put a protective arm around her shoulders as Nate approached. "Nate, I'd like you to meet Georgina Ellers, also known as Ginny. She's Hilary Stone's daughter."

Nate stared at Ginny. "You don't say!" Nate turned and looked at Derek in the rowboat. He walked to the edge of the platform. "Let's go, Derek. It's all over."

Derek looked up at Nate. "Thank you," he whispered.

Nate extended his hand and Derek, hesitating a moment, grasped it and climbed up. "Turn around. I'll have to cuff you," Nate said.

Derek's shoulders were slumped. He had given up any struggle. "Where's Sylvia?" he asked.

"Right outside, waiting for you." Nate turned back to Lucky and Ginny. "You ladies all right? Anyone in need of medical attention?"

They answered in unison, "No."

"Great. Follow me. Let's get out of here. It's finally stopped raining."

Lucky glanced down. She was soaking wet, covered in mud and pond debris from head to toe. They stood and left the boathouse. Ginny stumbled but managed to climb the log steps. Lucky followed. As Nate passed by with Derek in tow, Sylvia struggled against her bonds and began to scream insults at her husband. Nate ignored her and pushed Derek up the road to where the cruiser was parked.

When they reached the top of the rise, Lucky saw Elias's car turn onto the road. He climbed out and hurried toward her. "Nate called me on his way over. Are you all right?"

"Yes. And I am very glad to see you." Elias reached out to hold her but she pulled away. "I wouldn't do that if I were you."

"I don't care." He wrapped his arms around her and held her tight.

Nate looked down to the road below where Sylvia still

sat. "I hate to mess up my car. Bradley'll be here any minute. He can take her in. Ginny, you ride in the front with me. Hang on a minute though." Nate opened his trunk and pulled out two heavy blankets. He handed one to Lucky and draped the other over Ginny's shoulders.

Ginny climbed into the front seat of the cruiser. She was silent, her eyes blank. The shock of what she had been through was taking its toll.

They turned at the sound of another vehicle approaching. "Ah, here's Bradley now," Nate said.

Bradley pulled to the side of the narrow road and climbed out, picking his way gingerly toward Nate.

"One more down there," Nate said, indicating Sylvia trussed up at the wheel of the rental car. "Make sure you cuff her first. Don't take any chances with that one." He turned to Lucky and Elias. "Lucky, if you want to go home and get cleaned up, you can meet me at the station in a little while."

"Thanks, Nate." She had begun to shiver, but she wasn't sure if it was from standing in cold wet clothing or the aftermath of her fright.

"I'll drive you back," Elias said.

"But what about my car?" Lucky protested. "It's stuck in the mud."

"We can come back for it tomorrow. Your car's not going anywhere."

Lucky hesitated. "I'm disgusting right now."

"You can say that again." Elias laughed. "Get in before you catch pneumonia."

"If you insist." Lucky sat as gingerly as possible on top of the blanket in Elias's passenger seat.

He climbed in and, reaching over, wrapped the ends of the blanket around her. Then he backed his car up and pulled onto the road, allowing Nate to exit. He hit the brakes and turned to her.

"Why are we stopping?"

Elias took a deep breath. "I've been trying to find the perfect moment for the past two weeks, and it never seems like there is one, so I'm not waiting any longer." He reached over and wiped mud from her face.

"What are you talking about?"

He pulled the small velvet box out of his pocket and held it open in front of her. "Lucky Jamieson. Will you marry me?"

Lucky tried to speak but the words caught in her throat. Elias watched her anxiously.

Finally, she managed to croak, "Of course."

"You will?" Elias grinned from ear to ear.

"Yes." She flung her arms around his neck.

Chapter 61

ELIAS HAD WAITED while Lucky returned home and cleaned up. She bundled her mud-soaked clothes in a kitchen garbage bag. They were ruined. She stood under the shower, the heat soothing her aching muscles. A shower had never felt so good. She dressed in a fresh pair of jeans and a sweater and slipped on her flats. Elias waited at the kitchen table, a cup of hot tea ready for her. He looked up and smiled. "Will you promise me something?"

"What is it?" She smiled.

"That you're going to wear this." He kneeled on the kitchen floor and removed the ring from its box. "I think I should do this right." He smiled up at her. "Letitia Jamieson, will you be my wife?" he repeated.

"Absolutely," she replied.

Elias stood and slipped the ring on her finger. "I just wanted to make sure you weren't going to change your mind."

"It's so beautiful, Elias. I'm afraid to wear it."

"I *want* you to wear it. No matter what. It's meant to be worn." He hesitated. "It was my mother's. Are you sure you like it?"

"Like it? It's incredible. Never in my wildest dreams did I ever imagine having anything like this." She gazed in awe at the diamonds sparkling on her finger

Elias pulled her close and held her tight. She wrapped her arms around him. Neither spoke for several moments. Finally, Elias took her by the shoulders and said, "I better get you to the station before Nate wonders what happened to us." She thought she saw tears in his eyes.

WHEN THEY ARRIVED, Nate was on the phone with the State Police. Derek and Sylvia were being held in the two cells that the station boasted and Bradley was busy manning the phones at the front desk. Ginny sat alone on one of the long oak benches. She had been given a spare deputy's outfit to change into, but she still clutched the blanket around her shoulders as if she couldn't get warm enough. Lucky sat next to her and touched her hand.

"How are you feeling?"

Ginny looked up blankly. "I'm fine. I'm still in shock, I guess. I really don't feel anything just yet." Ginny swallowed nervously. "You know?"

"Yes. I can imagine."

Ginny closed her eyes and took a deep breath. "I guess it will all come out now. I know I wasn't honest with Barbara."

"Why, Ginny?"

"I wanted to . . ." Her eyes filled with tears. She could barely choke out the words. "I just wanted to meet her. To tell her who I was. To ask her why."

"Why she gave you up?"

"Yes." Tears filled Ginny's eyes. "It's impossible for anyone to understand. I still needed to know why. I've always needed to know why. Was I so ugly or terrible or disgusting that my own mother couldn't love me even a little bit?" She pulled a tissue from her pocket. "I'm sorry. You'll think I'm crazy. Maybe I am crazy. I don't know anymore. I was trying to find the courage to speak to her. Ever since I was little . . . when I lost my parents . . . the Ellers . . . that's how I found out I was adopted. When they died. They had never told me. After that I ended up in one place after another. People blamed me. I know they did. For what happened to them that night. But I never caused that fire. It was a spark from the Christmas lights and I was too afraid to run upstairs and tell them. I was so scared they'd think it was me. That I had done it. No one wanted me after that. I can't tell you how many times I fantasized about my real mother coming for me. Taking me to a real home. Loving me and wanting me back." Ginny shot a glance at Lucky. "You must think I'm pathetic. A grown woman crying about her mother. But when I saw how glamorous and self-possessed she was, I was ashamed. Why would she want me? She didn't want me then. Why would she want to meet a daughter who's nothing but a maid, a waitress? I tried, Lucky, I tried, but the words kept chocking in my throat. I couldn't do it. And then . . . it was too late. Too late to tell her who I was and ask her why." Ginny wiped her eyes quickly. "Now everyone will know."

"Ginny . . . honestly, I don't think anyone in town will think any less of you. I really don't." Lucky reached over and grasped her hand. "I can't make any promises. I'm afraid the whole story will come out. But people will understand why you came here. Why you felt the way you did. You haven't done anything wrong."

Ginny looked up and smiled ruefully. "I think being born was the one thing I did wrong."

Lucky heard Nate's office door open. He came around the counter and sat next to Ginny on the bench. "You feel up to giving a statement?"

Ginny nodded. "I'm all right."

"Good. Come on back. You too, Lucky. I'll make this as quick as possible."

They stood and followed Nate into his office. On the way in, he told Bradley to bring three cups of coffee in to them. Bradley turned, and watched them curiously. Lucky knew he was dying to find out all the details. She knew the news would spread through town in no time at all.

Nate sat behind his desk and leaned back in his chair.

Ginny's hands were shaking slightly. When Bradley arrived with the coffee, Ginny held the cup between her hands as if to warm them. Lucky was grateful for the hot beverage. She still felt as if she hadn't warmed up since her struggle in the pond.

"Near as we can figure out, your doctor, Dr. Cranleigh," Nate said, nodding in Ginny's direction, "Dr. Cranleigh knew that you'd try to find your mother. She must have been worried about you and went to the Drake House to try to talk to Hilary Stone. By the way, how did you find out Ms. Stone was your biological mother?"

"I . . ." Ginny swallowed, her voice was constricted. "I applied to the Adoption Registry. My mother had never tried to keep her identity secret. That's how I found out her maiden name, and then after that, it was easy to follow her trail. I was in therapy with Dr. Cranleigh, but when I saw the advertisements in all the papers . . . that she was coming here, I knew I had to take a chance. I knew it would be my only chance to meet her."

"I see," Nate said. "Well, I imagine Dr. Cranleigh suspected you might be planning to do that very thing, that you might have located your mother at the Drake House. What she did, trying to talk to your mother, was highly unethical, but it sounds to me as if she was worried about you. Maybe she was hoping to ease the way."

"I never knew she had been there. I wasn't working that day and no one ever mentioned it."

"She never did get to talk to Ms. Stone. According to Barbara Drake, she spoke to Phoebe very briefly but I think Derek interrupted them. When I first questioned him, he told me she was just a fan hoping to meet his mother. Now he's admitted he suspected it was about you trying to make contact. He had to keep Dr. Cranleigh away from his mother . . . your mother, so he arranged to meet her outside of town, with Sylvia, and you know the rest."

"How did Derek find out that his mother had given a child up for adoption?" Lucky asked.

"Derek's completely broken down. He's admitted he and his mother had been fighting for weeks, since his marriage to Sylvia. I would guess his mother told him about his half sister to punish him. She told him she was disgusted with him and she was trying to locate her daughter. When Dr. Cranleigh turned up, Derek figured she had information she might give to your mother." Nate nodded to Ginny. He says he asked her to meet him at the pond, but he denies he killed her. He said Sylvia did the deed. They just used the same murder weapon in *Murder Comes Calling* to be clever, or so they thought. Maybe they figured it would look like a crazed fan, imitating the book. Derek claims that was Sylvia's bright idea."

"Oh." Ginny held her hand to her mouth. "It's all my fault," she sobbed. "Dr. Cranleigh was trying to help me and it caused her death."

"When you knew it was your doctor we had found at the pond, why didn't you come and talk to me?" Nate asked.

Ginny shook her head. "I couldn't. I just couldn't do it. I found out from the Partridges one day that a doctor from Salisbury had been killed. Then when I read the newspaper and learned it was Dr. Cynthia . . . I was devastated. But believe me, I never in a million years imagined it had anything to do with me."

Lucky shifted in her seat. "Nate, I'm curious. Who hired the private investigator?"

"The one who was asking questions at the Salisbury Retreat?"

"Yes."

"Hilary herself did. Or rather her lawyer. He turned to Ginny. "She wanted to find you."

"She did? She was looking for me too?" Ginny cried.

Nate nodded. "That's right."

Lucky reached out and put a comforting hand on Ginny's shoulder. "Ginny was right here in an agony of indecision, afraid to reveal herself to her mother, and all the while her mother was searching for her."

"I've been in contact with Hilary Stone's attorney in New York. Hilary changed her will when she couldn't buy Sylvia off. Her lawyer hand-delivered the investigator's report to her New York office, but Hilary was already here in Snowflake. Audra received it at the office and brought the package with her when she came to town."

"That's right," Lucky said. "I remember Audra handing Derek an envelope to give to his mother the night of the book signing."

"Derek was already suspicious his mother intended to cut him out, so he was curious about the package. Hilary unfortunately never got to see the report. Derek kept it from her. There was even a picture of Ginny's driver's license. Derek read the whole report, realized his mother was serious about cutting off the money and told Sylvia. They knew they had to get rid of you and your doctor; otherwise they'd lose everything. He . . ." Nate looked at Lucky. "He had the same idea you did. Find the daughter. But he had the advantage of the investigator's report. And he saw the sign-in sheet on the front desk with Ginny's full name, but he didn't need that since he already had her picture on the license. They were just biding their time. Derek made sure Ginny's car was out of commission and offered her a ride home. The irony is they had no way of knowing Hilary had already changed her will and left instructions with her attorney."

"So Derek and Sylvia committed murder for nothing."

"Right. I don't think Derek planned to kill his mother that night, but there was an argument. That was the one Ginny heard. He said he didn't mean to do it, but when she turned away from him, he grabbed the nearest thing—the telephone cord—and strangled her in a fit of rage. On his own, I doubt Derek would have had the wherewithal to do such a thing, but Sylvia controlled him completely. She's vicious. She was determined to get her hands on Ms. Stone's money."

"Nate, the photo of Hilary's assistant, Phoebe, that I saw in the newsletter. I called you because I thought Phoebe must be—"

"Hilary Stone's daughter?" Nate asked.

"Yes. Why else would Phoebe be there?"

"According to Hilary's attorney, Phoebe, her assistant, was the only other person Hilary had taken into her confidence. When Hilary learned Ginny was receiving treatment at the Salisbury, she sent Phoebe up here two months ago to learn what she could. This was weeks before she became so angry at Derek. Phoebe didn't learn much. She never got to meet Dr. Cranleigh. Maybe she was hoping to connect with friends of Ginny's, or she was hanging around to talk to people who might have known her there."

"Why did Phoebe run away?" Lucky asked.

"She found the envelope that contained the attorney's report. She was alarmed and frightened of Derek so she decided to go straight back to New York to bring it to her boss, Hilary's husband."

"How did she find it? You must have searched their rooms."

Nate shook his head. "I did. Derek shoved it into a stack on Phoebe's desk when he returned to the Drake House that night after the book signing. Later that night when Phoebe was busy, he brought it to Barbara Drake and asked her to keep the envelope in her safe. He told her it contained an important contract. Barbara remembered it yesterday. In all the commotion, it slipped her mind. She reminded Phoebe about it. Phoebe was confused. She knew nothing about any contract. She read the report, put two and two together and realized she wouldn't be safe staying at the Drake House with Derek and Sylvia."

"Who inherits Hilary's estate now?"

Nate's eyebrows rose. He turned to look at Ginny and nodded once.

Ginny sat quietly, tears streaming down her face.

Chapter 62

LUCKY LOCKED THE front door and moved around the restaurant, turning off all the lamps but one. Horace, with Cicero at his feet, sat quietly at the large table. Sophie and Sage were in the kitchen clearing up for the night. Meg too was quiet as she moved around the front room, straightening chairs and wiping down the tables for the next morning.

"What's taking them so long?" Meg called out.

Lucky grabbed her cup of tea from the hatch and carried it over to the table where Horace waited. "They'll be here any minute." Lucky pulled a napkin out of her pocket and slipped a large hunk of chicken to Cicero. He gobbled it down and licked her hand.

"What do you say, Cicero?" Horace asked. Cicero gave a small yelp.

"You're welcome," Lucky replied, absently scratching the top of the dog's head.

"I'll bring some beers out," Sage said.

Meg finally joined them. "I'm so glad all those people have gone back to New York. Phoebe seemed kind of normal, but the rest of them . . ." Meg trailed off.

"Well, Phoebe and Audra are back in New York, but Derek and Sylvia won't see the light of day for a long time, if ever," Lucky remarked.

Sophie, carrying a tray loaded with several bottles of beer, joined them. Sage followed a moment later with chilled glasses and napkins.

Lucky turned to Meg. "I think you should do the honors tonight."

Meg's face lit up in a broad smile. She looked around at all of them. "Thank you," she said.

"For what?" Sage asked.

"For letting me join in. For not shoving me out of the way. This is the most exciting thing that's ever happened in my life."

"Let's hope it doesn't happen again, Meg," Sophie replied drily.

"Tonight's important. This is the very last meeting of the Murder Investigation Club," Meg announced.

"Here, here." Sage raised his bottle of beer in a toast.

Lucky looked up when she heard a knock at the front door. She rushed over and unlocked it. Barry entered with Hank following on his heels. The group at the table erupted in applause. Lucky joined in.

Hank's eyes were tearing. He cleared his throat. "Thank you. I owe all of you. I know I was an idiot to take off the way I did. But I can't thank you enough for all you've done in trying to clear me from any suspicion."

"Grab a seat, you two," Lucky said. "I honestly don't think Nate truly suspected you, Hank. I think he was just mad that you were avoiding him."

Hank sighed and sat in the chair that Horace pushed out for him. "Well, he did find my eyeglasses in Hilary's room. I was there. I did have a loud argument with her . . ." Barry took a seat between Hank and Horace.

"And I saw you leaving the Drake House that night," Horace remarked, "although I didn't tell Nate, but I'm sure other people spotted you too."

"Right." Hank nodded, straightening his new pair of

pince-nez glasses on his nose. He sighed. "I was so furious Hilary had come here. All these years I've been able to live a quiet life, able to put all that upset behind me, and what happens? She turns up again, like a bad penny."

Sage rose and delivered two glasses and two bottles of beer to Hank and Barry. Barry nodded his thanks.

"Nobody can blame you for feeling that way," Lucky offered.

"Well, it all came up again for me. The hurt, the anger, all these feelings I hadn't had for years, but then to try to bribe me to write *another* book giving her the credit after what she had stolen. To be honest with all of you . . ." He looked around the table. "I have a horrible admission to make. I *felt* like killing her. I really did. She was a maddening woman, a complete narcissist. I let her have it in no uncertain terms. And you know what she did? She just sat there and looked at me as if she simply couldn't understand why I would be so upset." Hank fell silent for a moment, staring off into space. "That really brought me up short. I realized I might as well have been speaking Chinese to her. She just didn't get it. Couldn't get it. She wasn't wired the way normal people are. That's when my anger dissipated and I realized there was no point even talking to her and"—he looked up and smiled—"and no point in carrying around all that anger anymore. It was just a moment, but it was the most freeing moment in my life. I felt like a huge weight had been taken off my shoulders. It doesn't excuse my running off to Bournmouth, I know, but I just needed some peace and quiet and time to ruminate over what had happened."

"So what do you plan to do now, Hank?" Lucky asked.

Hank smiled shyly. "I have a great idea for a new book. Something totally different. I'm going to start writing again."

"That's wonderful!" Sophie exclaimed.

"What's it about?" Meg asked excitedly.

Hank shook his head, "Uh-uh. Can't talk about it yet. I'm still working it out. But I'll let you all know when it's finished. Give me another year."

Lucky tapped a spoon on her teacup. "Hank's neglected to mention the most important thing of all." She glanced at Hank and smiled.

"What's that?" Sage asked.

"Wait just a minute, everyone," Meg interrupted. "There's something Hank and Barry don't know yet."

Barry raised his eyebrows. "What's that?"

Meg smiled from ear to ear. "Lucky and Elias are getting married!"

"That's wonderful!" Hank beamed. "My congratulations. I couldn't think of any better news."

"Ditto that," Barry said, smiling widely.

Meg shoved Lucky's elbow. "Show them the ring!"

Lucky blushed furiously and laid her hand on the tabletop. The diamond sparkled in the low light.

Barry reached over and squeezed her hand. "Couldn't wish for anything better, Lucky. Good luck to you both. When's the happy day?"

"Oh, maybe next spring or maybe June. We haven't quite decided yet."

"Well, I'll be there with bells on!" Barry exclaimed. "Did you know about this, Horace?"

Horace nodded. "Yes, Sophie told me yesterday. Isn't that wonderful? I can't think of two nicer people."

"Thank you all," Lucky replied sincerely. "But there's even more good news." She looked around at their faces. "Hank hasn't had a chance to share the news. It turns out that Hilary's husband is a very ethical man. When Nate told Derek Stone, Senior, that Hilary's ex-husband, Hank, claimed the manuscript for *Murder Comes Calling* had been stolen, and stolen by his own wife, he was horrified. He instituted a search and found Hank's original manuscript in Hilary's safe. He's promised to turn over all the royalties that would have been due to Hilary, to Hank, and he has dibs on Hank's next book."

"That's fantastic!" Sophie exclaimed.

Meg's brow was furrowed. "I don't know about all that, that's great, but I think you should get the credit for *Murder Comes Calling*," she said to Hank.

Hank shook his head. "I don't want it, Meg. It's really not important to me anymore. What's happened is water under the bridge. Mr. Stone might be afraid I could sue him and make this a public fight, but I have absolutely no intention. Besides, I really have no way to prove it *was* my book. Most of all, he did nothing wrong. I have no desire to embarrass him or his company. Think how bad that would make Lexington Avenue Publishing look." Hank took a sip of his beer. "No. What he's voluntarily offered is incredibly generous, and more importantly, he'll give my next book a fair reading. That's all I ask for."

Chapter 63

JACK STARED AT the contents of the tray in front of him. He had been moved out of the Coronary Care Unit and now occupied a private room. He shook his head. "Look at this. This is the saddest excuse for food I've ever seen." He swirled a spoon around in a bowl filled with a viscous beige substance. "These people need to pay a visit to our restaurant. Maybe if they tasted some decent food, they wouldn't try to foist this off on poor, unsuspecting sick people."

"I'm sorry, Jack," Sophie replied. "I should have been thinking. I could've asked Sage to pack something up for you. It'd be easy enough to sneak it in."

Jack's face brightened, "The good news is, they're lettin' me out tomorrow." He turned to Lucky. "How soon can I leave?"

Lucky shrugged. "I'd guess four bells. I think the cardiologist will want to see you when he makes his rounds in the morning and I'll come over early and get your paperwork all straightened out."

"Good. I'll be up and dressed and ready to go. Can't see

hanging around here another day. I'd lose my mind. And worst of all, I've missed all the excitement at home."

"Hey, there." Nate's voice boomed from the doorway. "How ya doin', Jack?" Sophie and Lucky turned and smiled. Lucky stood and pulled a chair close to Jack's bed for Nate.

"Fit as a fiddle. I'm getting out of this joint first thing tomorrow."

"That's good news." Nate stood at the foot of the bed. "Sorry I couldn't stop by sooner, Jack. But I guess you know I've been busy."

"And I've been a damn fool, so don't feel too bad," Jack replied.

"Some good news on that front." Nate turned to Lucky. "We've retrieved the cash that was stolen. Nanette Simms—whose real name is Rita Magnus, by the way, and is anything but a Southern Belle—and her husband, Earl, are cooling their heels in a jail cell in Bournmouth."

"Wow! You found them?"

"Yup. Turns out there were warrants for their arrest for similar crimes all over the state."

"Where are they really from?" Lucky asked.

"Right here in Vermont. Both of them."

"I knew it. I knew that accent was phony." Lucky smiled.

"They've certainly conned a lot of people." Nate turned to Jack, "I guess you're not the only one. Mostly low-level stuff but enough people have sworn out complaints against those two and have been able to identify them, it wasn't hard to locate them. The State Police caught them just as they were trying to cross the line into New York. They were thinking they'd leave Vermont and lay low for a while, but their luck ran out."

"Good!" Sophie exclaimed. "I hope they get the book thrown at them."

Nate smiled. "I think they will. They'll be sent away at least for a few years, more I hope." He turned to Lucky, "You'd be willing to testify?"

Lucky glanced at her grandfather. "What do you say, Jack? Maybe you should be the one."

"Happy to. I've come to my senses. To think that woman coulda led me down the garden path . . ."

Nate smiled broadly. "So I'll see you tomorrow night at the Spoonful then, Jack?"

"You bet you will. I'll be at my cash register before eight bells have rung."

"Good to hear," Nate called back as he left the room.

Lucky stood. "Sophie and I need to get back too, Jack. Sage and Meg are on their own today. Oh, I forgot to tell you, I've hired Miriam to help out."

"Janie's mother?"

"Yes. She was thrilled when I called her. She'll be part-time, just for the busiest times for now, but it'll take the weight off Meg's shoulders."

"Good decision, my girl."

"Bye, Jack." Sophie leaned over and kissed his cheek. "I'll see you tomorrow then."

Jack smiled and patted Sophie's hand.

Lucky and Sophie headed down the corridor to the elevator bank. Sophie stopped in her tracks. "Uh, Lucky, can you wait a minute?"

"Sure. You okay?"

Sophie's complexion had blanched. "I'll be right back." She turned and hurried toward the restroom sign.

Lucky followed and hesitated outside the door. She gave Sophie a few minutes, then entered. Sophie stood at the sink splashing water on her face. Lucky crossed her arms and stared at her friend. "When were you planning to tell me?"

Sophie stood up straight, and wiped droplets of water off her face. She groaned, "How did you know?"

"Oh, maybe the fact that you didn't touch your beer the other night at the Spoonful. Maybe the fact that Sage mentioned you weren't feeling well one morning. Maybe that . . ." Lucky smiled.

Sophie burst into tears and buried her face in her hands. Lucky rushed forward and wrapped her arms around her friend.

"I'm so scared, Lucky!"

"It's a big change."

"I never thought about it. I never thought it would happen to me," Sophie cried. "I can't get my head around it."

Lucky hugged her friend tighter and felt Sophie melt into her arms.

"When I think of Hilary Stone giving her daughter up for adoption, I can't imagine anything like that. I feel like there's a soul hovering around me, around me and Sage, learning to love us, waiting to be loved, waiting to be born." Sophie pulled back. Her eyes were full of tears. "But I'm *so* scared."

Lucky smiled widely, certain her eyes were full of tears as well. "You'll be a great mom."

"You think so?"

"Yes." Lucky nodded. "I know so." She reached for a tissue and wiped Sophie's cheeks. "Come on, let's get out of here." Lucky held the door as they stepped out to the corridor. "Has it occurred to you how much things have changed in just a few short years? Time is such a strange thing, isn't it? When we were kids, we felt as if it couldn't pass fast enough and now it seems to fly. It wasn't that long ago I had absolutely no thought of ever returning to Snowflake."

Sophie took a deep breath and linked her arm through Lucky's as they headed for the elevator. "And I was so mad at you for leaving for college in the first place." She pushed the button for the lobby. "I didn't even want to speak to you when you came back."

"And never in a million years did I think I'd have a chance with Elias. Now we're engaged and you and Sage are about to start a family."

"It's because of you that Sage is still here. He could have gone to jail for the rest of his life for a crime he didn't commit. Both of us owe our lives to you for figuring out who murdered that winter tourist."

"Don't dwell on that," Lucky said as they stepped into the elevator. "Everything's wonderful now. Jack will be back on his feet soon and the Spoonful . . . well, we'll keep on serving soup just as always. You and Sage are going to have a baby and Elias and I"—Lucky took a shaky breath—"will be getting married."

Sophie smiled. "You'll be Mrs. Letitia Scott."

Lucky laughed. "Now *I'm* scared. It feels like a new identity. I don't want to be different, I want to stay the same, I just want Elias and me to be together, for real."

"But this is a good change. And I'm going to be your bridesmaid, right?" Sophie narrowed her eyes.

"Of course, who else? You'll be my one and only."

"Well, unlike you, I can't sew, but promise me I can help pick out your wedding dress?" Sophie asked as they stepped out of the elevator.

"Yes, absolutely. I'll definitely need help with that," Lucky agreed. "Have you thought about any baby names?"

"Yikes! No! I'm still trying to get used to the idea I'll be a mother! And you'll be a godmother." She hesitated. "But maybe . . . if it's a girl, I'll call her Letitia."

"Oh," Lucky groaned. "Don't saddle the poor kid with that name."

"Why not? It's a beautiful name. It means happiness."

The glass entrance doors released and they stepped out into the warm spring sunshine. "Why don't you follow me back to the Spoonful and we can continue this argument there."

"What argument? We're not arguing. I've already decided."

"Well, if I'm going to be a godmother, don't I have a say?"

"I'll think about that," Sophie replied.

Lucky hugged her friend. "Let's get back to the Spoonful. I know we'll have some very hungry customers waiting for us."

Author's Note

Adoption laws, which vary from state to state, play a large role in the plot of *A Clue in the Stew.* Although records are always confidential to the public, in certain states information is made available to birth parents, adoptees, siblings and even descendants of deceased adoptees. In Vermont, the official site for adoption records is: dcf.vermont.gov/fsd/vermont_adoption_registry.

A Clue in the Stew references a site called connectadopt.com. This is purely fictional, although the name is based on a real site—the Worldwide Adoptee and Birth Parent Search Database, which can be found at: adopteeconnect.com.

If you are someone seeking information about a birth parent, a sibling or a child given up for adoption, you can register at adopteeconnect.com, provide any known information and receive notifications if another's search matches your parameters.

Recipes

CREAM OF ASPARAGUS SOUP

1 bunch asparagus
1 tablespoon butter
2 leeks, green part removed and white part thinly sliced
1 large potato, peeled and cubed
3 cups chicken broth
salt and pepper to taste
1 cup water
2 tablespoons lemon juice
4 tablespoons crème fraîche

Trim off thick ends of asparagus and chop stalks into 1-inch thin sections. Reserve 4 asparagus tips for garnish and set aside.

In a large pot, melt butter, add sliced leeks and sauté for 5 minutes. Add potato and chopped asparagus stalks, and sauté for 5 minutes more.

Add chicken broth and season with salt and pepper. Bring to boil over medium heat, reduce heat to low, then cover partially and cook about 15 minutes, until vegetables are tender.

In the meantime, add water to a small saucepan, bring to boil and add reserved asparagus tips and lemon juice. Cook on medium heat for 3 minutes just until tips are tender. Drain and let cool.

Purée the soup in a blender in batches, or with a wand, then reheat the soup over low heat. Garnish each serving with crème fraîche and asparagus tips.

Serves 4.

ASIAN TOFU NOODLE SOUP

3½ cups chicken or vegetable broth
1 cup water
2 tablespoons soy sauce
2 teaspoons minced garlic
1 tablespoon ginger root, freshly grated
2 cups shiitake mushrooms, stems removed and caps sliced
handful of rice noodles or whole wheat spaghetti, broken in half
1 cup carrots, chopped
2 cups snow peas, fresh, trimmed and cut in half lengthwise
8 ounces firm tofu, cut into ½-inch chunks
½ cup green onions, chopped into ½-inch pieces

Heat broth almost to boiling, and add water, soy sauce, garlic and ginger. Add mushrooms, noodles (or spaghetti) and carrots, and cook 5 minutes. Add snow peas, and cook 2 more minutes.

Add tofu, and cook until vegetables are tender but still crisp, and noodles are al dente, about 2 more minutes. Remove from heat and stir in green onions and serve.

Serves 4.

FENNEL AND DATE SALAD

3 tablespoons pumpkin seeds
½ cup chopped walnuts
1 head romaine lettuce, washed and thinly sliced on the diagonal
3 celery ribs, thinly sliced on the diagonal
1 bulb fennel, cleaned, outer leaves removed, cut in half and sliced very thin
1 cup fresh parsley
5 ounces hard Parmesan cheese, shaved
10 dates, pitted and thinly sliced on the diagonal
juice of ½ lemon
salt and freshly ground black pepper to taste

DRESSING

juice of ½ lemon
2 tablespoons walnut oil

Mix ingredients for dressing and set aside.

Toast pumpkin seeds and chopped walnuts in a small skillet for 2 minutes, remove and set aside. Mix lettuce, celery, fennel, parsley, cheese and dates. Add lemon juice, toasted nuts and dressing and toss again. Add salt and pepper to taste.

Serves 4.

TOMATO PEPPER SOUP

2 teaspoons butter or margarine
1 sweet green pepper, seeds removed and diced
1 yellow pepper, seeds removed and diced
1 medium onion, finely chopped
1 clove garlic, minced

2 cups chicken broth
2 cans diced tomatoes, puréed in blender with juice, or 1½ pounds fresh tomatoes, chopped
2 teaspoons maple syrup or sugar
4 tablespoons uncooked white rice
2 basil leaves, torn in pieces, or ½ teaspoon dry basil
¼ teaspoon dry thyme, or small sprig fresh thyme
2 bay leaves
dash cayenne pepper
freshly ground pepper to taste

Melt butter or margarine in a large pot. Add green and yellow diced peppers, onion and garlic. Cook on medium heat, stirring, for 5 minutes or until onion is soft. If mixture dries, add a little broth. Add remaining ingredients except black pepper: broth, tomatoes, sugar, rice, basil, thyme, bay leaves and cayenne pepper. Bring to a boil, then lower heat and simmer about 15 minutes or until peppers are tender. Turn off heat, cover and let sit until rice has softened, approximately 20 minutes. Reheat, and add freshly ground black pepper to taste. Remove bay leaves and serve hot.

Serves 4.

CORN AND CHEESE CAKES

½ cup yellow cornmeal
½ cup all-purpose flour
½ teaspoon baking soda
½ cup grated cheddar cheese
½ teaspoon salt
dash black pepper
1 large egg
¼ cup half-and-half
1 cup yellow corn kernels
½ cup chopped green onions

nonstick vegetable oil spray
¼ cup (approximately) spicy brown mustard

Mix cornmeal, flour, baking soda, grated cheese, salt and pepper in a large bowl. Whisk egg and half-and-half together and add to dry mixture, blending well. Stir in corn and green onions. Spray large nonstick skillet with vegetable oil spray. Over medium heat and working in batches, drop small amounts of batter on skillet, pressing down lightly and turning over. Cook until each cake is golden brown, about 1½ to 2 minutes. Top each with a dab of mustard. Serve warm.

Depending on size, makes approximately 20 small cakes.